A CROWN OF FELLING

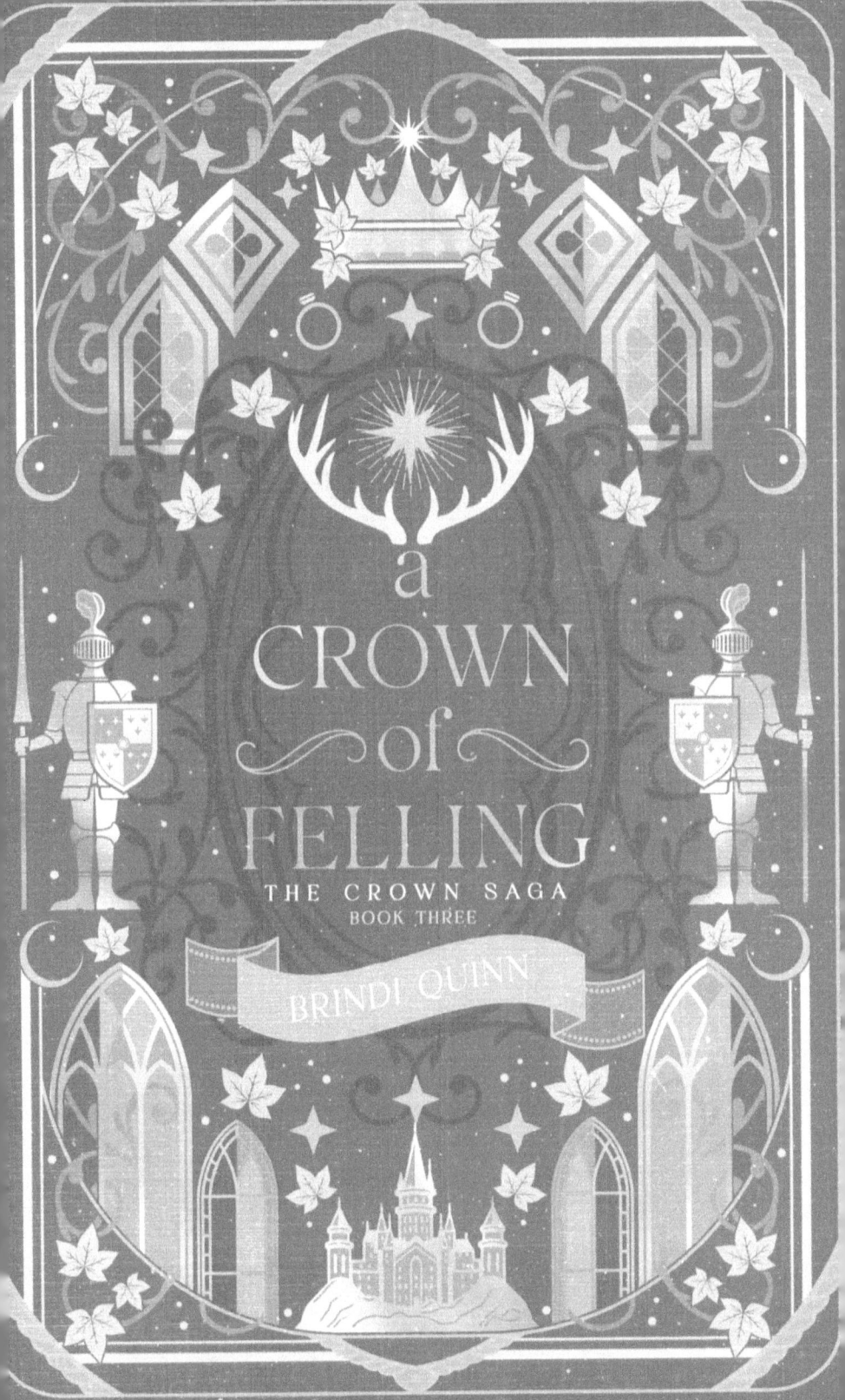

a
CROWN
of
FELLING

THE CROWN SAGA
BOOK THREE

BRINDI QUINN

A Crown of Felling
Copyright © 2021 by Brindi Quinn
Re-Crowned Edition, 2025

N & E

Published by Never & Ever Publishing | @neverandeverbooks
Edited by Meg Dailey | @thedaileyeditor
Cover and title by Saint Jupiter | @saintjupit3rgr4phic
Artwork by Natascia Mora | @moranatascia
Maps by Centaur Maps | @centaurmaps
Interior by Brindi Quinn via Vellum

ISBN (Paperback): 978-1-967709-01-4

Originally published February 19, 2021.
Lovingly revised, refreshed, and re-crowned in 2025.

SERIES READING ORDER

Book One: *A Crown of Echoes*
Book Two: *A Crown of Reveries*
Book Three: *A Crown of Felling*
Book Four: *A Crown of Dawn*

To every woman who learned to stop asking permission.

CONTENT WARNING

The Crown Saga contains references to child abuse, child trafficking, and exploitation, which—though not depicted in graphic detail—may still be distressing for some readers. The series also features moderate to graphic violence, large-scale battles, and occasional body horror, including monstrous transformations. Romantic and sexual content ranges from mild innuendo to explicit scenes. Additional sensitive topics include coarse language, alcohol use, magical coercion, emotional manipulation, and pregnancy depicted under perilous circumstances.

DRAMATIS PERSONAE

THE QUEENS & THEIR COURTS

- **Merrin Iralore (22)** — Queen of **the Crag**.
  Compassionate, irreverent, irrepressibly daring;
  harbors the power of creation and an alchemist's
  deft touch. Bona fide Nemophilist and feast for a
  devil.
- **Beau Lysavere (23)** — Queen of **the
  Clearing** and Merrin's sister-in-crown. Regal,
  freckled, unfailingly composed. Expecting a child
  with a grumpy knight.
- **Sestilia of the Cove (nearly 26)** —
  Tempestuous sea-queen with silver hair to the floor
  and a mind as mercurial as the tides. Equal parts
  lonely and lethal. Swears Merrin is her best friend
  —consent optional.

KNIGHTS & ALLIES

- **Sir Windley of the South (25)** — Beau's most
  infamous guard, reckoning with his newly
  remembered past. Hair shifts with whimsical
  magic; charm masks a storm-dark core. Obsessed
  with his lion-hearted queen.

- **Sir Rafe of the North (20)** — Fire-sheathed blade at Merrin's side. Sword now flares with heat; newly pacted to Soleil, goddess of the sun. Queen Beau's lover—missing his true queen more by the hour.
- **Sir Albie (looking grayer by the day)** — Merrin's senior knight. Weather-worn, fatherly, fretting endlessly while his queen's away.
- **Mother Poppy (ancient)** — Royal tome-keeper, former regent, grandmother in all but blood.
- **Meraflora "Flora" (late-20s)** — Warm-hearted herbalist who hid Windley after his escape. Honey-voiced, braver than she seems. Looks suspiciously identical to Merrin—and has no idea why.
- **Sir Saxon (27)** — Knight of the Crag. Can drink an army under the table; in charge while Sir Albie's away.

FOES

- **Charmagne "Charm" (mid-20s)** — Windley's rose-haired Spirite sister, all burnished-copper beauty and razor-edge temper. Merrin still regrets not ending her the first time they crossed blades.
- **Edius "Edi" (late-20s)** — Broad-shouldered Spirite mimic who can wear any face he drains. Fresh from betraying his rag-tag kin, he now scours the realms for allies willing to gamble on his secret agenda.

- **Pip "Pipsqueak" (looks ~18)** — Moon-pale prodigy with cotton-candy hair that changes to each heartbeat he "tastes." Endlessly re-memory-scoured, he wavers between puppy-loyalty to Windley and dread of the wide, hungry world beyond his leash.
- **"Master" Ascian (deceased)** — Lavender-eyed puppeteer who once owned Windley. Hex-weaver, life-leech, collector of pretty things; met an untimely end at the hand of the Nemophilist.

OTHER POWERS & PRESENCES

- **The Widowbirds** — Long-tailed messengers bonded to royal blood; summoned by a filigreed whistle, each note attuned to one of the Ten Northern Queens.
- **The Echoes** — Shadow-hands that obey only the Nemophile's Crown, glimpsed behind closed eyes and heard at the mind's edge.
- **The Scarlet Wood** — Living forest of blood-red leaves.
- **The Emerald Wood** — Night-bright sister-forest.
- **Gwen (age unknown)** — The quiet mystery Edius calls his *fiancée*. Saving her is Edius's every motive—even when he cannot find the words to explain why.
- **Bobbin** — Mysterious monster tied to Pip's soul. Said to resemble a spider with "a few extra legs."

THE FOUR GODDESSES

- **Luna** — Goddess of frost, tides, and the silver moon. Once sworn to Rafe, she now drifts overhead like a jealous satellite, stirring trouble whenever the clouds part.
- **Soleil** — Goddess of sun-fire and relentless dawn. From her rainbow-sherbet sanctum she has branded Rafe with her flame and now waits to see whether his heart can survive the blaze.
- **Exitium** — Goddess of Destruction, recently pried from Merrin's soul. Ravenous for ruin, she roams for a new royal host, offering power that always costs more than it gives.
- **Vita** — Goddess of first breath and seedling green; creation embodied and Exitium's eternal counterweight. Gentle is not harmless—where Exitium devours, Vita overgrows, and either can bury a kingdom.

Nemophilist

Noun. A wanderer drawn to the enchantment of forests; one who finds solace among trees and deep woods.

THE
Queendoms

SNOWY
NORTH

QUEENDOM
OF THE
CLOUDFALL

QUEENDOM
OF THE
CACTI

QUEENDOM
OF THE
CANYON

DESERT

QUEENDOM
OF THE
CRATER

WILDERNESS

QUEENDOM OF THE RYSTALLINE

THE CRYSTAL SEA

QUEENDOM OF THE COTTONWOOD

QUEENDOM OF THE CURRANT

THE SCARLET WOOD

FOREST FORTRESS

QUEENDOM OF THE CLEARING

QUEENDOM OF THE CRAG

INN

QUEENDOM OF THE COVE

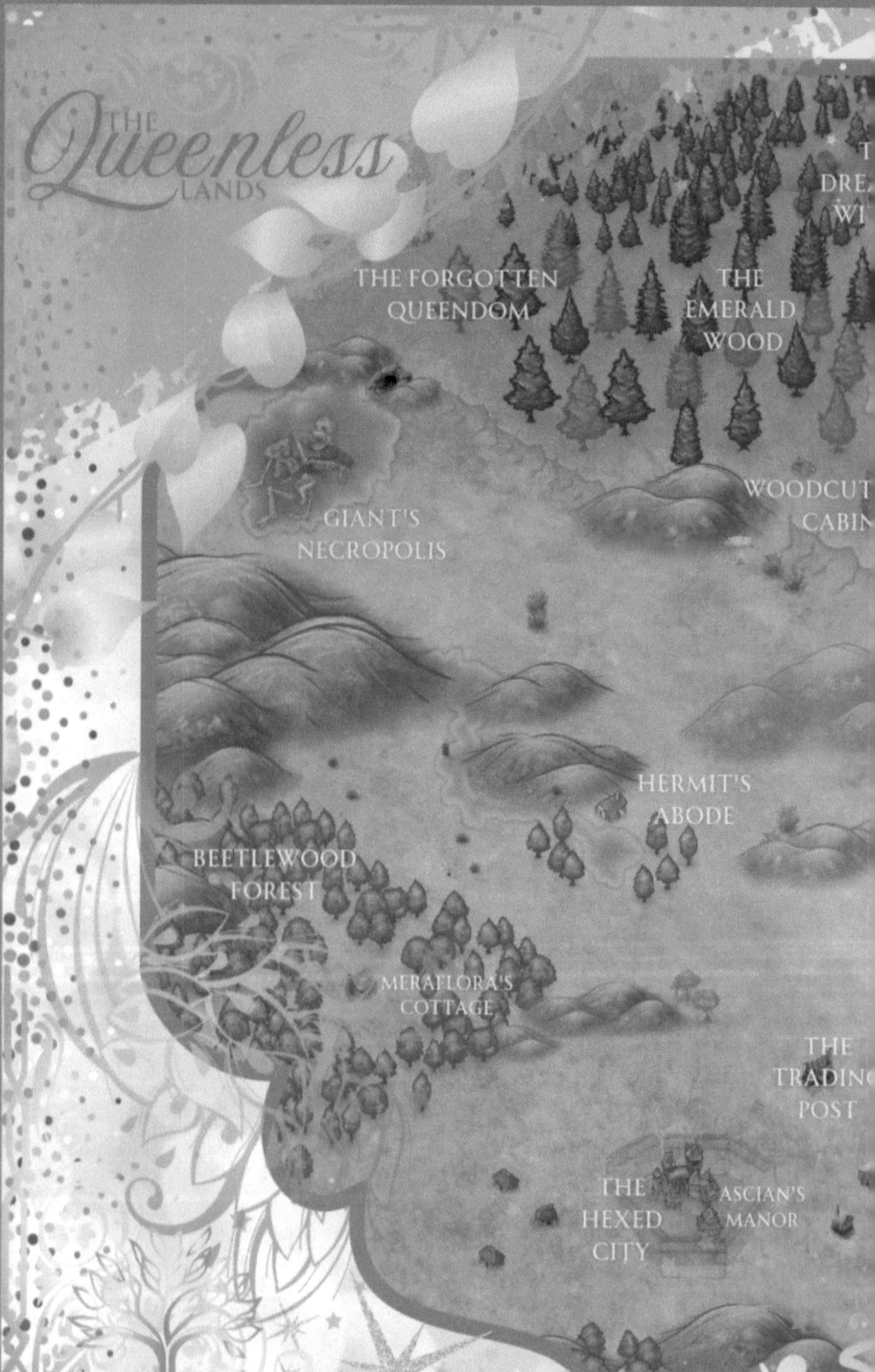
THE Queenless LANDS
THE FORGOTTEN QUEENDOM
THE EMERALD WOOD
WOODCUT CABIN
GIANT'S NECROPOLIS
HERMIT'S ABODE
BEETLEWOOD FOREST
MERAFLORA'S COTTAGE
THE TRADIN POST
THE HEXED CITY
ASCIAN'S MANOR

THE
WILLOW
GROVE

THE GOLDEN
FIELDS

THE
EDGE OF
NOWHERE

THE BLUE
FLOWER
FIELDS

SOUTHERN
SPIRITE
CITIES

CONTENTS

PREVIOUSLY IN A CROWN OF REVERIES...

When I returned to the physical realm, it was as though the world had taken a deep, rejuvenating breath.

A dawn-lit thrum stirred beneath my collarbone —Vita's muted resonance settling where Exitium's shadows once coiled. Life, not ruin, now coursed bright in my veins.

My feet felt lighter, as if brushed by wind. Everything sprang sharper, more vibrant—the gleam jittering across the waves, the weather-bleached driftwood, even the charred crater my fury had gouged into the sand.

Only Windley, Rafe, and a few irritated crabs remained. The others were gone, though their footprints betrayed them: Charmagne and Pip had fled one way, Edius another.

Windley spotted me and lunged across the beach, eyes glassy, face streaked with soot from the darkness I'd unleashed. Before he could speak—before I could fully grasp all that had happened—he swept me into his arms as if he'd never let go.

"Your Majesty."

Windley's embrace went beyond love, beyond gratitude—

deeper, incandescent, a wonder language could never cage. I surrendered to it: the cadence of his heart against my cheek, the living current racing in his veins, the low hymn of creation in the very air. Vita's power was unlike anything I'd known—radiant where Exitium had rasped their cold, ruinous hiss.

When Windley finally released me, he flicked a wary glance toward the crater where Ascian had fallen—his form half-crumbled into ashy remains. I, however, turned to the wavy-haired, amber-eyed magician who looked as though he'd been dragged through hellfire.

"Rafe." I laid a hand on his shoulder. "You made it. I was so worried about you. Thank goddess—not *that* goddess, though. Maybe you'll fill me in later?"

He hesitated, then did something unprecedented: he patted my back with a stiff, awkward motion—like a distant relative mustering the faintest show of affection. For Rafe, it was monumental; for me, unexpectedly tender.

That brief relief died at once.

Behind me, Ascian's body finally collapsed the rest of the way. Windley stumbled across the scorched ground, dropping to his knees near the charred debris. He sifted frantically through the cinders, ignoring the heat as he scooped and scattered handfuls of soot.

"Where is it?" he muttered, voice tattered. "No, no, no..."

His fingers plunged uselessly into the dust again, and a strangled groan escaped him.

"Ascian's ring—it's gone!"

Alarm jolted through me. I hurried over, my bare feet quickly layered in ash. "What do you mean?"

Windley shook his head, frustration blazing in his eyes. "If Charm took it, she'll have access to every hex he ever stole—including that monstrosity inside Pip!"

Ice pricked along my spine. We had toppled one tyrant

only to hand his stolen souls to an even less stable heir: *Charmagne.*

Worse, the echoes were on the loose—slinking across the sand, sniffing for a fresh royal to corrupt. Let them latch onto someone wilder than I'd ever dared, and everything we'd bled for could unravel before dawn.

Unfortunately, they would find *her.*

Although we didn't know it yet, Exitium had already chosen her next victim—a royal as volatile as she was wrathful. A queen beautiful, mercurial, and *magnificently* mad.

With Albie and Beau's whereabouts unknown...

With Edius's true intentions still uncertain...

With magical twins nestled inside Beau's belly...

With an ancient, monstrous creature bound inside Pip...

With Charmagne wielding the might of a hundred hexes...

And with at least three of the four goddesses furious at us—

I, the Great and Mighty Merrin, alongside a flame-wielding magician and a dangerous rogue with a surprisingly tender heart, set out to save the world from destruction's capricious grasp.

Simple enough, right?

I

VITA

T his story would be better if Flora were the one telling it —beautiful, warm, honey-voiced Flora—but alas, captive ones, you're stuck with me, your favorite rantipole queen.

It feels like eons since last we spoke; I've missed you terribly, and I lament knowing we're tumbling toward the end of our journey together—but we won't reach that end today. There's more road ahead, and there's something I should confess now that we've come this far.

Would you believe, this is my second time telling this story? The first time...well, it didn't end so well.

You'll see what I mean. Strap in. It'll go quickly.

With the mess we'd left ourselves in, Windley, Rafe, and I had a difficult choice to make.

In the blackened crater of the beach, Windley gazed silently after Charmagne and Pip's footprints, leading toward a city he had once helped corrupt. His dulled eyes ached with dread for what might come now that Charmagne possessed Ascian's ring—and with it, access to whatever lingering hexes it still contained.

Meanwhile, Rafe had been staring longingly in the opposite direction for some time now: home. More than anything, he yearned to return to his lover queen, who carried two of his children within her womb.

Behind us, the sabotaging sun painted the waves in lusty hues of orange. If Soleil had kept her promise, the echoes would still be trapped safely within my soul, rather than roaming free, searching for another royal foolish enough to let them inside. None of their future hosts would have Beau's guidance, her hushed warnings about the danger lurking beneath their surface.

Without the echoes whispering at the edge of my awareness, my head felt strangely empty. Yet, though my ears were clear, my vessel wasn't vacant. Something new had begun to unfurl within, spreading from my heart to my fingertips with the warmth of a creator's embrace.

"*Are you all right, Merrin? You have been still for quite some time.*"

"I'm...overwhelmed," I murmured to the warm flutter now nesting in my chest—the steady, insistent pulse of Vita herself. "Windley is pulled west, Rafe north, and both of them keep looking to me for a command I no longer know how to give. When I finally admit the echoes are gone..."

"*You fear weakness? Do not. Creation is just as powerful as destruction—it must be, for the world to maintain its balance.*"

"Then show me. I need a way to fight."

"*You have one already, though you cannot wield it as you are now. Your body lacks vitality. No hume possesses an endless well. You must replenish what you have lost before all else.*"

She was right. My body felt hollowed-out, brittle as the crab-less shells scattered at the water's edge, drained by Charmagne, nibbled at by Edius, after a night of feasting from Windley.

But there was hardly time to rest. Not with an all-powerful cupcake on the loose. Not with a goddess of destruction barreling toward the queened lands.

Yet Vita pressed on with soft insistence:

"The beastling made a promise, did he not? To return to the girl in the cottage?"

"You mean Flora?"

"A suitable place to rest. And surely you miss her, too."

Miss Flora? No. I wasn't particularly eager to see her reunited with Windley.

Vita let out a soft sound—something suspiciously like a giggle. *"Humes are curious creatures, aren't they? It is why they're so beloved. Trust my breath inside you; the cottage is the best place for you now, little royal."*

"You're serious, Vita? But what about Exitium? Surely a bodiless deity can reach the north faster than mortal legs can run. Do you truly favor pursuing Charmagne first?"

"I do not care about the beastling."

But Flora's cottage was on the way to the hexed town. Why else would we go there, if not to chase Charmagne?

"It is imperative you seek out the girl in the cottage, for only then will you understand why I have placed my hope in you. Only then will you wield my light."

And with that, the goddess's presence tinkled away like distant chimes.

I stood alone, gazing out at a world that was terrifyingly vast.

And beautiful.

With Vita's life flowing through me, I felt every wave's

gentle push and pull at my back, heard the wind's whispered intentions as it brushed through the trees, sensed each individual grain of sand beneath my feet, shaped and weathered by eons of salt and sea. I felt Rafe's heart yearning for Beau. I felt Windley's heart—tight, guarded, braced fiercely against the world.

Until he turned, and his eyes found mine. Then, I felt it warm, loosen, and race.

"Lion queen?"

"Wind." His name left my lips, and his heart sped faster. "I have something to tell you. I have something to tell both of you."

"Phooo. Damn, lion queen. That's...a lot to take in."

An understatement of unfathomable proportions. Windley scratched absently at his indigo hair.

"So my lore was right? Two halves to the Nemophile's Crown, Exitium really a goddess—*the* goddess who ends things —and Vita's been riding shotgun inside you all along?"

"Since my feet first touched the Emerald Wood," I said, watching his face. "She claims her power equals Exitium's, but she won't let me wield it until I've rebuilt my strength. And she's adamant we go to Flora's cottage."

Windley frowned slightly. "Flora's? Why there? Couldn't you just rest at camp?"

I shrugged, relieved his heartbeat stayed steady at the suggestion.

But someone else's heart was racing, though his face remained as unreadable as stone. Because I hadn't previously told Rafe about Exitium, the truth he absorbed was significantly heavier.

"The echoes will find another royal?" Rafe asked, staring off northward, ancient amber eyes distant.

"Yes. And if Pip truly can decimate entire cavalries at will, he and Charmagne could pose just as great a threat."

Windley folded his arms. "Not just to the south, either. Charm has always harbored a certain loathing for the north. I shudder to think what she'll do now she's untethered." He nodded slowly, gathering resolve with each passing moment as he considered his piece of the puzzle.

"Alright, you two. Charm's my burden. I'll never rest easy until either she or that ring is destroyed. Judging by the tracks, she and Pip went straight back to Ascian's manor."

He gave me one of those lingering looks of his—as though it might very well be his last.

"Merrin—"

"Don't. You know I'm coming with you. It isn't even a question."

A breath hitched—equal parts ease and regret. "You're as ever hopelessly incapable of staying put."

"Multiple birds, one stone," I added. "I still have half the Crown, and it's urging me west too. If Exitium's aim is to end the world, Vita's our best hope of stopping her. I have to follow her guidance—even if that means revisiting Flora."

A grin tugged at his mouth, and relief slid in behind it; the tired dullness in his eyes lifted at last.

But Rafe's heart remained tethered elsewhere.

"I won't order you to come with us, Rafe. Your position is complicated—I understand," I said gently.

Though Rafe's flame would be invaluable against Charmagne, I wasn't the royal he truly sought to protect—not while other evils hunted royal blood elsewhere.

"My vote?" Windley kicked dismissively at the ashes where Ascian had once stood. "Chap should go north."

"So you can steal the queen again?" Rafe retorted dryly.

"Among other reasons." Windley shot me a glance before turning to petition Rafe seriously. "Think practically, mate. The quickest way back to Abardo is by prancelope—but I can't charm one separately for you. You'd only slow us down."

Yet a part of me suspected he was thinking primarily of Rafe's heart.

I pressed further. "Actually, Rafe, it might be best if you warn Beau and Albie of Exitium's arrival. Beau's lineage has long held the echoes at bay—maybe she'll know how to stall Exitium until we reach you. And if you decide to go, you should take this."

I slipped the filigree whistle from my neck and pressed it into his palm. "Give it a single blast when you're close. The widowbird comes to any call—the tune you play only tells it *which* royal to seek. Tie on your message, and it will follow Beau's blood-scent straight to her. You know her melody by now, I'm sure."

Rafe stared down at the whistle resting in his palm. "But this is a royal relic."

"And I'm a royal, entrusting it to you."

Rare indeed, a faint flush climbed Rafe's ochre-brown cheeks. "Thank you, Your Majesty. I'll keep her safe."

"Take this too, chap," Windley tossed over the bag of coin we'd collected from Edius, Flora, and the charmed shopkeep. "Buy yourself a stag from the first farm you pass. You can't expect to chase her on foot."

Rafe seemed unsure how to accept the kindness.

"Besides, best save your stamina for your reunion with the queen—I trust a bounder like you will put it to good use."

"Ugh. Good luck, Your Majesty."

We exchanged muted farewells, parting ways on a shore

painted by sunset's dwindling embers. Afterward, Windley watched pensively as Rafe disappeared into the distance.

I nudged him. "Who knew you were secretly so kind-hearted, sacrificing a sun's worth of power for the sake of its vessel?"

"Just an act, mostly. Did it work? Are your defenses lowered?" Windley's smile sharpened, one wicked fang catching the light. "Let's hope Lady Life's claims about her power hold up, lest I end up protecting you again."

"'Again' implies you ever protected me to begin with," I teased.

"I must have, at least once." He tapped his chin. "Between all that drinking and canoodling?"

"Protecting me from yourself doesn't count."

"Oh. Then no."

I met his smirk with my own, though softer. "In any case, whatever Vita's power is, I can already feel it moving inside me...like amplifying the earth's pulse."

"Pulse of the earth? If you say so, tree whisperer." He tossed a playful wink my way. "You can explain that poetic nonsense once we're away from this cursed place. Let's see if Dandelion's still around, shall we?" With that, he started whistling cheerfully, patting his thigh as though calling a dog.

If he harbored any worry, he hid it well.

Turning my back, I stared into the shimmering sea, vulnerability creeping in now that our magician was gone.

A hush blossomed behind my ribs—Vita's voice, warm as summer loam:

"This weight isn't yours to carry alone. I teased the first leaf from the soil—surrender now, and know peace; the dark will not devour you again."

Relinquishing control had never come easily.

However long I'd gazed toward the fading horizon, it had

been enough time for Windley to charm a prancelope—though whether this was the original "Dandelion," I couldn't say. The beast clung to his side lovingly, much like every creature he bewitched.

"I'm okay."

"That's not what I asked," he pressed with added warmth. "You're crying. Why?"

"To be honest, I don't know whether it's sorrow or joy."

"Maybe strain, then." Windley enfolded me in his arms. "Your spirit's weak, love. Just how much did Charmagne steal? That gannet. Come—I'll hold you steady while you rest."

Windley helped me onto the lovesick prancelope, then settled close behind, exuding a quiet devotion as we rode away from the lonely beach, both of us exhausted and filthy.

Unlike before, I no longer had fallen echoes to draw upon for energy. The journey from coast to cottage became a blur: flat fields giving way to rolling hills, night dissolving into day, our bodies pressing onward through autumn's chilled breath. We traveled beneath a moon that scorned us and a sun that had turned away. Whatever Vita's power might be, I hoped fervently it would restore what I had lost.

Enough to stop a goddess of destruction.

Enough to defeat a hundred latent hexes.

Enough to keep pushing forward.

"Trust me, Merrin."

But faith was rarely simple. And while this path promised its own set of hardships, I would soon discover the greatest challenges often rose from within.

As I said, Windley and I were exhausted and filthy.

Which is likely why we never noticed we were being followed.

And the one following would soon cause my heart greater pain than I had ever known.

2

THE SECOND TIME

"You awake, lion queen?" murmured lips blazing against my ear. "We're nearly there."

I stirred just as Windley's heart did. The ride had flown by, thanks largely to how snugly he'd held me, fencing off the chill the whole way.

"A promotion may be in your future," I teased, voice a near whisper. "You make for an excellent backrest."

He hauled me tighter. "Surely you can find more enjoyable uses for me."

Surely I could.

"Thanks for letting me rest, my knave. I know you needed it, too."

"Naturally. It's the most uninhibited access I've had to your neck all journey."

"Sniffer."

He chuckled. "Glad to see you're feeling lively." A cool palm settled against my forehead. "Feels like your spirit's replenishing...slowly."

He was right. Only now, with a surge of vitality, did I fully realize how perilously thin my life force had been back on that beach.

Vita's concerns were more than warranted.

"You can rest more once we reach Flora's," Windley said, his voice low. "It's just down the way."

I recognized it immediately. But as we rode up her walkway this time, my emotions were no longer clouded by something dark and slithery. I saw it in an entirely new light.

Tucked away in a wooded alcove branching from a busier road and wrapped lovingly in roses, Flora's cottage was precisely the sort of place songbirds might choose to court. Ivy climbed the trees along the path, hosting beetles that shimmered like tiny gems, flickering vividly as they darted among emerald leaves. Only the sharpest winds penetrated the barricade of trunks and thistle, rustling chimes and glass bottles delicately strung along her porch.

Flora was a tinkerer at heart; half-woven baskets baked in the sun through the canopy's opening overhead, while bundles of drying flowers dotted the charming yard.

It was a place for painters to paint, for writers to write.

For lovers to love.

A fetching woman in a cozy white sweater was drawing water from a moss-stained well when we approached. I braced myself, prepared to be gracious as her eyes filled with unmistakable delight upon seeing Windley, and as he flashed her a grin typically reserved only for me.

A perfect maiden in a perfect setting, who most certainly harbored feelings for Windley—even though he never seemed to notice.

Whatever jealousy brewed within me, Vita quickly detected it.

"Wait, Merrin. Look at her with your heart unsoiled. You should begin to feel it."

I didn't grasp Vita's warning—until a bright, startling warmth flared beneath my ribs and the world seemed to cant ever so slightly.

As Windley swung me down from the prancelope and stepped forward to greet our host, that warmth blossomed into something startlingly tender. The longer I watched him trade quick, easy words with the barefoot maiden in the grass, the more a wholly new affection took root—growing, spreading, until it filled my chest:

Love.

But it wasn't love for Windley.

It was love for *Flora*.

In fact, it was a love so compelling, I couldn't stop myself from rushing forward through the grass, shoving Windley aside, and pulling the startled girl—who looked uncannily like me—into an embrace.

Much to her bewilderment. "O-oh! Queen Merrin! It's so nice to see you again!"

And much to Windley's confusion. "Merr?"

There was no denying it—I loved Flora. The feeling struck as clean and luminous as first morning light, yet it bore no resemblance to the devotion I carried for Windley, Albie, or even Beau. This was different: a love that wanted nothing but her safety and happiness, that ached to shepherd her toward every gentle thing the world could offer. It wasn't romantic, nor sisterly; it thrummed with a fierce, protective instinct that felt almost...maternal.

While Flora graciously endured my sudden embrace, Windley darted in circles around us, certain I'd been bewitched.

Forcing myself away from the confused girl, spitting strands of her silky hair from my lips, I turned sharply and called out to the one responsible—

"Vita! What was *that*?"

"*A creator's love. Is it not grand?*"

Not the word I would've chosen.

Windley rested a cautious hand on my shoulder. "Merr?"

"I—I can't explain it," I hissed, clutching Windley's sleeve. "I love her."

He blinked. "Pardon?"

"Not like that," I rushed on. "It's...protective. I'd step in front of a blade for her without thinking."

"Oh. Of course." He cleared his throat—then: "*WHAT*?"

I couldn't resist glancing over my shoulder to ensure she was still okay. "Meraflora, you're well, aren't you? Healthy? Content? Is there anything at all you need? I'd love for you to ask me. Anytime. I'll always be waiting."

I pawed affectionately in her direction until Windley swiftly forced my hand down.

"Give us a moment, would you, Flora darling? It seems the queen is experiencing something...Nemophile-related."

"Certainly! I'll prepare some tea!" The darling girl looked all too relieved to retreat at once into her cottage.

"I'm so proud of her," I gushed dreamily to Windley. "Aren't you? Such a sweet, gentle, loving soul. Such goodness in her! Though I wish she'd find herself a mate soon. Do you know anyone suitable?"

"What in goddess's green earth has gotten into you? Last time we were here, you practically despised her!" Windley shook me with careful restraint by the shoulders, but I was too busy admiring the charming little home Flora had crafted for herself.

In my ear, Vita released a tinkling laugh.

"*I suppose it must seem unusual for a hume. There is nothing so potent as a creator's love—and you're the very first to feel it.*"

Fighting the instinctual urge to run after the wholesome girl, I gave Windley an apologetic laugh and quickly said, "One moment," before closing my eyes and stepping into Vita's light.

"What's going on?"

"I dearly wished to tell you during our previous visit. I felt your sorrow over her appearance, though the irony wasn't lost on me. After all, she was created in your image."

And with that, I disappeared from Flora's lawn.

What Windley's face must have looked like. Yelling my name through clenched teeth, frantically searching the soil where I'd just stood. Surely, he thought it was my doing. Surely, he was cursing me for disappearing without a trace. And surely, Flora watched worriedly from her window as he clawed uselessly at the empty ground.

This was mere speculation, though. When I vanished from Flora's lawn, Vita whisked me somewhere beyond the earthly realm.

It was a shimmering place that smelled like spring.

"Where are we?" I marveled, feeling vernal, floral, safe.

"Your soul. It is better now, is it not? Now that the dark is gone?"

My soul?

Indeed. The place felt peaceful—a far cry from the shadowed ravine where I'd last found myself under Exitium's sway.

"Do you like stories, Merrin?" Vita's voice reverberated around me like silver chimes rippling through mist.

I scoffed, studying my hands through the wispy air. "So long as it doesn't involve an otter and a crane."

"Good. It will help if you think of your life as a story. Or rather, as a series of stories."

That was easy enough. Life was nothing if not one long, imperfect story. Flawed characters, uneven pacing—each change of heart or circumstance birthing a fresh chapter.

Vita continued, *"Many stories have been written of this life, each replacing the last."*

I stopped marveling. "Are you saying time repeats?"

"That is one way to think of it."

She tried explaining other ways I might see it—one involving a shape neither line nor loop—but none were as simple as time repeating.

"In order to ensure the right conclusion to this story, you must first know how the last one ended."

A heavy book fell into my lap, opening midway.

It seemed to be about me, for therein lay my image.

Yet it was a different version of me.

My hair was slicked back in a royal bun, I wore a tight corset and gown, and in my hand rested a curl of shadow as I gazed boredly from the window of the treetop fortress.

I would never dress so formally within the forest fort.

"This is real?" I asked. "This is how I looked in another iteration of time?"

"No two stories are exactly the same."

The page flipped, revealing another scene:

Rafe entered the room alongside a guard I had never seen before—one who wore the colors of Beau's court. The unknown guard handed me a scroll. I read it.

The darkness in my palm grew.

The page turned again.

I was racing across fields atop a stag that wasn't Ruckus, alongside Rafe, Albie...and Saxon?

Following Beau's cavalry through the Emerald Wood, toward the base of Giant's Necropolis.

This was a story I knew.

It was a retelling of the day I'd gone to rescue Beau from the southern mountain.

Only, in this version, Saxon was with us. I already possessed the echoes...

And Windley was nowhere to be seen.

Another page flipped, and now I was in Luna's palm while the cavalry battled her spectral warriors—the moonbeams—below.

This was the part where she demanded Rafe's heart in exchange for Beau's freedom.

But where I'd expected to see myself blasting her away, the storybook version showed me bowing instead, gazing helplessly downward—

To where Rafe lay clutching his chest.

Afterward, the moonbeams shrank into the earth, and Beau appeared, washed upon shores surrounding the lake of bones.

Beau was saved.

The mountain remained intact.

And Windley was still absent.

Pages flipped rapidly, landing on an image of Beau in the treetop fortress, cradling a beautiful child with eyes like hers and skin like Rafe's.

And she was sobbing.

Great, silken moondrop tears.

Windley's favorite chair had been replaced by a rocker.

"What is this, Vita? Why didn't I destroy Luna's body? Why is Beau crying?"

"She weeps, for despair has consumed her, having birthed the child of a conjurer who no longer possesses the heart to love."

"You mean literally?" I questioned sharply. "Rafe lost his heart?"

"It was bartered away."

"By...me? I gave Rafe's heart to Luna? Why would I ever do that?"

"Because you did not understand what was truly at stake."

The book fluttered toward its end, displaying an older Beau seated alone at her desk, sealing a document with a black clover —a symbol of war.

Then the second-to-last page.

Beau's cavalry at the threshold of my queendom, launching flaming arrows into the market, while I stood at the palace windows overlooking the city, draped in a gown of blood-red, shadows filling every corner.

A wave of darkness rippled across the Crag and the Clearing, destroying stone and flesh alike, blanketing the queened lands in wrathful shadow—

Before spreading to devour the entire world.

The book slammed shut, quivering in my hands. A hollow ache swelled in my chest, and I struggled to breathe through it.

"That's the end?"

"That was the way your last story ended. When the neighboring royal discovered you were responsible for the loss of the conjurer's heart, she laid siege upon your nation to reclaim the dark half of the Wood's Crown. You unleashed the destroyer's power in defense of your sovereignty, but it consumed you. The darkness overtook everything. The world fell."

My pulse slammed against my ribs. Surely I hadn't—

I dug my nails into the leather, resisting the urge to hurl the cursed book, yet the images seared themselves behind my eyes: marketplaces flattened, queendoms throttled in shadow, everything I loved drowning beneath the fury I'd unleashed.

Ascian wasn't even there. Windley wasn't, either—no midnight abduction, no reckless laughter in the woods, no hushed confession of his heart. With nothing to check the dark, it simply swept in, and I alone gave it shape.

"But time is fluid, as I am fluid. In the darkness, you called out to me, begging we undo what was written. You surrendered all the Crown's power so we might create a being to rewrite your story."

"A being?"

Another book fell into my lap atop the first. It blew open, revealing a smoother, gentler version of me.

No, not me. "Flora. But why Flora?"

The pages turned backward to show a boy. A Spirite boy, hugging his knees in a dark cell behind a hidden door. My hand shot to my mouth. It was worse than I'd ever imagined—the despair in his eyes, the bruises on his back.

I brushed my fingers across his image. "Windley."

I never wanted to see him like that.

"When you gave the conjurer's heart to the moon goddess, you did so because you didn't know love. We created this girl so the next time you faced Luna, you wouldn't repeat the mistake. This was the page you hoped to rewrite."

"We created Flora...to free Windley?"

"There were many you might have loved, but none so desperate as this beastling's soul. It called to you from the void. We created the girl to release him from his shackles, so he could find his way into your story."

Because knowing love meant I wouldn't squander another's heart. A rewarded effort. Windley had been vital in my decision to defy Luna, and it was only through Flora's existence that he had reached the north at all.

"When your story began anew, the destroyer noticed the shift and waited to seed you until certain she'd find a new outlet for your rage. But you withstood, for your heart is stronger now, as I knew it would be. A thousand stories have ended in ruin. Together, we'll stop this cycle. You will wield the Crown as intended. You will exile the

destroyer to the end of days. In you, I place my hope, little royal."

An of-the-people, for-the-people type. Or so I tried. But I was quickly realizing how one misstep could alter everything. How could I be certain each choice was correct? That I'd craft my story to a happy end?

Not to mention, saving the world was no small feat.

Much greater than saving one friend.

Much larger than ruling a queendom.

Far beyond anything I'd ever done.

"Have faith, Merrin. My power is great. Once your vitality is restored, you'll feel it. Rest now. I'll soften your creator's love so it doesn't consume you. You needed to experience it fully to embrace my light. Now, you'll have the strength you desire."

Vita offered nothing more, fading away as I returned to the physical realm, feet rooted in Flora's soil, my destined one frantically patting my cheeks.

I opened my eyes to his, blurred with concern. "Wind... ley?"

"Finally! Where the hell did you disappear to? And why are you suddenly infatuated with Flora? Is it Lady Life? Thinks you could do better than a *beastling*, does she? Seeded you with new affections, has she? I've about had it with these damned goddesses."

He was wrong, of course—but before anything else, I had to know—

"Windley, what does 'wyrdbound one' mean?"

His ears twitched. "Where did you hear that term?"

A boy with a beast in his belly.

If you're really his wyrdbound one, he'll come for you.

I said nothing, only held his gaze—regal and *predatory* as ever.

He hesitated, rubbing a hand along his jaw. "It's just a fairytale. A southern one."

"Tell me."

"In stories, they're the ones who change fate. When a tale's bound for ruin, the wyrdbound one steps in and turns the tide." His voice softened. "For Spirites, it's...something else."

"How so?"

His throat worked around an answer. "I've mentioned Spirites love only once—truly. Some believe that 'once' is predestined." His fingers flexed restlessly. "Not that it matters. They aren't real. Just a way for storytellers to explain things that make no sense."

I traced my thumb along his jaw, watching an ember dance in his eyes.

It mattered.

Then, without another word, I took his face between my palms and kissed him deeper than I ever had before.

In that breath I tasted destiny—sharp as winter air, sweet as stolen wine—and knew there was no turning back.

3

MOVING BLOOD

"The shape of time? Draw it for me." Windley handed me a pointed stick and motioned toward the ground.

"I literally cannot." I pushed his hand down. "And that's your biggest takeaway?"

"Of course not. It's just the easiest place to start. I'm still struggling with the rest. Like how you and Queen Beau could ever become enemies. That seems far-fetched."

More far-fetched than me using the Nemophile's power to create a person?

"It's true we've long been friends, but...over these last eight years, you've been involved in nearly all our merriment and mischief. You've always given me space to be myself. Maybe I'm a completely different person because of you. I mean, you should have seen me in those pages—I was *kempt*. And Albie looked at least ten years younger."

Windley fell silent, harboring something thick and unspoken in his throat.

"Wind?"

"If it's true," he said at last, staring at me harder than ever before, "then I have you to thank for pulling me away from Ascian's clutches." He paused a long while before adding, "I owe you my life, Merr."

On the steps of Flora's porch, Windley and I took each other in as though there were secrets waiting to be found, as if a nose might somehow mean more than a nose.

"Are we really that ingrained in one another?" I whispered.

Had I truly created Flora as someone to nurture Windley, to set him free? And was Windley truly the catalyst that had prevented me from succumbing to a path of ruin?

Truly—I wouldn't have been able to keep from loving him even if I'd tried.

Vita's revelation lodged between us like a river-stone—cool, unyielding, impossible to ignore. Windley's gaze swept over me, eyes distant, as if weighing a world where I'd never existed; I did the same to him, drawing in the smoke-and-salt of his skin with new, uneasy hunger.

As he swept a knuckle along my cheek, the curtain at Flora's window fluttered, her tea surely cold by now.

Embarrassment spiked at the thought of what else she'd seen—me suddenly reappearing on her lawn and mauling Windley like some rabid creature, and him desperately trying to contain my frenzy to avoid revealing our location to Charmagne.

I loved him terribly.

"We should go inside," I murmured. "Flora's watching."

"Or we could simply stare at each other until nightfall," he offered with a casual shrug.

"You'd get bored. Notice imperfections. Is one of my ears lower than the other?"

He feigned a dramatic gasp. "Is one?"

I swatted at him lightly before reaching for the door, hesitating briefly. "Do you think she saw me maul you?"

"Unquestionably."

"I assure you, I'm normally not so unbalanced," I told Flora over lukewarm tea, grateful that my motherly impulses had finally ebbed. "Perhaps I can visit again when I'm in my right mind."

"If I'm honest, I can't quite picture Windalloy with someone...perfectly steady," Flora admitted, cheeks flushing. "I swear I don't mean that as an insult, Your Majesty."

Windley tapped his chin, giving me a sidelong look. "Wholeheartedly agree."

"None taken," I said.

I was quick to accept Flora's hospitality—food, a bath, a bed. This time I slipped away before Windley; my first duty was to rebuild my strength and feel the edges of Vita's gift. And Windley was...

Well, he was something of a distraction, wasn't he?

It was evening when I woke again, alone.

The bedroom window was cracked open, letting in the fresh coolness of night and the hushed chorus of insects that came with it.

I found Flora in the living room, by the fireplace, grinding dried petals with a pestle and mortar—one of the loveliest sounds.

"Your Majesty!" She quickly set the bowl down and rose to her feet. "Do you need something?"

"No, I'm quite rested now. Thank you. What are you making?"

"Dye," she answered. "For thread."

"If you have any left over, mix it with vera. It's excellent for the skin."

"Oh! I—I shall. I suppose you're looking for Windalloy? He's out back, feeding your prancelope."

But when I didn't move right away, she tilted her head curiously. "Queen Merrin?"

"You've done well, Flora. Thank you for tending him in that dark place—and for turning the key when no one else would. Whatever it cost you, you have my deepest gratitude."

Flora's cheeks pinked. "So he told you."

Then, with disarming candor, she said, "I suppose you could say I helped loose a killer and suffered nothing for it. But Windalloy was a lantern in my own night. Opening that door—letting him end what I couldn't—was the brightest thing I've ever done. I'm grateful every day that our paths crossed."

Kind. Warm. I cupped her jaw, pressed a kiss to her cheek, and let my thumb linger there—an unspoken vow—before slipping outside to find Windley.

With my vitality restored, the clearing was unrecognizable. Dusk glazed the world in deep blue, and the grass—cool, slick—seemed to breathe beneath my bare soles, every blade stretching toward the sky. Night itself thrummed, a living current skittering under my skin. I halted, shivering.

"You'll grow used to it, Merrin," Vita promised.

I stole quietly around the cottage's side, past the walls of roses and thorn, feeling the veins inside the petals pulsing, roots beneath the dirt stretching eagerly.

I cupped one of the blooms, surprised to find it hotter than it should be, nestled delicately between my palms.

But I was swiftly distracted by the radiant heat of another body standing inside the stag pen, feeding an apple to a spotted beast, who appeared absolutely delighted by his attentions.

"Merrin!" Windley turned, the apple falling forgotten to

his feet, and left the prancelope gazing longingly after him. "How are you feeling?"

"Better," I replied.

"Good—you're humming again." He drew his hand from my forehead, shoulders loosening. "Thank the stars. Never letting you run that low again—curse Charm for even trying... What? Why are you staring?"

Because each steady beat seemed to ripple through the air and straight into me.

He guessed wrongly. "Look, I think we should just carry on as though nothing's changed. Whatever Lady Life told you, this is the only version of time either of us knows. We're still the same people. You don't have to look at me like...however it is you're looking at me."

Far off base.

Yes, it was remarkable, what Vita had revealed.

Yes, it was unfathomable to think we'd rewritten time to be together, and that I'd lived at least one life without him.

But right now, all of that came second to—

"Windley, can I touch you?"

A confusing question, yet the corner of his mouth lifted playfully.

"Now, you don't ever need to ask something like that."

"I mean, like I did before...in the bed?"

"You want me to remove my shirt?" He searched my face for a motive. "Not that I'm disappointed, but behind darling Flora's cottage, at the fall of night? A bit scandalous for you. Does this have something to do with your new powers?"

Yes, and the rhythm beneath his skin mirrored the hum beneath my feet.

Beating. Throbbing. Pulsing.

I placed my hand softly at his throat. "You feel good, Windley. I sense your heartbeat, your rushing blood, the life coursing through you...I'd like to feel it closer."

I felt his throat move beneath my grip.

"*Ffffuck*, lion queen. Aren't we trying to avoid draining you?"

I released him quickly. "Sorry. It's Vita's power, making everything feel throbby. She said I'd get used to it, but..." My eyes drifted hungrily over him—the loose top button of his shirt, the swell of energy beneath it.

He gazed at me, amusement and confusion mixing enticingly with desire—

"Come here." He drew me to the cottage wall, just out of sight of the windows, and guided my hand to the hem of his shirt.

"Go on, then."

"What?"

He dipped to my ear, voice a low rasp that skimmed along my skin. "If you want this off—take it, lioness."

Straightening, he set one hand on his hip and waited, brows lifting in dare-bright amusement. Deliberately, I slid my palms up his flanks, the fabric peeling away beneath my fingers, baring the heat of his body inch by glorious inch.

Lean. Firm. Delectable.

And many other savory descriptors tempting me to dig my lion claws straight into him.

His skin prickled at the chill of night, at the brush of my fingertips. All the while, I felt his life force swimming beneath my touch, speeding faster the higher my fingers climbed.

When the fabric reached his chest, he took over—peeling the shirt the rest of the way off—then simply watched, curiosity glinting in his eyes, as I pressed my palm to the steady thrum of his heart.

I traced the veins of his arms, slid my fingertips hot along his muscle, rode the air as it lifted through lungs and throat, then down the simmering ridges of his abdomen.

"Whoa! Y-you sure about that, queenie?"

Distracted by the flow of his blood, my hands had wandered to the button of his trousers.

Embarrassed, I spun away from him, suddenly mousy over my boldness.

But he seized my hips, pulling me back against him, settling his chin upon my shoulder.

"No need to skitter, love. I only stopped you because my instincts were starting to act up." His breath trembled deliciously as his hands slid up and back down my waist. "While I would very much like to steal you away into these dark woods, my job right now is to protect you—not prey upon you."

Rousing.

I turned slightly, pressing my cheek to his. "Where would you take me? Somewhere comfortable, I hope."

"Shh. Don't indulge them."

"Who?"

"The instincts."

For once, it was my mouth's corner that twitched with mischief.

"Little minx." He backed off in a smooth, disciplined motion. "How about you stop toying with me and tell me what it feels like—this pulsing-of-the-earth business—while I valiantly *fight my very nature* and redress myself?"

Indeed, he appeared deeply at odds with himself as he frowned thoughtfully at the shirt in his hand.

I drew a long breath, fully savoring the hum of creation around us.

"It feels like the ground has a heartbeat and the trees have lungs," I told him wondrously. "The world seems like the belly of a great beast that's swallowed us whole, and I can sense life inside everything. Strange, isn't it, how we're all given a starting breath and then we simply run on it? Like we're enchanted. Is life really just self-sustained magic?"

Windley fiddled distractedly with his sleeves, rolling them halfway up his forearms.

"Well, I can tell you this: life becomes something tangible when you pull it from another person, much like magic..." He stopped abruptly. "You're doing it again."

He meant looking at him like I wanted to split him wide open.

"The beat of your heart is like watching the Emerald Wood awaken at night," I murmured.

"I see," he replied quietly, giving up on his sleeves and gently capturing my hand.

"Does anything happen to my pulse when I do this?"

He pressed his mouth soft and hot to my wrist.

"It...does."

"And this?"

He tugged me closer by the hand and placed a lingering kiss on the sensitive hollow inside my elbow.

"Yes," I breathed, feeling the wave surge powerfully through his chest.

He released me, pleased.

"And to think you once worried I lacked a heart."

"It's a different sort of heart, though, isn't it? I felt Rafe's beating back on the beach. His was bigger, warmer. Yours comes alive, but when it's dormant, it's..."

"Like the pit of a cherry," he mused.

"Like the pit of a plum," I corrected prudently.

"Hmph. I prefer cherries." He tilted his head back, drinking in the night's first scattering of stars. "Yes, mine differs from yours or Rafe's. Humans tend to keep theirs in constant motion, snowballs rolling downhill—easier to pick up debris that way. My kind keep ours hardened when not in use. Less easily damaged."

He caught the way I looked at him and sighed.

"No, that doesn't mean I stop loving you when I'm away from you, if that's what you're thinking."

Precisely what I'd been thinking.

He set both hands firmly on my shoulders.

"No, your scent clings to my senses long after we've parted —enough to drive a person mad." His gaze settled smoldering on my lips. "When my heart hardens, it does so with you tucked safely inside, my queen."

The blue of evening blanketed us.

The chill of oncoming night breathed gently through the clearing.

And as Windley leaned forward to claim my mouth once again, I realized—

His wasn't the only heart I could feel vibrating through the trees.

4

FRESH WOUNDS

"Merr?"

Windley saw me stiffen, our faces mere inches apart.

"Is Flora expecting a visitor?" I asked.

"Definitely not." He swiftly pushed me behind him, scanning the darkened treeline. "You hear someone?"

"I *sense* them. Where are your hatchets?"

"Inside. Shit. Nobody should know about this place—the only reason I did is because she mentioned it when we were young. Run inside the house, queenie. I'll see what they want."

"It is a beastling, Merrin," whispered Vita.

"Vita says it's a Spirite."

"All the more reason for you to *run along now*." Windley nudged urgently at my shoulders.

But I scarcely heard him, already dipped inside Vita's light.

"Can you see who it is? It isn't Charmagne, is it? Windley shouldn't face her alone. Please, tell me what to do!"

"You have the power to give and take life, Merrin."

"How?"

"Your intentions. Before, you wielded them to destroy. Now, use them to nurture life. Bid the earth to grow or wither, and it will obey."

Well, if that wasn't clear as dirt.

"Dirt. Yes," Vita replied calmly, reading my thoughts. *"I formed you from dirt, and through dirt I shall deliver you. Place your hand upon the soil and speak your intent."*

But that was hardly enough to go on, and I still doubted whispering my intentions at dirt would ever rival destroying mountains with a single word.

"Creation answers destruction in equal measure. The earth already knows the song—your will is the conductor. Set your hand to the soil, trust the pulse inside you, and let it answer. Nothing moves if you don't believe it can."

I thought back to when I felled the blood stags—how I'd first used the echoes. Then further back, to when I'd wielded the Crown to thaw Rafe's frozen heart.

I hadn't done either because I knew they'd work.

I'd done them because I believed they would.

I dropped to the dirt at Windley's boots. "Intentions," I whispered, pressing my palm to the cracked autumn earth.

"Alright, lion queen—work your wild. I'll keep whatever it is off your back."

The trespasser hovered just inside the trees. I slowed my pulse until it matched the ground's hidden beat—

Glow. A clean, emerald flare spread beneath my hand.

"That light—just like the Emerald Wood!" Windley breathed.

I poured will into the soil. The earth answered with a quiet shiver, then whoomed upward: blades of grass speared sky-high, weaving together into a living wall that dwarfed the treeline.

For one glorious heartbeat it felt powerful—dangerous.

Then the stranger simply shoved the stalks aside and stepped through as though parting laundry on a line.

"Grand trick, highness," the figure drawled, brushing burrs from his cuffs. "Should I applaud, or tremble?"

The spell had been spectacularly pointless.

"We will work on it," Vita assured, cool as dew.

Windley bared a fang. *"You!"*

I eased around his shoulder. "Edius?"

Indeed, it was the brawny, sphinx-eyed lackey whose heart thumped small and cold, like Windley's when he shuttered it. He slapped seeds off a slate-gray travel jacket, half his dark hair knotted back, the rest spilling loose against his neck—a style northern women favored, but our men almost never wore.

"Heya, Merrín."

"Goddess damn it!" Windley spat bitterly. "Now Flora will have to move!"

"Move?" I questioned.

Windley scowled deeper than ever. "Charm got a taste of her when we were young—she'd rather the coven not know where she lives."

"Easy, Windalloy. I'm not planning on telling Charm a goddess-damned thing. No need to get bent."

"Excuse me, *bent*?" Windley repeated through a brittle smile.

But I remembered how Edius had left my mouth uncovered during the fight with Ascian.

I gently guided down Windley's arm, which sought to separate us.

"What are you doing here, Edius?"

"Came for you, highness."

Windley bristled instantly, surging forward as though his mere presence could erase me from Edius's view.

"Relax," Edius amended. "I don't mean came for her like that. I came to make a deal with her."

Windley turned up his palm sarcastically. "My advice? Say exactly what you mean the first time. It could make the difference between keeping or losing a limb. Not that it matters—we're not interested."

But he groaned when—

"What sort of deal?" I popped out from behind him again.

Edius glanced at Windley, then back at me. "I'd rather discuss it privately—just the two of us."

"Oh, I'm *sure* you *would*." Windley crossed his arms firmly, all hot arrogance. "Absolutely not."

"Fine." Edius released a long, gravel-rough exhale. "I want your help freeing someone Ascian hexed."

"Nice try," Windley scoffed. "Even if it were like Ascian to cast his own hexes, any curse he laid would've fallen when he did."

"Oh, right, because you know exactly who he hexed and didn't hex while you were off playing knight?" Edius shot back. "And no, this particular one didn't drop because Ascian never kept it on himself. He stowed it inside that ring, which means Charm has it now. Which is...a gods-damned nightmare. I figured if anyone can get her to release it, it's the Nemophilist."

"Who?" challenged Windley.

Edius blinked. "Huh?"

Windley flexed his fingers, instinctively reaching for absent hatchets. "Who," he growled, "did Ascian hex?"

Edius flicked his gaze between us. "Oh. My...fiancée."

"Bullshit," said Windley immediately. "What would be the point in hexing another Spirite?"

"Did I say she was Spirite?" He looked at me again pointedly. "She's human, like this one."

"I highly doubt that."

"Why?" Edius shrugged. "You're with a human. The south's gotten more progressive these past few years, Windalloy. You'd know that if you hadn't run away."

Windley bared his canines in a fierce glower, while Edius openly displayed his own with smug satisfaction.

"What about you, Edius?" I asked. "Does Charm still have access to your hexes as well?"

"Gods no. I dropped them the moment Ascian fell. Ask your boyfriend if you don't believe me."

"Windley?"

Windley rolled his eyes dramatically. "So what if I don't smell any hexes on him? All it means is he's freed up to hex someone else—like, oh, I don't know, *you*, lion queen."

"Sure, if I felt like being turned into ash," Edius retorted.

Because he didn't know I'd lost the echoes and that my current power was limited to growing vegetation.

I studied him closely, searching for any tell of deceit.

"It's true we intend to pursue Charmagne before returning north," I said slowly, "but surely you understand our hesitation in assisting you, Edius."

"Because of the whole kidnapping thing, huh?" he muttered.

"The kidnapping, the forest ambush, holding me hostage while Charmagne nearly drained my life away..."

"Buuut," he interjected, "I did pack all that stuff for you."

"Which you promptly tried to take back."

"And when Ascian showed up, I intentionally left your mouth free so you could invoke your witchcraft or whatever."

That much was true.

Maybe releasing you helps me, maybe it gets me whipped. Either way, it's leverage.

He had said that too, after urging us to go north to avoid Ascian.

This was what he meant by leverage.

"A word, lion queen?" Windley pulled me aside, gripping my elbow. "You aren't actually considering this, are you?"

"It's not the first time he's mentioned needing me to save someone."

Ever wonder why I might run errands for Ascian?

Maybe he's got someone I care about in chains...

Maybe I don't have a choice.

And then there was—

We could've skipped all this mess... Freed her and left these idiots behind...

"A lie repeated is still a lie, Majesty," Windley warned. "I don't blame you for wanting to believe him. My kind excels at deception, and your heart is the sort that tries to embrace everyone you meet."

"Then let's take emotion out of it," I said. "If you're truly worried about him telling Charmagne or others about Flora's cottage, wouldn't it be safer to keep him close until we're sure he isn't a threat?"

Windley shrugged darkly. "Or we could gut him right here and spare ourselves the trouble."

But he knew me better than that.

"Ugh. I know, I know," he dragged a weary hand down his face, "and yes, that reasoning of yours does hold some irritating logic."

Edius must have sensed our softening.

"Look, Merrín." His voice carried from the shadowed yard. "You're my last shot. The last plan blew apart. The one Ascian hexed is someone I'd trade my freedom for—that's why I ran with those bastards this long. I can fight, I know the south, and I know Charm. If you're hunting her anyway, let me tag along... as your bodyguard."

"Ha!" Windley loosed a dark, incredulous chuckle. "A

bodyguard? For her?" He shook his head, canines glinting. "Precious."

Edius raised his palms placatingly. "Take it or leave it, hon. But it's all I've got."

Windley's amusement vanished instantly. "That's *Highness* to you, berk."

I caught his gaze mid territorial standoff—prompting him to tilt his head skyward, silently petitioning divine patience, before exhaling in defeat.

"Very well, Edius," I decided, "but at the faintest hint of foul play, I won't hesitate to unleash the full fury of the unseen world upon you—that is, if Windley doesn't gut you first."

Edius gave a low whistle. "Scary. Not him. You."

We'd let him believe I could still turn my enemies to dust.

Windley glanced toward the cottage. "I can't guarantee Flora will allow him inside."

"I can sleep out here on the ground," Edius offered.

Windley met my eyes again, pinched the bridge of his nose, then let out a second, heavier sigh.

"Fine. Come along, you berk."

Edius trailed after us to the porch like a stray pup.

"Go in and explain things to Flora," I told Windley. "I'll wait out here with him."

Windley arched an eyebrow. "And leave you with a green thumb as your only defense?"

"He doesn't know that," I whispered. "And I'll keep my distance—stay on the porch."

"For the record, I hate all of this. But he does look...desperate. Pathetic, almost."

"There's that overactive heart I'm so fond of." I showed him my sweetest grin.

"Flirting will get you—" He broke off with a melodramatic sigh. "Everywhere. It always does, lion queen."

Edius still loitered twenty paces away, propped against the old stone well, pretending not to eavesdrop.

Windley raised his voice so it would carry. "If I sense even a flicker of beguiling..." His eyes narrowed. "On second thought—step closer. I'm tagging you myself."

Edius grimaced. "Hard pass."

"Oh, it's happening." Windley's tone purred like silk across a drawn blade. "If you run off with the Nemophilist, I need a way to track you."

When a Spirite beguiles another, it leaves an imprint that resonates whenever power is used.

The closer you are, the stronger it feels. Too far away, and you sense nothing at all.

Ambiguous when Windley first explained it.

Clearer with a live demonstration.

Once Windley beguiled Edius, he'd sense Edius's "ripples."

"Or—shit. Forget it. Charm'll sniff it out. You're safe till we clear Flora's. Savor it while it lasts."

With that, Windley disappeared into the cozy cottage, leaving me alone with our newest ally—who immediately cast his flinty gaze over me.

I returned it, cool and dangerous, until he looked away.

"I was telling the truth, you know," he said.

"For your sake, I certainly hope you *are*."

"I'm not planning any double-cross. All I care about is setting her free. After that, I'll be outta your—ah!"

He doubled with a sharp grunt.

A trick?

I braced myself to grow more ridiculously tall grass.

"Sorry. Gotta get this off; it's killing me."

He shrugged out of his traveling jacket, flung it onto a stump, then craned to peer at his own back.

"Shit. Can you see this? Is there blood coming through?"

Turning, he showed the back of his shirt—soaked in both dried and fresh crimson.

"Edius! What happened?"

"Ah, nothing. Don't worry about it."

I leapt off the porch, seizing his shirt—he jerked away.

"Back off—gods, it stings!—you damned little mirefox!"

I had never heard of a mirefox.

I halted. "Explain how you got that."

"My fault. Rode like hell to keep up with you two—ripped it open. Then I climbed a tree for moonfruit while I was waiting—must've torn again."

That still didn't explain what caused the wound to begin with.

"Show me."

"Nah."

"If you're going to be my bodyguard, I'll treat you like any other guard. Show me so I can tend it—my family's remedies are famous across the queendoms."

"Bossy," he grumbled—yet he turned and peeled up his shirt.

Beneath the fabric lay a back far too like another I knew—heart-wrenchingly so. Clusters of three scars, the freshest only days old. I hovered a hand over them and knew:

"Ascian did this."

Worse: he'd done it because of me.

Edius gave a dry, pained laugh. "Payment for your getaway—trust me, I've taken worse."

That was only the first time Edius made my heart ache.

5

WORTH EVERY HEARTBEAT

Flora also possessed a heart inclined to embrace everyone she met. Despite her misgivings, she overcame her fear and helped me tend to Edius's wounds, blending vera from the surrounding woods with tanger root from her own garden.

Edius passed out beside the fire before Flora and I had even finished wrapping his bandages.

"Did I say pathetic?" Windley remarked. "I meant *pathetic*."

"They're the same word."

"Astute." He tapped my nose playfully.

"Are you sure you're okay with this, Flora?" I inquired in a hushed tone.

"I can't say I feel entirely comfortable," she admitted, "but he's never harmed me directly, and I can hardly abandon someone who arrives injured on my doorstep." She moved carefully, lifting a knitted blanket over him. "Besides, it isn't a stretch to think he may not have aided Lord Ascian of his own free will. After all, Windalloy, you didn't. And neither did

Pipsqueak. Even Charm...well, she has her reasons. We know Lord Ascian preyed upon those strong in might but weak in spirit. Why should his latest victim be any different?"

Wiser insight than I could've offered—from one who was kindest and gentlest among us.

Despite Vita having dulled my creator's love, pride welled within me at Flora's compassion.

"Good goddess, lion queen, you look like you want to kiss her." Windley hooked an arm around my neck. "Kiss me instead."

Tempting—but not in front of Flora.

With my vitality restored, I could sense it clearly now—the way her heart quickened whenever she glanced his way—though she was far, far too sweet to ever act on it.

I felt guilty for that.

Guilty for helping create someone who would love him yet never see that love returned.

The sooner we left, the better for her delicate heart.

"You take the bed tonight, Flora. We'll keep watch to ensure Edius doesn't cause trouble," I offered.

"Oh! Are you sure?"

"Yes, I slept plenty through the day, and Windley can take the sofa."

Windley's arm lowered slowly from my neck, confusion flickering in his eyes at my willingness to surrender the bed after our previous exploits there.

I took his hand and guided him onto the sofa as Flora wished us goodnight. Then I slipped down onto the floor in front of him, my cheeks warmed by the lazy fire chewing through a thick log.

"Sorry, Wind. I can't bear to flaunt it in front of her."

"Flaunt what?"

I took his cheek and gave him the kiss he'd asked for earlier.

Windley let out a low groan. "I told you there's nothing between Flora and me."

"For you, perhaps." I closed my eyes, sensing Flora's presence fading silently down the darkened hallway.

"What?" He looked at me as if I were mad. "I'm like a kid brother to her."

"No, Windley, you're much more than that."

And I was feeling luckier by the second that he was mine.

He scratched at his hair, now a stormy gray in the firelight. "Humans. Always so complicated."

Perhaps because we left our hearts lying open.

"You never joined me in bed earlier. You must be exhausted after riding all that way," I shifted the conversation with gentle tact.

"Mm. I've been savoring what I stole from you earlier. Making it last."

"Vampire."

"Vixen."

"Queen chaser."

"Knave kisser."

I bumped my shoulder against his, and his devil's grin shone brighter in the fire's glow.

Afterward, silence descended comfortably between us as he twisted coils of my hair around his fingers, the delightful crackle of flame turning the room from cozy to cozier still.

The dancing shadow of firelight against the wall was beguiling in its own right, and Flora's cottage smelled like a bakery and library tangled together inside a flower shop.

I nodded toward Edius, curled in a pathetic lump on the rug.

"However much we distrust him, he certainly seems to trust us, passing out like that at the mercy of former enemies."

"Who's to say it's voluntary? Lashings drain a person,"

Windley replied quietly. "I understand not fighting back if you're a defenseless kid—but a brute like him?"

"Maybe because his story is true," I offered. "He has something more precious to lose than strips of flesh."

Windley made a low, contemplative noise.

"You'll give him a chance, at least, won't you?" I turned slightly to look into his eyes.

"We'll take him to Abardo tomorrow, pry Pip from Charm's claws. If he proves himself, he stays. If he doesn't—your choice: my blades or your...sprouting sorcery."

"Ass." I elbowed him. "Vita said we'll refine it. I'm sure I'm capable of more than just lawn-sprouting."

"Oh, I know you are, my queen—capable of anything." He curled a hand behind my neck and drew me closer. "Now, join me up here."

"There's hardly room."

"There's room," he insisted.

"You won't be able to lash about in your sleep the way you like."

His eyebrow twitched. "Lash about?" He shook the thought away. "Come on, queenie. Let me hold you." His voice was a touch pouty, a touch demanding, entirely endearing.

"You want to cuddle?" I teased softly.

"I want to cuddle."

A rather unsoldierly thing to say.

A very Windley thing to say.

I gave in, nestling up beside him on Flora's small sofa, while the fire crackled, Edius rested, and the outside world kept its steady cadence beyond the cottage walls.

"Better," he murmured, though his eyes remained open, thoughtful.

"Are you apprehensive about tomorrow?" I asked in a low voice, searching his gaze for hidden worries.

He needed no clarification. "It's just a town."

"And the house?"

I waited patiently for him to admit what I could already see hiding behind his eyes.

"Yeah, the house will be..." He hesitated. "It still feels like Ascian's out there somewhere. Like a shadow of him lingers. Maybe that shadow is Charm."

I squeezed his arm comfortingly. "Ascian is gone, Windley. What I did to him—it was true destruction. His soul was burned from our world. And soon his ring will be, too. And after that..."

There's no path back to the life we knew.

"Whatever comes next will be worth every heartbeat we wait."

I didn't dare list the thousand fears behind that promise— he felt them anyway in the hush that followed.

"Turns out reality beats daydreams," he murmured, his palm warm at the small of my back. "I used to invent excuses just to brush against you, and now..."

He kissed me—first a brush of lips, then deeper—our breaths slipping into the same rhythm.

It took every shred of discipline not to climb over him.

"Regret surrendering the bed?" he teased, trailing a leisurely line along my arm while the log hissed in the fire.

"I regret surrendering the bed."

"There will be others." He tucked himself closer, resting his forehead in the hollow of my collarbone.

My wyrdbound one—hair paling at the roots, heart a locked chest with me sealed inside.

His fingers had only just threaded through mine when the lump of Edius on Flora's rug shifted and groaned. Over Windley's quiet breathing and the fire's low crackle I could barely catch it, yet I could have sworn the wounded Spirite whispered one name:

"Gwen."

Windley didn't hear it, already slipping securely into sleep, knowing his hatchets were within reach by the sofa's headrest, believing I possessed the strength of a goddess. And it was that very goddess I heard when I cleared my mind.

"Your soul glows near him, little royal. It is intriguing to feel love for a beastling. I have not experienced it before."

"Because their foremothers are something else?"

"Horrid things. The reason beasts desire to devour one another."

The Drakaina. Could they truly be so terrible if they'd created someone like Windley?

"The beastlings are only the least feral of their creations. Lucky for humes, children often diverge from their parents' whims."

True enough. I tucked it away for now.

"Hopefully Edius proves the same," I said.

"I do not sense malice from the new beastling."

Neither did I. But hearing it directly from a goddess eased my nagging doubts.

"With him showing up, I didn't get much chance to practice your powers. I worry about facing Charmagne tomorrow, but we simply can't spare another night here. Exitium may have already found a new royal by now."

"Indeed she has."

"What?" I jerked in Windley's arms. "Why didn't you tell me sooner?"

"It was necessary for you to come here, to feel the joy of creation and awaken fully to my light. The time was not wasted."

I realized then Vita had known Exitium's new target all along. Had she told me sooner—

A life might have been saved. A precious, precious life.

But I didn't know yet.

In the space behind my eyelids, Vita showed me a crescent-shaped spire atop a familiar castle. I knew that castle. I knew that crescent. And of all the queens in all the lands, Exitium's choice was simultaneously best and worst. Best, if you hoped for destruction; worst, if you hoped to prevent it.

"That's the Queendom of the Cove! You mean Exitium is headed for Sestilia?"

"It is as you say. But fear not, little royal. She is bodiless now, forced to cling to the living. Just as she followed you from the Scarlet Wood, she now follows the conjurer."

"Rafe? But I sent him north! Why didn't you warn me? Had I known, we could've kept her here, away from any royals!"

"You felt his heart, did you not? He would have gone all the same. Yet all is not lost. The conjurer's journey north will take days, and even then, the destroyer will need passage to the spider queen. She must be given reason to surrender fully, as you nearly did. Surely, even with this detour, even with tomorrow's delay, even with the uncertain journey north, you will reach her in time. It is what I am counting on."

She spoke with such assurance that I almost believed her.

"Even if that's true, Vita, it implies we'll defeat Charmagne tomorrow. But what if I'm not strong enough to fight any of them as I am now? Using your power isn't intuitive like the echoes were. What if I'm not suited for it?"

The glow in my chest spread, calm and sure. *"Look around, Merrin. This cottage took care to build, yet destroying it would be easy enough."*

"So creation is harder to wield than destruction?"

"Not harder so much as requiring more thoughtful intention. Anyone can destroy, but not everyone can create. Use this time to ponder how you might breathe life into the soil to aid your combat."

I blinked, trying to process that. "You want me to fight Charm with dirt?"

"Mud works particularly well. It's excellent for crafting golems."

Vita's words echoed in my mind, mingling with visions of mud-born warriors and whispered assurances of strength. But exhaustion eventually blurred the edges of thought, and despite myself—despite everything—I drifted into sleep near dawn, hearing no plotting from Edius's lump.

When I awoke, I was alone on the sofa. Flora, her hair in two dangling braids, served breakfast to a visibly uneasy Edius at the table, while Windley sulked in a corner, patching a hole in his cloak.

"Good morning, queen of the lions." He tilted his head toward the kitchen table. "Unfortunately, it wasn't all a dream."

My first instinct was to rush to Windley and tell him immediately what Vita had said about Rafe, Sestilia, and Exitium. But I decided it best to let him handle one enemy at a time; the coming fight against his former siblings would be emotional enough.

"How are you feeling, Edius?" I asked instead.

Windley caught the slight stammer in my voice and narrowed his eyes, but I swiftly turned away, feigning great interest in Edius's answer.

"Stiff."

"Oh! But his wounds have closed nicely," chimed Flora. "I reapplied the salve you prepared, Queen Merrin."

"Thank you, Flora. Keep that recipe handy. Add honey if you ever suffer a burn. And willow bark for pain relief."

She eagerly scribbled down every detail with her quill.

Little else needed noting that morning as we gathered our things and prepared to leave Flora's cottage. Edius stayed quiet, like an envoy dispatched from a hostile queendom. Flora remained visibly nervous with one of Ascian's former lackeys loitering in her hideaway. Windley, meanwhile, seized every possible opportunity to size up Edius, dramatically moving his hatchets around, ensuring Edius never missed a glance.

Was he issuing a silent warning or simply peacocking?

Edius stepped up beside me and folded his arms as Windley and Flora said their goodbyes on the porch.

I did my best to ignore the obvious flutter of her heart as she reached up, laying a tremulous hand against his cheek. "When will you come again, Windalloy?"

Perhaps Windley sensed it now, too. He searched her eyes for a beat, realization rippling across his features before he caught her hand, guiding it from his face with moth-wing delicacy.

"Meraflora, darling, you know I owe you everything—"

But.

He was going to say *but.*

And it wasn't of his own volition. It was because of what I'd told him—because of what he now sensed on his own—and it occurred to me, painfully, that I shouldn't have been the one to mention it.

After everything Flora had done for us, I would not allow him to break her heart for my sake.

"We shall have you up north for a visit soon, Flora, if you don't mind making the journey," I quickly interrupted.

Windley caught my eye, understood, then gave Flora a reassuring nod. "Soon."

Flora clasped her hands at her heart, radiant with happiness.

"Interesting," Edius muttered under his breath, arms still folded.

When I turned to ask what was so interesting, he poked me right in the forehead and turned away.

"E-excuse me?"

"What?" Windley was at my side in a heartbeat. "What did he just do to you?"

But Edius had already moved away, attention deliberately elsewhere, so I quietly assured Windley it was nothing.

It wasn't nothing.

But it would be quite some time before I understood what that little poke meant.

6

THE HEXED TOWN

All the way to Abardo, I tried not to think about the fact that Exitium was trailing Rafe northward, or about how we'd given him money for a stag to hasten his journey, or that he'd ride through night and day to reach Beau. Instead, I focused my energy on visualizing how I might wield dirt and mud against Charmagne.

I imagined hurling clumps of earth—which she swatted away effortlessly.

I imagined creating a barrier of bushes—which she simply stepped through.

I imagined summoning a golem-like creature from mud—which she promptly crushed beneath her heel.

I felt painfully unprepared to face the hexed city, and Vita hadn't provided the detailed instruction I desperately needed.

Then again, neither had the echoes.

With them, I'd always found creative solutions—spreading their shadow across the ground or unleashing them from my hands or mouth.

Why was the power of creation so much harder to grasp?

Perhaps because Exitium had only ever asked me to embrace what was already inside me.

Now, I was tasked with mastering something external, something foreign.

"Trust, Merrin."

To worsen matters, the day was absurdly sunny for late autumn. As we rode—me clinging to Windley and Edius beside us on his own charmed beast—I struggled to ignore Soleil's warmth upon my neck, knowing she'd had relations with Rafe, that she'd abandoned us in our direst moment, that Beau carried her child.

Goddesses.

It seemed only the unlucky ones became entangled with them.

I was still considering uprooting a tree to drop onto Charmagne—which she would surely evade—when Windley commanded Dandelion to slow.

"We're here already?" I asked, nerves spiking.

"Yes, lion queen."

Windley helped me down a short distance from the moss-strewn walls of the silent city, where no movement stirred aside from ours.

I was far from ready.

But however well I thought I hid my panic, Windley saw right through it. He gently lifted my chin with a knuckle.

"Don't worry. You're staying here. You need more time to master this whole 'pulse of the earth' business. Your sweat last night betrayed your nerves. The brute and I will scout the house. I discussed it with him already."

"But—!"

"You forget, Majesty, I made it through life just fine without your shadow tricks." He patted his belt where his hatchets hung, giving me his mischievous wink. "I'll manage."

"But aren't the people here hexed—"

"To capture me. And if it looks like I've already been caught..." He gestured toward Edius, who was absently scratching his prancelope outside the gate.

Even with Soleil blazing bright overhead, the city beyond that gate appeared dimmer than the rest of the world. It was neither a place of light nor life, for both had been drained away by a young Spirite forced to swallow a spider-like creature, whose master had been replaced by the foulest cupcake of them all.

Windley caught my paling expression.

"We don't intend to confront Charm just yet, Merr. Our goal is just to separate Pip from her. They don't know the brute's made a deal with us, so we have surprise on our side."

"You trust him, then?"

"He won't cross us if he believes you can do to him what you did to Ascian. I haven't told him your power's changed. He thinks you're staying out here in case they run."

Defenseless.

Weaponless.

I despised the idea.

"Here." Windley pressed something into my hand—a small knife with an intricately carved handle.

"When I get back, you can tell me whatever it is you've been hiding from me this morning. Deal?"

Frustratingly insightful incubus.

He kissed my forehead quickly before jogging off toward Edius, who waited impatiently, hands tucked in his jacket pockets, long hair swept to one side.

"Ready, Edmond?"

"It's *Edius*."

I hurried forward, intent on protesting further, but Windley tossed me a reassuring wave before slipping through the gate into a city eager to deliver him to the most detestable creature I'd ever known—

Leaving me outside with two prancelopes who disliked me and a pile of dirt I hadn't the faintest idea how to control.

"Perfect. Just perfect."

"*Faith, little royal.*"

Faith in what, exactly?

But Vita didn't answer.

I crouched to the ground and concentrated on the earth's pulse, feeling Windley's heartbeat grow more distant as he and Edius moved deeper into the hexed city.

"Faith," I repeated, aligning my breathing and heartbeat to the rhythm of the soil beneath me, my skin prickling as the ground began to glow the vivid green of the Emerald Wood. "Go!"

The dirt around my knees lifted—a mere few inches—before collapsing again.

"Argh! I don't understand, Vita!"

"*You fail, Merrin, because you only picture your creations faltering. Do not imagine how they might fail—envision how they will succeed.*"

But how could I make myself believe in something so uncertain?

"*The world runs on the same breath—the breath I bestowed. You feel it, even if you cannot see it. Manipulate my essence. Bend it to your purpose.*"

Vita's breath.

True enough, I could sense it flowing through grass blades, clover roots, even the songbirds flitting overhead. It was exactly as I had described it to Windley—a starting breath from which everything drew life, as if enchanted.

And if that breath could sustain countless creatures over countless ages...

I focused harder, drawing that sustaining energy up through the earth and into my lungs. Beneath me, the ground swelled brighter than ever, illuminated with Vita's emerald power.

"Vita! It feels like something's happening!"

My fingers moved instinctively, strumming invisible threads like a harp, weaving Vita's breath through the air. Then I scooped it into my fist—and a small mound rose from the dirt in front of me.

Only anthill-sized, but still something.

"I did something!"

But Vita's reply offered no comfort. *"Something's wrong, Merrin! I sense unrest in the city! Your beastling called out your name!"*

"What? Windley did?"

Heart racing, I bolted to the entrance, straining to catch sounds of trouble.

"There are many voices!" Vita urged. *"They surround your beastling!"*

Echoes gone, Vita's power unsteady, and armed with a dagger fit for paring fruit—I still wouldn't abandon my wyrd-bound one.

With that resolve burning in my chest, I plunged into the bleak city.

Abardo was just as lifeless as before—overflowing rubbish, tightly shuttered windows, and clouds swallowing the sun the instant my foot touched the city's cobblestones.

"That way!"

"Windley!"

I followed Vita's directions until I heard the chaos firsthand —two Spirites battling something large and charged.

"Is that a mob?!" I shouted, racing into the housing district and sliding to a halt.

At least sixty glassy-eyed civilians swarmed Windley and Edius, wielding whatever came to hand—shovels, skillets, even a loaf of stale bread.

"Lion queen! What are you doing here?" Windley spun his hatchets in a defensive circle, careful not to cut anyone. Edius stood beside him in a boxer's stance, knocking back attackers with practiced jabs.

"Vita said you were in trouble!" I yelled. "I thought they believed you were already captured."

"Fuckin' Charm!" Edius snarled, ducking a hurled bin-lid. "She flipped their hexes on me. Must've guessed I'd bolt—hated that scorpion from the start!"

"They're not after me?" I blurted. The mob swarmed past as though I were smoke, fixated on the two Spirites.

"Probably figured you'd smoke 'em in a blink," he panted between swings.

I flinched. *No longer.*

"You're pulling every blow," I observed.

Windley caught three attackers in one sweep. "They're spell-bound, Merr—no will of their own."

Just like the ones he'd once hexed.

"I know," Edius grunted, weaving through fists like he was born to it. "Someone I care about's tied to one of these hexes—gotta keep 'em breathing."

"Then run!" I urged.

Edius scoffed, dodging a rusted spade aimed at his head. "And get swarmed before I clear a path? Easier said than done without breaking spines."

Frantic, I flailed my arms. "Over here!" But the mob paid no heed, fixated on the Spirites alone.

"Listen, Merrin. Do you hear it?" Vita pressed in my ear, her voice taut with urgency.

I strained harder. Murmurs, metal clashing, fists striking—
"They're speaking nonsense!"

"Not that!" Vita insisted. *"Listen deeper!"*

I focused on the pulse beneath the earth, Windley's steady heartbeat, Edius's cautious rhythm—and then understood.

Those were the only two heartbeats I sensed in the entire market.

"I—I don't feel their hearts beating!"

"Their breath has been stolen."

"Windley!" My voice cracked. "They have no heartbeats!"

"Damn it," Windley snarled. "They're sustained only by hexes. When those break, these people will fall. Ascian didn't just drain them—he forged them into living wards for himself! Sick bastard."

Horror filled me as I spotted a child in the crowd. Barefoot, expressionless, a doll hanging limply from her fingers. And no heartbeat.

Oh, goddess.

"Aw, shit," Edius muttered. "Then there's no choice." He punched an elderly man, who staggered back with a sob.

"They still feel pain?" I cried.

Absolutely not.

I wouldn't witness an innocent slaughter!

Windley locked eyes with Edius. "Merrin. Go. We'll handle this."

But Windley wasn't immune to trauma—his past still haunted him, memories of innocent lives lost to similar hexes raw and aching.

You have the power to give and take life...

My breath snagged. I didn't truly know how to wield that power—or if I should. But instinct surged to the forefront, compelling me to drop to the ground, palms splayed across the dirt threading through cobblestones. Every connected thread of life echoed in me, the townsfolk bound to the earth's pulse.

A pulse of insecurity flickered in my chest. Then I drew Vita's breath from deep beneath the soil, braced myself, and exhaled my intention back into it.

"Lion queen?" Windley shouted. "What did you do?"

Emerald light erupted, spilling across the market in a single, blinding surge. It pooled under Windley, Edius, and every frozen onlooker while my heartbeat hammered its command into the soil.

Then—silence.

Sixty-odd bodies drooped at once, life leaking away in green motes that corkscrewed into the sky like dying fireflies. Dread cinched my ribs: I'd meant to rouse the earth, not reap it.

"Their souls," Vita observed, her whisper circling me like distant windchimes. *"Well done."*

In mere breaths, the once-animated figures revealed their true state—lifeless husks, robbed of everything by Ascian's hexes. I had extinguished them, mercifully perhaps, but the burden crushed me all the same.

My strength failed. I crumpled, overwhelmed by exhaustion. Two Spirites rushed in to support me, but I could hardly feel their touch.

Killing—even out of mercy—left scars.

A hollow sob tore from my throat, and I buried my face in the nearest shirt, tears coursing hot and bitter.

"Ah—" A clumsy hand patted my head awkwardly.

"I've got her." Windley pulled me away protectively. "Go check the house—though I doubt you'll find them."

"Nah," agreed Edius, "Doesn't even seem like they've returned. Probably controlled the hexes remotely."

Their words barely reached me through my anguish.

"Come here, love." Windley lifted me in a sure, tender

sweep, carefully siphoning bits of his power into me. "No use hiding now. Let me numb this for you." He carried me out through the desolate streets as tremors wracked my body—fueled by thoughts of stolen futures and extinguished breaths.

"You did what you had to, Merr," he soothed. "I've witnessed enough hexes to know. Without you, we'd have had to cut through them one by one. You granted them peace."

Yet taking life never came without consequence, justified or not.

"I'm proud of you," he murmured. "You summoned your strength swiftly, and your new power is incredible." He set me down against the city's cold outer wall, tilting my chin to study my eyes. "Majesty?"

"I acted without thinking," I admitted through tear-blurred vision. "What if there was another way?"

"No." He spoke with unyielding certainty. "They were beyond help. Even if Pip released his hex, their fate would have been the same. Now, open your mouth."

"Why—?"

Windley placed his thumb against my bottom teeth. "Take what you need. It'll ease the pain. Let you float awhile."

"Take?" My tongue brushed uncertainly against his skin.

His fingers twitched slightly. "Draw."

I hesitated, confused.

"Suck," Edius clarified, maddeningly nonchalant.

Windley flushed scarlet. "Not helpful, Edmond."

But I'd already complied instinctively, lips closing around Windley's thumb, *drawing* him in. Heat bloomed inside me, silky and soothing, unraveling tension in a way that made my mind feel weightless. I enjoyed the weight of him, the subtle sweetness on my tongue.

I felt a sudden, primal urge to sink teeth into his flesh.

Windley froze, eyes wide as he realized his terrible miscalculation.

My tongue lightly grazed his thumb's underside, and he jerked away as though burned, staring at his own hand in disbelief. His throat bobbed.

"Gods, that escalated," Edius noted. "Why not just drag her off and have your way already?"

"More erotic than intended," Windley muttered. "Talk about her like that again, Edmond, and you'll be one limb short of a matching set."

"It's *Edius*." He dropped traveling packs beside us, indifferent. "Charm and Pip haven't been back. Likely took off right after switching the hexes. Grabbed what I could from the house —whatever I withheld from our little thief last time."

I was still too dazed to retort, warmth making my thoughts delightfully muddled. Instead, I focused on simpler sensations: the lingering scent of late summer, nostalgic and bittersweet.

Windley composed himself, running fingers through silvering hair. "I have a theory," he admitted reluctantly, "but I hope it's wrong. For now, watch for ripples. Speaking of—"

"No." Edius scowled immediately.

"As I said: whisk her off and I'll need a trail. Stand still for the imprint, or—"

A muscle ticked in Edius's jaw as the meaning landed. He looked past Windley to me—then to the wilds where Pip waited—and sighed. "Fine. Get it over with."

"Look away, queenie."

Naturally, I disobeyed. What I saw next flooded me with conflicting emotions.

It wasn't exactly common to see your lover kissing another man—especially one with rugged features, striking eyes, and a perpetually brooding mouth.

Windley gripped Edius by the throat and kissed him.

Quick, firm, clinical—and enough to briefly ignite Windley's eyes sapphire-blue.

"Satisfied?" Edius drawled, as if it were their thousandth kiss.

"Not yet," Windley said, tight-voiced. "Use your power."

"On who?"

"Not on me—I don't need another tracker."

Edius's gaze swept the clearing, finally fixing with predatory focus on—"Dandelion."

"A beast? No, it would be stronger on—" Windley's eyes cut to me in reluctant apology. "Your Majesty, do you mind? He can't imprint on you the way he can on me. I just need proof it worked."

Still foggy from everything, I scrubbed a sleeve across my face. "It's fine."

I resisted the impulse to lean away as Edius prowled nearer, his feline eyes narrowing thoughtfully; my hesitation only drew him closer, until his minty breath stirred the hair at my temple.

"Ah." His mouth quirked. "Now I see it—missed it at first."

A soft electric tingle skated beneath my skin as his fingers skimmed my arm. He blinked, slow, deliberate...

When his eyes opened, I sucked in a breath: they shimmered like ancient gems—bright, pulsating emerald, the exact shade Windley reserved for me.

I tried to glance at Windley behind him, but Edius held me steady, touch careful—as if I were spun glass.

"Well?" he murmured over his shoulder.

"Yeah, it took. Off her—*now*," Windley snapped.

Edius lingered for a single breath...then flicked a finger against my forehead—the same insolent tap as before. He pivoted away, unreadable as ever.

"Really?" I huffed, rubbing the spot.

I caught Windley's eye, but he ignored the gesture and offered a knightly hand for balance.

"So, what's your theory?" Edius asked, facing Windley. "Where'd they run off to?"

"North," Windley sighed.

"Why?" Edius pressed.

"You know some of Charm's history, don't you?" Windley said.

"Some," Edius allowed.

"What history, Winsley?" I asked, still shaking off the last of the beguiling haze. "Windley."

Windley cracked a rakish grin at my intoxicated tongue, though it faded almost instantly as he grew serious. "Remember when I mentioned I'd visited the Emerald Wood before? The second time was to flee captivity. But the first time was to retrieve Charm."

"Retrieve her?" My brow furrowed. "She was in the north?"

I'd questioned it before—how Charmagne knew so much about my homeland, and how she'd recognized my royal blood by scent alone.

"No. Charm's from the south, but she was trafficked north as an infant. Humans raised her, and not kindly," Windley explained. "It's why she hates your kind—and the northlands."

Charmagne, too, was merely trying to survive Ascian.

"Ascian heard about her, had her smuggled to the Emerald Wood, and went to retrieve her himself—with Pip and me along. She never told us the whole story, but she'd reveal enough to assert dominance over us. Sad, really. After her childhood, Ascian's demands seemed mild by comparison."

Noting my troubled silence, Windley assured, "I won't repeat any details."

"Revenge," Edius said coolly. "Given her power, I'd probably do the same. Any idea where exactly?"

"No," Windley said thoughtfully. "But northern currency is different. She'll eventually use her power again—leaving us a trail."

"We have business in the north anyway," I decided, thinking of the echoes traveling toward Sestilia even now. "Unless either of you objects, that will be our destination."

"Either of us?" Edius repeated skeptically.

"You chose to spare the innocents of Abardo, and you allowed Windley's imprint without resistance. Henceforth, I consider you my guard. That doesn't mean you have my full trust—but you've earned a fraction. Don't break it, Edius, or you'll never regain it."

He looked mildly amused. "Am I expected to bow?"

"No."

"Good."

"Wonderful," Windley grumbled, steering me aside possessively. "Exactly what we needed—another predator around. Give us a minute, *predator*. There's something I need to coax from the queen while she's feeling loose-tongued."

Edius scowled slightly but turned away to ready our things. Windley guided me around the city's curved stone wall, cornering me gently against it.

"Alright, lion queen." Windley spoke dangerously close. "What have you been hiding from me?"

I hesitated—had my own joke about interrogations all those days ago given him ideas?

"Don't act cute. You're already cute, and you're still hiding something. I see it hovering above you like a tiny storm cloud." He wiggled fingers near my head to illustrate. "Let it out. That's why I'm here."

"I didn't want to worry you—especially not before facing Pip—but..."

I drew a shaky breath and spilled it all: the goddess's vision of Sestilia, Exitium tailing Rafe, the spider queen's looming danger—every swirl of dread I'd swallowed since Flora's hearth.

Windley's reaction was swift, furious, and loud.

"THAT FRUITCAKE?"

Edius appeared around the corner, shoulders tense.

"Fruitcake," Windley repeated, shooing him away with a flick of his fingers. "You're fond of those, aren't you, *Edmond?*"

"No," Edius said flatly.

Windley bent to my ear. "Our little secret—for now."

Then, with a sharp whistle, he summoned cantankerous Dandelion II—or III, or whichever.

"Northward, my queen. Time to collect the pastry."

7

DOES EDMOND
SEEM A BIT...?

I t was no small feat that I managed to push thoughts of lovely Sestilia, shrouded in smoke as black as her nails and gown, from the forefront of my mind. Indeed, only Vita's persistent assurances—that we would reach her in time— allowed me to focus on anything else.

After all, Vita had witnessed a thousand iterations before ours, countless threads of fate. If I was the author of this story, could there be a better editor than the divine herself?

Practically speaking, our return northward would surely be swifter, thanks to Dandelion's tireless hooves thundering against the earth's steady heartbeat. With each stride, reaching Rafe before he made it to the queenlands seemed increasingly plausible.

But no great tale exists without its share of subplots, and ours certainly wouldn't be without detours.

The first began with the moon.

Luna had returned to her place in the sky after Exitium's departure. Perhaps because she believed I was no longer a threat, or because Rafe had ceased to be fair game. Yet, as we made camp in the foggy fields of blue flowers on our first night's stop, Windley made a startling observation.

"Is it me, or is Luna looking rather..."

"Oblong?" I finished, noting the moon's stretched, egg-like shape.

"Luna?" Edius questioned, straightening from the boulder he'd been leaning against to peer upward.

"We have history," Windley replied casually.

"With the *moon*? Of course you do." Edius shook his head and slumped back against the rock, lapsing into the quiet brooding he'd maintained ever since we'd left Abardo. My imagination, perhaps, but I suspected he was deliberately avoiding conversation—though more than once I'd caught him staring at me, as if there was something he wanted to say.

Windley, meanwhile, had been unusually demonstrative throughout the day, his pulse quickening deliciously each time I tightened my hold around him on Dandelion. Naturally, I tightened it every chance I got.

Now we'd stopped in the same rolling fields we'd crossed on our journey south, only tonight they were blanketed in fog so thick it felt like wading through whipped cream. I'd witnessed mist like this at sea on chilly mornings when the court slept in, but seeing it spread so thickly across the land was mesmerizing.

Sitting down meant sinking waist-deep in soft clouds, prompting Windley to build the fire extra large, burning away enough mist to create a small, cozy clearing. Edius, meanwhile, wrestled with a tent he clearly didn't understand.

It was oddly amusing—watching the man who'd once ambushed us now struggling to make sense of guy-lines and poles.

"What are you doing?" Windley scrutinized Edius's chaotic progress after several clanking minutes.

Edius lifted what was unmistakably the tent's *floor* and tried to fasten it halfway up a rod.

"Does this go here?"

Not even remotely.

My eyes widened with realization. "Edius, do you...not know how to pitch a tent?"

He dropped the canvas, surrendering it to the fog. "How hard can it be?"

Windley snorted gleefully. "Offering yourself as a body-guard and you can't even manage fabric and sticks. You *do* know how to catch a meal, don't you?"

Edius narrowed his eyes dangerously. "What's that supposed to mean?"

"He's a city boy, Merr." Windley folded his arms smugly. "Explains the jacket. And the hair."

Scowling, Edius jammed a tent pole deep into the mist. "Oh yeah? And your hair? You look like a gods-damned flamingo."

"Queenie likes it." Windley tilted his head toward me with exaggerated pride. "Don't you, queenie?"

I did like it, though it undeniably drew attention.

"You two seem rather bubbly," I intervened. "But I refuse to take sides. We don't have time."

Edius ignored me. "Humans trust you more if you stick to a single color, *Windalloy*."

"A human who trusts based on hair color isn't a human worth knowing, *Edmond*. I conserve my energy for far more important matters."

Like canoodling.

Windley shot me a rascal's wink.

"Ha! Is that a joke?" Edius scoffed bitterly, rapping the embedded pole with his knuckles. "You put all that effort into landing a royal, and you don't even put her to use? Shame. If she were mine, I'd make damn sure she knew it."

A rogue hatchet cleaved the earth inches from Edius's boots, slicing neatly through fresh grass that had sprouted beneath my fingertips.

"She's not a piece of meat, you cad," Windley growled, expression darkening. "Disrespect my queen again, and you can say goodbye to her aid."

"He's right," I added evenly. "I may not need a title from anyone, but I won't tolerate being thought of as a 'pet.'"

Edius exhaled bullishly through his nose, dragging a weary hand over his face. "Fuck, Merrín." His palm lingered at his jaw, tense. "Didn't mean it that way."

I studied him carefully. He looked genuinely regretful, as if unaccustomed to the rules of civility.

Letting out a slow breath, I thawed. "Here, let me help you."

Under Luna's watchful gaze, I knelt to gather the scattered poles near Edius's feet.

"Hold this piece?" I offered kindly. "It goes here. Easier once you've done it properly."

He said nothing, just watched me, gaze direct and searching.

"I take no offense," I murmured as we fitted the final beam. "We're from different worlds, I know. But Windley and I see ourselves as equals. I imagine it's the same with you and your fiancée."

It was meant as a neutral observation, an olive branch to soothe earlier tension. Yet something in him shifted visibly.

Edius's grip tightened on the canvas until his knuckles blanched. When he finally spoke, the words came rough, scraped from somewhere unsteady.

"Can't say it's the same," he murmured. "Didn't mean any

slight, highness." Another breath. "Some folk choose the tether. Choice turns a collar into ribbon."

That should have ended it, yet a low pulse spilled from him —the familiar Spirite thrum Windley carried—now tangling with Vita's fresh, bright current inside me. The two magics crackled in the fog, quickening my blood.

Fire-glow carved hard planes across his face; spice-and-timber scent drifted from his skin, edged with something unmistakably enchanted. My gaze, more instinct than will, caught on the slow parting of his lips.

"If it were you and me, *lion* queen," he said, voice hushed and vibrating with that lure, "I'd make sure the ribbon sat easy."

Heat flared up my spine—part magic, part me. I drew a steadier breath, searching for an anchor. "What's her name?" I asked, prying the conversation toward safer ground. "Your fiancée. The one Ascian hexed."

"Oh." His throat worked; the shimmer in his eyes flickered but didn't leave my lips. "Gwendol. Gwen for short."

"What's she like?"

"Small."

"Small?"

He cleared his throat. "Normal-sized. Shiny hair. Glowing."

"Glowing?"

"Her...smile."

Strange. A clumsy description that made me wonder if she was even real.

The diversion did the trick. His shoulders eased—only a notch—before he turned away, voice dropping back to its usual gravel. "Think I've got it now, highness. Appreciate the lesson."

Freed from the spell of his stare, I hurried to Windley, who was stirring dinner. He'd noticed, of course, how my eyes had lingered a shade too long on the wrong Spirite, but—mercifully —he let it pass.

Instead: "Fetch me a spoon, love?"

Grateful for the excuse, I darted over and prodded him with the utensil. "Your favorite weapon."

"Har, har." Windley snatched it, forcing a grin. "Keep that spoonery private, please. Poor Edmond's already over-stimulated."

My banter fizzled; the fog-draped field felt suddenly hushed. Edmond—no, *Edius*—stood by the half-finished tent, silhouette silvered by moonlight, hands loose at his sides.

"Are you really a queen, Merrín?" he asked, studying the canvas we'd wrangled. "You're nothing like the ones in stories."

"Oh! You read stories?" I tried, reaching for lighter ground.

"No." The single word shut like a gate. "Windalloy, I...need some air."

"That's the spirit," Windley drawled, giving a jaunty wave. "Don't hurry back."

Edius vanished into the mist, slipping between the ghost-blue flowers until he merged with the tree line—one shadow among many.

I lowered beside Windley. Cool, silken fog swallowed me to the waist; it tasted faintly of moss and distant rain.

"I can hear your heart from here," Windley teased around the spoon's handle. "Feeling flustered, lion queen?"

"No!" The denial came too fast. "I didn't—he just—"

Windley chuckled, warm and unbothered. "Relax. He's a Spirite; you're human; and an extraordinary one at that. Of course the lure gets messy. I'm not worried about you in the slightest." He flicked his eyes toward the dark where Edius had gone. "Him, though...that one's still learning how to keep his fangs to himself."

I glanced quickly behind us to ensure Edius was still far

enough away. "You don't think he'd try to steal me again?" I whispered.

Windley set down the spoon. "Second-guessing your little rescue project? Afraid the predator who's already *kidnapped you once* might strike again? You're the one who insisted we take him in like a half-tame wolf cub."

Whatever look crossed my face, it made him sigh in surrender.

"No," he offered. "I don't think you need to worry. It's just his instincts flaring up. Truthfully, he's done rather well considering what happened earlier."

He handed me a bowl of porridge he'd finished cooking.

"What do you mean?"

"Today's mercy kill was..." He pressed his fingertips together, kissing them dramatically, as if savoring the memory. "So compassionate, so humane—it was a perfect showcase of your spirit. And for creatures attracted to spirits, you may as well have been dancing around in your frilliest underthings. Probably why he's been quiet all day. Trying to compose himself."

"You're joking." But he clearly wasn't. I nearly wondered if there existed fabric thick enough to shield a spirit.

But better for him to avert his eyes than for me to hide my soul.

"Your spirit's always delicious, Merr, but today it was next-level enticing. Even I've struggled with it—on account of my *affections*. He, on the other hand, is still acclimating to you. It should ease once he adjusts to your scent."

I took a spoonful of Windley's porridge—about as exciting as porridge ever gets—and frowned.

"If I didn't trust you, I'd have whisked you away myself."

He angled a contemplative look toward the dragon-shaped trees. "Spirite instincts are strong, Merr. He's already tasted how good it feels to steal you once. But fantasy's easier than reality. He knows what you can do—and that supposed fiancée of his is still in danger. He won't risk it."

"Supposed?" I blinked. "You don't believe he's engaged?"

"Not for a second." He tilted his head pensively. "I believe he's fighting for someone, yes—but not some human fiancée he's deeply in love with. I suspect he invented her to make you trust him more. A little emotional manipulation, since the unchanging hair wasn't quite enough."

My spoon slowed, porridge cooling while I wrestled with the thought. Compassion never did have an off-switch.

Windley sensed my unease. "You've done nothing wrong, queenie. The weakness lies with us. I don't think he'll act, but if he does, I'll gladly defend your honor—assuming you don't get to him first."

He moved a comforting hand to my back.

"More importantly—how are you feeling after earlier?"

After draining the life from a city full of innocents?

"Better," I lied.

He gave me a knowing look. "If you'd like to talk—"

I silenced him with a soft kiss. "You're always the one I'd talk to, anyway."

"Shivers," he hummed, easing back just far enough for me to catch the ember-quick spark in his gaze. "Want a dose?"

The answer, as always, was yes.

Windley's smile went fox-sharp as the Spirite heat slid into his voice. "Or," he whispered, leaning close, "shall I show you what he could only *dream* of?"

The air hummed. His eyes smoldered, equal parts promise and dare.

"Being a pet can feel exquisite," he crooned, words dripping like amber over a blade. "Let me collar you for one night, my lion—no crowns, no titles—and I'll have you *purring* at every command."

He might've been teasing, but every syllable slid from his tongue as if slowed by honey, trapping me in place, igniting a longing deeper than I'd ever known.

My heart, already pounding, bolted into a wild stampede.

"How'd I do?" he asked.

I swayed, pulse skipping. "You flubbed the script."

His smirk widened, wicked and bright. "Close enough."

The charm he'd loosed wrapped around me like warm surf, tugging me forward. Heat shimmered through my skin.

"I...want you, Wind," I whispered, closing the space between us. "Have me."

"A-ah. Shit, worked a little too well." He swallowed thickly, breath hitching.

Yet I pressed a heated kiss to his throat. "Touch me, Windley."

"M-Merrin, you can't say things like that." With effort, he brushed a whisper of a kiss against my cheek. "Not out here, my queen. But soon."

He made a strangled noise just as footsteps approached through the mist.

"Edmond!" Windley blurted, relief flooding his voice. "Just the berk I need—escort her to the tent *before I lose every ounce of restraint*."

But as Windley nudged me forward, Edius hesitated, looking just as wary of taking me.

"Er, what?"

"Take her," Windley insisted, voice strained. "I...did something profoundly stupid."

Edius held his hands out awkwardly near my upper arms without making contact. "I'm not going in there with her. Unless you want me to..."

"No! Just put her inside." Windley groaned, covering his flushed face with one hand. "Get her away from me. Goddess, after riding pressed up against me all day, each gallop bouncy and warm, then seeing her soul utterly bared in Abardo..." A tremor-laced breath escaped him. "I'll end up doing something I regret. Tuck her away, safely out of sight. We'll both sleep out here."

He peeked through his fingers at me, eyes bright yet pleading.

"N-night, Merrin. Be a good little lion and stay put."

It wasn't until Edius pushed me carefully into the tent and sealed me off from Windley's pheromone-laden aura that I regained my senses.

"S-Stars, Windley! I didn't mean to be so forward!"

"Nothing to apologize for, darling. Just please—*for the love of all the goddesses*—stay in there!"

Then, quieter, almost to himself:

"For once, I actually miss having that grumpy, cockblocking conjurer hanging about. Instead, we've adopted yet another wolf. Perfectly safe scenario for the queen's innocence. Sir Albie would certainly approve."

I heard Windley rise, his footsteps heavy.

"I'm taking a walk," he growled. "Edmond, if you so much as glance at that tent, I'll cut off—well, whatever I can find first."

Edius hovered outside, his silhouette shifting uncomfortably against the glow of the campfire. His voice came low, clear but uncertain, through the canvas:

"Merrín? About before, I..."

I sank onto my bedroll, pressing my palms hard against my flaming cheeks. "It's fine. Windley explained."

"It's not fine."

A beat of silence.

"Look, I need you—your help, I mean."

The next words tumbled out before he could choke them back.

"Maybe we should...share the tent tonight? Just—to blunt this attraction."

I shot upright. "Blunt what?"

"Wrong phrasing—gods." His shadow scrubbed both hands over its face. "I don't mean anything improper. I just... The closer I stay, the faster the instinct fades. I don't want you thinking you need to fear me. Whatever this—pull—is, it isn't how I usually am."

It wasn't normally like this for Windley either.

What in goddess's name was happening?

Vita's voice sparkled inside my head, bright and unrepentant. *"The destroyer was dampening your spirit before, Merrin. Now, with darkness purged, you shine brighter than ever."*

Oh, no.

This was Vita's doing.

That night, I slept surrounded by very, very tall grass.

8

THE WHITE TADPOLE

I awoke alone in the tent to murmured voices just outside —two Spirite guards who sounded like they hadn't gotten much sleep.

Stepping outside quickly confirmed the theory.

"You two look..."

"Dashing?" Windley grumbled.

I tossed him a vial of vera and rose, taken from Flora's. "Rub this under your eyes. Both of you." My focus bounced between the exhausted men. "Are you...composed?"

"Yes," Windley muttered.

Edius sat with elbows propped on knees, his face buried in his palms, as if attempting to hold his brain inside his skull. A long breath escaped him—one of those deep, steadying exhales that failed to actually steady anything.

"It's Vita, Windley," I said. "Or rather, the lack of Exitium. My spirit feels...abnormally clean now, or something. I think that's why you can sense it more clearly."

Edius rubbed his temples, still staring blankly at the ground. "Lack of Exitium? Wasn't that your invocation?"

"A goddess, actually," Windley supplied. "The queen's lost half of the Nemophile's Crown—the wicked half, apparently—and it's currently en route to possess another royal. A terrifying little vixen with a penchant for offing relatives."

Edius's hands fell from his face, eyes narrowing at Windley as if he'd misheard.

When exactly did we decide we trusted him enough to share all that?

Edius whirled toward me. "That's your business in the north?" he rasped. "So, you're only half as powerful as before?"

"Hardly," scoffed Windley. "As you clearly saw yesterday, she's still perfectly capable of ending life at a whim. So, best behavior, Edmond."

Edius half-rose, then sank back down.

Fingers raked through his hair, gripping hard at the roots while he tried to absorb the news.

"The Crown is split," I went on. "I still wield creation. Destruction's half is with Exitium for now, but we'll reclaim it—equal forces, two sides of one power."

"The hell?" His voice flattened. "As long as you're strong enough to pry that ring off Charm, the rest is background noise."

He might pretend indifference, yet the tight edge in his tone told another story—the same strain I'd heard in Rafe when he spoke of Beau, in Windley when he spoke of me. Love or not, Gwen was what kept him moving.

"I'm going to wash in the spring we passed yesterday," I told them. "We'll need to travel through the night if we want to catch Rafe, so get some sleep. You have one hour."

A short distance from camp, a clear spring shimmered among blue-flowered trees whose roots gripped rocky earth warmed by the mild soil of the foggy fields. After ensuring I was safe from wandering eyes, I undressed and slipped into the tepid water, breathing deeply the cool haze around me—mist that looked like steam but tasted of dew.

Truthfully, I didn't need a bath—I'd just had one at Flora's. But this was more for contemplation. Soulmates, second lives, thirsty Spirites, Charmagne's troubled past, the rhythm of the earth, and the souls I'd sent to the sky...

I was nowhere near sorting through it all when something slick brushed my calf. I yelped, kicking up a panicked splash that slapped the bank.

"An eel!"

Not an eel.

"*A tadpole,*" corrected Vita, amused. "*We can use it.*"

Before I could fathom what we might possibly use a tadpole for, the pool around me began to bubble with green light. An orb of water lifted from its surface, surrounded by a shimmering emerald glow, suspending a tiny white winter frog tadpole directly before my face.

"Use it how, exactly, Vita?"

"*You have already practiced taking life. Now, learn to give it.*"

"It's already alive."

"*Grow it.*"

"How?"

"*Wrap your hands around it and whisper your intentions.*"

I hesitated. Whispering to a tadpole while nude in a spring seemed exactly the sort of thing mad queens might do.

Whatever expression crossed my face as I cupped the water orb, it earned me a tinkling laugh from Vita.

I leaned closer, near enough to kiss it, and cleared my throat. "Grow, little tadpole."

"*As if you mean it.*"

"Please grow into a beautiful winter frog with white skin and lovely jumpy legs."

"You do not need to compliment it, Merrin. Froglings cannot understand humes. Envision its growth. Desire it from your heart."

Easier said than done when I couldn't bring myself to care much about the creature. But as I'd often discovered, sometimes simply closing one's eyes could solve ailments no potion ever could.

So, I closed mine, allowing myself to feel the earth's pulse rippling through the spring, the breathing life of trees whispering through petals, the swell of tiny organisms inhabiting the surrounding water.

"To create is to be fulfilled."

Vita's power expanded in my chest—warmth spreading, tingling through my veins.

"Grow."

The word left my lips infused with Vita's essence, and I saw green radiance glow behind my closed eyelids. When I opened them again, the whole spring shimmered with emerald light, as though conjured by a masterful sorceress.

Suspended before me now was a fully grown winter frog—white-skinned and decidedly lovely-legged.

"Well done, little royal." Vita sent a pulse of warmth through me before slipping away.

This was how I found myself racing back to camp holding a frog, clothes hastily thrown back onto my damp body.

"Windley! Look what I did!"

I stopped short, discovering Edius now inside the tent and Windley passed out near the fire, curled snugly beneath a blanket like a child, hair slowly shifting from pink to blond.

I turned away, stepping through mist to return the frog to its spring home, when—

"Wait." Windley's drowsy voice rose from the fog. "Show me."

"You're awake?"

"I am now."

I crouched beside him and presented the frog proudly.

"Lunch?" he muttered, rubbing his face.

"We aren't eating it! I grew it from a tadpole. I gave it life."

Windley blinked drowsily at me. "You aged a tadpole into a frog?"

"Yes."

"Isn't that technically taking life?"

My smile faltered as the realization sank in.

Oh. Was it?

The frog chose this moment to spring from my palms into the mist, perhaps sensing our troubling conversation.

"Froglings cannot understand humes," Vita reminded lightly.

"Thank you, Vita. Very reassuring," I muttered.

"What's that?" Windley murmured.

"Nothing." I sighed forlornly, glancing toward the spring again. A tiny unease settled in my chest. If this was Vita's idea of creation, I still had much to learn.

"Well, congratulations on aging your tadpole," Windley drawled through another yawn. "You're quickly mastering your power. Perhaps you can turn Charm into a frog next."

"You truly didn't sleep at all last night, did you?" I remarked.

"No. I was kept awake by...primitive thoughts."

I, the glutton, wanted very much to hear what those primitive thoughts entailed.

He sighed theatrically. "Same as ever, queenie. Tying you up, taking you into dark caverns...only, perhaps, a bit stronger than usual. But fret not—I have it under control." A flicker of night shimmered behind his gaze, and his voice dipped low. "I would never harm you, Merr."

I knew that.

I brushed hair tenderly from his brow. "You look like death. Would you like some of my energy?"

He sat up on his elbows. "You don't have to do that. I can manage."

"But you won't ride long in your state," I said. "I'm not sure we can spare any more time to rest."

Windley chewed his lip as though imagining it were mine. "Tempting."

"We shouldn't fear using your power either—not until we know where they are. It might even draw them out, which could work to our advantage."

"*Tempting*," he repeated, voice rougher.

"But I don't want to worsen your instincts, so I'll leave it to your discretion."

He paused, thoughtful. "It wouldn't worsen them."

"It wouldn't?"

"No," he murmured, thumb grazing his lower lip. "It would appease them. They grow unruly when denied. The memory elixir helped, but once it wore off—and after I tasted you..."

He trailed off, flicked his head as though clearing fog. "I'm fine, Merr. You're under no obligation to satiate me."

Satiate.

Saaatiate.

I leaned closer, voice dropping to match his. "I don't think I need to remind you I enjoy it, too."

A slow, unholy smile tugged at his mouth. "Well, if it's for your sake..."

He rose, extending a blackstone-ringed hand, eyes brightening with invitation, chin cocked in arrogant promise—the faint points of his ears catching the light. "Play with me, lion queen?"

"Play?" I took his hand. "Well, it has been a while since we've enjoyed a proper game, so perhaps—"

Before I could blink, he scooped me up, sprinting away from camp into fields of hazy blue, invigorated, as if he hadn't spent half the morning looking like death warmed over.

"Yes," he purred, tightening his hold. "This feels good."

"Windley, are you trembling?"

"Only a little. Excitement, queenie." His voice dropped to a mischievous hush. "Let's pretend I'm stealing you, shall we?"

His heart raced wildly at the thought.

Mine matched his pace.

"I've never played this particular game, but I think I rather like it," I whispered, mock-protesting just enough to encourage him.

"Shush," he ordered softly, lips grazing my temple. "If I were really stealing you, I'd have ensured your silence. Where I'd truly like to take you is that hermit's abode—remote, abandoned, where we'd never be disturbed..."

Something in him coiled tighter, a restrained force beneath his words.

"But this will do," he said, slowing.

He carried me into a small thicket not far from camp, a natural enclosure wild with overgrown brush, tangled roots, and trailing vines whispering secrets in the breeze. He set me down like a prince, and my feet sank into damp earth, my back pressed against the rough bark of a gnarled, leafless tree whose twisted limbs clawed into the mist.

I traced absently along the aged grooves of its trunk. "Do you like this location because it's hidden?"

"I like it," he said, a predatory rumble curling beneath the words, "because *you're* hidden."

His gaze fixed on my mouth—hesitation fluttering for barely a pulse.

"May I take this further?" He held his hand just shy of my lips, awaiting permission.

Windley himself wasn't dangerous, yet the reminder of his primal hunger was—and I found that danger intoxicating.

"Yes," I breathed. "Take it further."

He closed the gap. Fingers—heat-slick despite the cool air—slid along my cheek, then sealed over my mouth, a velvet-iron reminder of who directed the moment. His other hand skimmed to my shoulder, easing my shirt downward in a slow reconnaissance.

Neck. Shoulder. Collarbone. His mouth traced a pulse-stirring route over each, leaving sparks that hummed beneath my skin.

A faint, helpless sound spilled from me; his heartbeat answered, drumming against my palm.

He dipped lower, dwelling at the hollow of my throat while he inched the fabric aside. Every brush—every breath—left me blazing.

Emerald eyes tracked the reveal as he bared more of my chest.

I flinched—a whisper of doubt.

Like an anemone sensing threat, he recoiled, peeling his hand from my lips as though scalded.

"You all right, queenie?"

The hesitation hadn't come from disapproval, but from something new and vulnerable: being uncovered, tasted, explored.

Warmth prickled across my skin, pooling beneath every place he'd touched—and every place he might yet claim. My breath hitched.

"Keep going."

His eyes darkened with relief and rekindled hunger. Yet he paused again, carefully cupping my breast, lowering his mouth with aching tenderness. A shiver rippled down my spine, heat spreading through my veins as his lips moved over me—unhurried, staking a slow, possessive path.

Here, hidden among quiet roots and tangled vines, alone in the hush with a predator—I welcomed primitive thoughts.

But Windley was noble—for a soul-stealing incubus.

With restraint that seemed to pain him, he slid my shirt respectably back into place, leaving my stomach tightened, veins heated.

Not entirely noble, though.

He spun me around, pressing me forward against the tree, one hand holding me firmly while the other trailed slowly, torturously, up my back beneath my shirt. Every vertebra ignited beneath his touch, baiting me with aching, carnal desire. I could feel him behind me, tense muscles, suppressed breath, his energy filling the spaces inside me left by my stolen strength—making me want to bite him, claw at him, crawl inside him.

When he reached the top, he hesitated again.

"I've...taken enough," he panted. "I should stop."

Yet he continued to hold me pinned there, our hearts racing in unison—loud, insistent, drowning out reason.

Edius was right; submission could be sweet—but so could dominance.

I turned swiftly, reversing our positions and pinning Windley to the rough bark, one hand snug at the nape of his neck—thumb grazing the live wire of his pulse—while the other braced his shoulder.

"L-lion—"

I swallowed the rest of his protest with a kiss, threading my fingers into his hair and sliding my palm over the hard planes of his abdomen. He answered with a low growl, hoisting me onto his hips and pressing me to a nearby tree. The bark scored my back in the best possible way.

"Goddess, Merrin," he breathed, rolling his hips against mine. "Out of every guard, every Spirite—how am I the bastard lucky enough for this?"

I meant to tease him in reply, but a shimmer of beguilement lit his eyes—dangerous, hungry.

He caught himself at once, easing me to my feet. "Damn it. Did I stop in time?"

"Only just," I said, collecting my breath.

His heat transformed to quiet vigilance as he brushed damp strands from my face. "I didn't drain you?"

"I feel many things," I said, decidedly content, "but 'drained' isn't one of them. You?"

"Say the word, and I'm yours all night."

"For travel, you mean?"

"What else?" His brow raised, inviting me to take it further.

We were just immature enough that innuendo would always be our shared language. Yet a sober warmth overtook his features. He tipped my chin with gentle surety. "You realize I'd never consider you prey, don't you? Pets offer themselves for feasting, but you, my queen...you're so much more."

I sealed my answer with a soft kiss.

All the way back to camp, he laced his fingers through mine, striding in with renewed swagger. At the tent he rapped the canvas smartly.

"Up and at it, berk—fruitcake awaits!"

When only groans answered, Windley gave the fabric a playful slap, laughter rumbling in his chest until movement stirred inside.

Edius finally emerged, looking worse for wear. His weary gaze ricocheted between Windley and me, a spark of envy and irritation flaring in his eyes before he masked it. A sleeveless undershirt hugged his frame—that drew the eye to broad shoulders and a tapered waist.

Windley sidled up beside me, waiting for the question I was still shaping in my mind.

"Yeah, yeah, go ahead," he sighed, already reading my intention. "But why even ask me? It's your spirit."

"I suppose I technically didn't."

"Spared you, then, did I?" He clasped his hands behind his back with mock formality while I decided just how loose I wanted to be with my own spirit. "It isn't indecent, if that's what you're wondering. Not in my reality."

"Is it safe?" I asked, voice pitched low.

"Safer than what we just did," he returned.

I cleared my throat, drawing Edius's attention. "Edius? Would you like a little energy—enough to travel comfortably?"

He stiffened for a beat. "No, thank you."

A breath passed. Then he tossed the tent flap aside.

"Wait. Are you sure you're all right with it?"

"I wouldn't have offered otherwise."

With a grudging glance at Windley, he muttered, "Do you mind?"—clearly asking for privacy, not permission.

"Not at all," Windley replied with a plastered-on smile, making no move to leave.

Edius rolled his eyes, then faced me.

"This'll be quicker—and easier."

He brushed aside my outstretched hand and hauled me into a seasoned bear-hug. His shirt breathed the same cologne I'd noticed the night he kidnapped me—and the arms caging me felt like braided cable. Power flowed in a steady pulse, far smoother than the jolt he'd dealt on the beach or in the manor.

He held me as though welcoming a long-lost friend.

"If you feel like clinging back, go ahead. That's just instinct talking."

I already was.

I waited, a bit awkwardly, hugging him fondly while Windley looked on.

"*This beastling harbors no malice,*" Vita murmured, and I felt the truth settle inside me.

Without his usual hungry edge, the moment felt oddly calming; Edius's oversized embrace was protective rather than predatory. So when he murmured, almost absent-mindedly,

"You taste better every time..."

I didn't recoil the way I might have moments ago.

Color crept up the rims of his ears. "Dammit—compulsion. Just...take it as a compliment."

A beat, then his voice dropped to a thunder-low whisper meant for me alone.

"And...sorry about last night."

"Vita's presence amplifies everything," I told him.

"Yeah, well..." His jaw ticked. "I'm usually better at control. I don't make a habit of forcing affections—especially not on marked humans. Won't happen again."

"Marked?" I echoed.

Edius's gaze flicked past me to Windley—held there a breath—then came back.

"Forget it," he muttered, slamming the door on the subject.

When he finally released me, the shadows beneath his eyes had thinned, and a new vigor hummed in his stance.

"Feel better?" I asked, curious at seeing this power play out.

Edius studied me, some unreadable emotion flickering behind his gaze. Then, without warning, he tapped a finger lightly against my forehead.

Windley didn't comment, simply ordering Edius to finish packing the tent so we could resume pursuit of Rafe along the coast—the path we assumed he'd taken.

With any luck, I thought, we would catch him tonight.

But luck wouldn't be with us that night—or the next night. Rafe, for his part, would soon find himself knee-deep in his own mess—both literally and figuratively.

As for the rest of us...

We had scarcely begun extinguishing the campfire when both Spirites stiffened simultaneously, rigid as if struck by some unseen blow.

I dropped the kettle I'd been holding. "What is it?"

Neither answered immediately; instead, they exchanged a tense, loaded glance.

"You feel Charmagne?" I guessed.

"Worse," Windley revealed, slowly turning northward.

"Ascian," Edius finished, expression grave. "We feel Ascian."

9

CONFESSIONS

It was impossible. Even Vita had confirmed Ascian's soul hadn't survived my spell. I reminded the Spirites of that as we rode swiftly north.

"It did feel different, didn't it?" said Edius. "Sorta hollow?"

Windley nodded. "Yeah. Like a phantom..." A sudden realization whetted his gaze. "Oi, Edmond, was Ascian wearing his ring when you beguiled him?"

"Well, yeah," said Edius. "He never took it off—" The same understanding flashed across his features. "You think that's it? We imprinted on the ring instead of Ascian himself?"

"It would make sense," said Windley, slowing Dandelion slightly. "The only reason Ascian had us beguile him was so he could summon us whenever he wished. But wouldn't he also want the option of using his powers unnoticed? Surely, I wasn't the first to betray him."

"You're right," said Edius, thoughtful. "That ring can hold power on its own, independent of him. If our imprint landed there, all he had to do was remove it when he wished to work magic in secret."

"Then it was Charmagne you felt," I concluded. "Using Ascian's ring."

"It would be just like her," said Edius. "Taunting us by wielding his power after sensing us use ours."

"And if she headed straight north from the beach," I reasoned, "then she'd naturally be ahead of us."

"Likely," Windley agreed, though tension still edged his voice.

I waited until Edius had trotted a safe distance ahead, then leaned close to Windley, murmuring quiet reassurance. "He's gone, Wind. I felt him vanish. Vita herself confirmed his soul crossed to the departed plane."

Windley's shoulders eased, and he squeezed my hand as if siphoning strength.

Whatever it was they'd sensed, it gave urgency to our journey north, hoping to catch Charmagne on our way to intercept Exitium.

With ripples as our guide, we rode through day and night, blue skies fading to gold, blinking away grass and wind and worry. The next time we stopped for camp, it was at the southern edge of the Emerald Wood.

A few significant things happened that night.

The first occurred the moment we set up camp beside a silver stream winding through the enchanted forest. Soleil painted the sky for Luna, sweeping vibrant oranges and deep golds across the canopy, bathing the leaves in apocalyptic beauty.

Bitch.

I was halfway through cursing her when Windley helped me down from Dandelion, but my complaints vanished the instant my feet touched the mossy ground.

Moving into the Emerald Wood had already been breathtaking. The earth's pulse, which I'd grown used to, now thrummed more vividly beneath my skin. Life stirred everywhere—creatures rustled high among the branches, vines stretched and twisted with each slow breath. Ferns swelled with their own subtle heartbeats, and even the leaves seemed to murmur, carrying whispers of blood through their veins.

Vita's power tingled through my body, syncing effortlessly with the forest's vibrant pulse.

But the moment my toes pressed into that emerald moss, everything magnified.

"Lion queen!" Windley reached promptly to catch me as I stumbled forward, momentarily overwhelmed by the surge beneath my feet. It felt as though the moss itself were breathing, rising and falling like a giant, sleeping creature.

"This green wood is hallowed ground," said Vita warmly inside my mind. *"It was my resting place for eons. That is why my power manifests so intensely here—even when you aren't actively wielding it."*

All along, the moss's nightly radiance had been Vita herself?

But why only at night, I wondered.

"My strength is most visible at night, when the forest wakes, alive and restless. In daylight, much of this wood slumbers."

"Merr?" Windley kept me upright, worry creasing his brow.

"I'm all right," I assured in a quiet undertone. "Vita's breath here is intense. It caught me off guard, but I'm adjusting."

He kept me upright, eyes still watchful. Neither he nor Edius would let me help with camp preparations.

So instead, I sank my fingers into the plush emerald moss, marveling at the hidden life trembling beneath its surface, enthralled by the intricate roots weaving deep through the loamy soil.

Windley chuckled, watching me with fond bemusement.

"We're off to fetch dinner, tree whisperer. Be good while we're gone." He dashed away before I could protest. Edius had already vanished quietly in another direction.

Soleil was gone, leaving a lingering rosy wash in her wake. Within this twilight hush, my feet began glowing their signature vibrant green—brighter, stronger than ever before.

"Vita...it feels so different now."

"Indeed, little royal. The destroyer dampened my power last time you walked this wood. Now, I am with you alone, in full."

I brushed my fingertip along the fluted leaf of a strange, waist-high plant, and at once, the entire stalk ignited in radiant emerald.

"Vita!"

Her laughter tinkled away joyfully.

Grinning, I grasped a cluster of vines hanging gracefully from a massive tree. They flared brightly at my touch, pulses of green magic dancing upward. As I moved on, enchanted handprints and glowing footprints marked my delighted passage, fading slowly behind.

So utterly captivated, I didn't realize I was backing right into someone crouched quietly by the streamside—a broadshouldered someone. A broad-shouldered Edius—elbows resting casually on his knees, attention downward, perhaps fishing for dinner.

"Oh!" I gasped, whirling around. "Edius! I'm sorry, I was lost in the magic. Isn't this incredible?"

But as his head lifted, I realized he hadn't been fishing at all. He'd been splashing water on his face.

And—for the first time ever—he'd swept all his long hair fully back, tied neatly in a knot, exposing every feature in crystal clarity.

That's when I saw it.

Edius's hair had always fascinated me—longer and

smoother than northern men wore theirs, usually half-tied back in some sort of shielded habit.

Now I understood why.

All this time, that style had hidden a secret.

Spirites resembled humans—aside from their overly alluring features, cat-like canines, and ears pointed at the tip, giving them a look of natural mischief.

Windley had those ears. Pip, Charmagne, and Ascian had them too.

But—

"Edius...don't all Spirites have pointed ears?"

Still crouched, he yanked the tie from his hair, shaking it loose over his shoulders. "They do."

The glow at my feet bathed him softly in green, illuminating the lines of his arms, the firm angle of his jaw, and the sharper edges hiding behind his usual veil of aloofness.

He knew exactly what I'd seen.

Maybe that was why he didn't flinch when I reached forward and tucked the hair behind his ear with deliberate care, exposing the severed tip.

I exhaled quietly. "Oh."

As I'd thought, Edius's ears had been cut at the points.

"Who—?"

"I did." His voice was calm, unbothered. "Long time ago, trying to fit into a life that wasn't mine."

The quiet rivulet beside him lapped in muted pulses, undisturbed by our presence or our pasts.

The chill of evening crept closer, whispering against my skin, but Edius seemed indifferent to its bite. He watched me from the ground in patient silence, waiting—for judgment, perhaps, or simply acceptance.

"That's all I'm going to say about it, so there's no point asking again."

I still lingered, studying him perhaps a heartbeat longer than he liked.

"May I at least ask if...you've healed from it?"

His mouth pulled into a wry line.

"Like I said, it was ages ago." He lifted one shoulder. "They'd mended before you were even born."

"Hardly." I scoffed. "You can't be that much older than I am."

"Oh?" His head tipped, wry mischief flickering. "Take a guess."

"...Twenty-five?"

Smirk. "Try again."

"...Twenty-seven?"

The smirk only grew.

"Alright, how old are you?"

"I know what you meant," he said, rolling the kink from his neck. "Just messing with you."

A breath escaped me, half-sigh, half-laugh. "I asked because—"

"I know." His gaze flicked to mine, a small warmth unfurling. "...Thanks for worrying."

A breeze stirred, teasing loose strands across his face.

"Does that mean you're starting to like me?"

I answered honestly. "Considerably more than the first time we crossed paths in these woods."

He rubbed the back of his neck, eyes dropping. "...Sorry about that."

I blinked; I hadn't expected an apology.

He pushed on before I could fill the silence.

"I was rough—no excuse. I got in deep, and they had leverage; I needed some of my own." His gaze slid toward the stream. "When you're desperate, what it does to your soul stops mattering."

His jaw tightened. After a breath he added, lower, "Easy to justify anything once you've sunk that far. Bet your boyfriend could tell you the same."

Everyone carried their scars differently.

"I understand, Edius. In a smaller way I've felt that pull—wielding Exitium, even now with Vita. I've made my share of gray choices—though nothing like what you and Windley endured. Or Charmagne."

"Nah. Don't waste sympathy on her. She's a bastard. And for the record, you should've killed her on the beach."

I probably should have.

"But I couldn't strike someone who wasn't even holding a weapon," I said, steady but gentle.

"I know, Merrín." A genuine smile—his first in days—tugged at his mouth.

I narrowed my eyes. "What's funny?"

"Humans like you are rare."

"I suspect you don't know many humans at all," I teased.

He shrugged. "I've eaten a lot."

I recoiled.

He barked a laugh. "Relax, little mirefox—kidding."

I squinted. "I am not...whatever that is."

His gaze drifted down my hair, amusement tugging at the corner of his mouth. "Mmm."

I flicked two fingers at the path. "Back to camp, Edius. Windley should have dinner by now."

He swung in beside me, voice looser than before.

"Edi."

"Hm?"

"It's Edi—if you like."

But it felt strange calling him that, so I simply avoided using his name throughout dinner. Dinner itself proved robust

—food offerings in the enchanted wood were abundant compared to the sparse fields we'd crossed earlier.

Windley was tearing meat from a bone when the night reached its peak. "That glow of yours is blinding, lion queen." He scooped my feet onto his thigh, though it did little good since the ground beneath me still shone brightly.

"I'll get her a blanket," Edius said, dropping one over me like a tent, his mouth twitching as I poked my head out.

We'd made camp in a clearing beneath a break in the trees, the better to see the stars guiding us home. Necessary, perhaps, but unsettling as it gave us a perfect view of Luna's eerie, newly egg-shaped form.

"Well, that's...spooky," Windley murmured uneasily.

I turned inward to the one who might offer clarity. "What's wrong with her, Vita?"

"*It seems she attempts to breach the celestial realm and reenter the physical plane.*"

"Can she do that?!"

"*Only if the splintered fragments of her body reunite. Such a body should never have existed. The moon and sun are astral beings, meant only to pass above, never enter the physical world. Alas, my sisters have long coveted the lower plane.*"

"Why?"

"*Long ago, they shared rule over the race of angels. But those fell, and with nothing left to rule, they turned their desires toward the hearts and flesh of those carrying angelic remnants—conjurers.*"

I nearly choked. "Wait—are you saying Rafe has angel blood?"

Vita's laugh trickled through my thoughts, honeyed and knowing. "*Not fully, no. But faint echoes of angelic lineage still dwell within him, granting him dominion over the powers of sun*" *and moon, much as your royal heritage grants you dominion over creation and destruction."*

I reeled slightly. Rafe—brooding, mysterious Rafe—carrying a sliver of angelic blood? It explained so much, yet raised a hundred more mysteries.

My mind swirling, I pressed further. "Then what exactly are royals descendants of?"

"The very first humes ever created," Vita answered with clear affection. *"They rested longest in my palm, staining their blood with divine essence—the same essence flowing through you."*

Divine essence. Was that why royals smelled different to Spirites and widowbirds? Did that mean…?

But before I could spiral further, Vita tugged gently at my attention. *"I enjoy speaking with you, little royal, but your companion grows anxious without your reply."*

She meant Windley, who'd apparently been shaking my shoulders for some time while I conversed privately with Vita.

"Oh!" I blinked back into the physical realm, cheeks warming. "Sorry, Wind. I was just—Vita explained about Luna, and…" I hesitated, my eyes drifting toward Edius and back. "And Rafe."

Windley tilted his head, curious. "And?"

My pulse quickened as I relayed what I'd learned.

Windley's eyes widened, then his lips quirked. "Our brooding conjurer's part angel? Well, that explains why wraiths always flock to him."

"And Vita says royals carry divine essence of their own—it's literally in our blood."

That earned a double-take from both Spirites.

"So now we know why I smell divine to your kind," I said, if Vita was right.

The grin froze on Windley's lips; his nostrils flared once, a pulse beating at his throat.

"It explains why you smell different, queenie—let's...leave it at that."

"What does that mean?"

"Nothing." The flush creeping up his ears said otherwise, and for the first time his gaze skittered away—as though afraid of what I'd see if he met my eyes.

Interesting. I'd keep questioning Vita in private—glean more, and spare the men another round of me staring into space.

"I'm going to relieve myself near the creek. And I'm taking this." I bundled the blanket around my shoulders. "Won't be long."

But while I started in the direction of the stream, I didn't make it far. Instead, I ducked behind a screen of ground foliage, spreading the blanket around myself to smother my glow. I settled within earshot of the camp, intent only on uninterrupted time with Vita.

I never meant to eavesdrop on two predator-blooded twenty-somethings, but the night had other plans. Before I could slip into Vita's glow, Edius's voice sliced through the dark —uncouth as ever.

"So...have you taken her yet?"

Windley scoffed. "I'm not answering that. She's a queen, you filth."

I smiled at his swift defense of my honor, already shifting to leave when—

"Heh. Like a book," Edius drawled, lazy and canny. "Let me guess—you fed her some noble line about 'giving it time,' said it was all for her sake?"

Windley bit down on whatever answer tried to rise.

I knew the line by heart—his vow to wait, to *take* me only

when everything was perfect. Now Edius was yanking the covers off that tidy *in-a-bed* excuse for both of us to stare at.

"Don't blame you," he went on. "Even I find it hard to stop, and I'm not the one in love with her." A breath passed. Silence, then—"Can't imagine what it'd be like if she loved you back."

Windley's silence said everything.

"Would be easy, wouldn't it?" Edius murmured. "A woman that sweet, that warm—could drain her before you realized. She'd slip right through your fingers if you weren't careful."

No. Windley had joked about devouring me, but surely he wasn't actually afraid of hurting me. I waited for him to scoff it off.

"I'm scared as shit, mate."

Windley's voice roughened, edges stripped bare. "We're not made for this love nonsense, yeah? Most days I can leash the hunger before it turns feral, but with her...goddess, it's like holding back a floodgate—like clenching the sweetest sweet between your teeth and never being allowed a bite. What if I can't let go?"

Vita forgotten, I went very still. For all his teasing, Windley was truly afraid he might drain the life from me the moment passion slipped its leash.

Spirites can draw life force from others. Steal it, repurpose it for ourselves. Passion, of course, being the strongest conduit...

Even now, a delicate balance remains. Lose control, and a Spirite could drain their partner in a single moment of ecstasy...

A cruel irony... A lingering instinct from what we once were...

I'd never taken that warning seriously—until now.

"Tough spot," Edius muttered, tone off-hand but not cruel. "Honestly, you'd be safer if you didn't love her at all." He scrubbed a hand over his mouth. "Still—she'd make one hell of a feast. Maybe I'll hunt down my own queen up north."

It was a predator-grade joke—a peace offering, even—and Windley rose to it.

"There's always that fright down south," he drawled. "Soul tastes of brine and bone—right up your alley. Or the northernmost queen; she'll take any warm body, so long as it's pretty enough."

"You?" Edius pried.

"Never another queen," Windley snorted. "Other royals, aye—though that thrill wore thin years ago. Tried to drown her scent in a dozen others, didn't work."

His voice dropped, unexpectedly earnest. "She doesn't smell like that because she's royal."

Really? But our first time through the Emerald Wood—

Maybe it's because you're royal—or maybe it's you...

Windley dragged a hand through his hair, searching for words that didn't exist.

"It's her, mate. The swing of her stride when she thinks no one's looking—all lion and sunrise. The crease that appears between her brows when she's solving some impossible riddle. The way her voice drops right before she decides whether to spare or strike—then lifts again, light as birdsong, as if the whole choice never just shook the stars."

He raked in a shaky breath. "And that scent—summer grass after rain. I taste it and my fangs ache. She walks by and the whole damned horizon tilts. How do I even pick one thing? She's...every bright fever I ever chased."

Edius whistled low and long. "Like sinking your teeth into fruit you know will crack them."

Windley's laugh was short, almost pained. "Yeah—and I'd still bite again."

Silence settled. Edius flicked a twig into the fire; embers snapped.

"Tch. If you were ever going to drain her dry, you'd have

managed it by now. You've hovered round a whole parade of royals and every one of 'em is still kicking, aren't they? No cause to start bungling it this late in the game." He lounged back, legs out, a razor-thin smile cutting across his face. "Unless you're softer than you let on."

The flames crackled.

Windley's reply came lighter, almost surprised. "You're a berk, but...can't remember the last time I talked to another Spirite." A beat. "Thanks, mate."

"Can't remember the last time I talked to one who wasn't nuts," Edius muttered back.

Their conversation ended there.

Windley had made a friend, and I was glad for him. Yet guilt pricked—I had eavesdropped. Stronger still was a new, needle-sharp fear of offering myself to him. Not fear *of* Windley—I trusted him—but fear of the cost. For the first time I truly grasped what loving me might take from him...and from me. I'd have to tread carefully—for both our sakes.

10

THE BLIGHTED ROOTS

I crouched in the woods, hiding my glow, practicing looking natural.

I would never harm you, Merrin. Never.

I believed those words. Believed Windley would never intentionally hurt me. My trust in him was sound.

...But what if it was out of his control?

Every time Windley and I had skirted innocence, he'd always been the one to pull back. Always.

Was it because he feared what might happen if he didn't?

For eight long years, he'd watched me, loved me, held me just out of reach—desired me in ways I'd only begun to understand. What would happen when he finally surrendered? If I let his teeth rest against my neck, could he savor me without sinking them in?

Besides, it was more than a little awkward knowing they'd all been discussing my taste. Windley was one thing—but Pip, Charmagne, even Edius?

Edius, who'd drunk of me twice since joining our mission,

and each time he'd handled me with such deliberate care, as if fighting to remain in our good graces.

With those troubling thoughts swirling, I returned to them feeling like a child caught somewhere I shouldn't be—perhaps playing in the castle armory.

Not speaking from experience, of course.

"Hello, guards." Too stiff. I quickly added a—"H-hope I'm not interrupting any guy-talk."—for good measure.

Windley narrowed his eyes, searching out my secrets—then widened them abruptly, as if he'd found every last one.

Oh no. He knew.

He sprang to his feet, drawing his weapons.

Well, that was a bit extreme!

"Majesty! Look out!"

One of his hatchets whizzed just above my head, slicing into something squishy. Equally squishy bits of plant matter fell onto my shoulders as I covered my hair, whirling around to find whatever Windley had targeted.

None of us had heard it coming.

None of us had noticed it gathering debris.

None of us had seen it amassing life from the surrounding woods.

But there it was, towering over me: a messy heap of rotting vegetation—very much alive.

"What is that?!" I stumbled back into Windley's protective grip.

"I—got nothing. Edmond?"

"Psh. Damn if I know!" Edius stood nearby, fists raised as though prepared to punch the mass, undeterred by its layers of wet peat and soggy leaves.

"Vita?"

"It is blight! Left by the destroyer! She has tainted my wood!"

"Will it attack us?"

The heap answered for itself, lashing out a vine-like tongue.

"Ah—!" Edius tried to punch it away. His fist met sludge; his skin hissed and smoked. "My arm!" A livid purple bloom spread up his forearm. He staggered back, cradling the burn. "I don't know about you two, but I'm getting the hell out of here!"

"Not without the queen, you aren't." Windley yanked me behind him as another tendril whistled past. "You're a guard now—the only way you leave is with her at your side."

Edius shot an anxious look from Windley to the creature to me. "Fine, but I'm not dying for this shit. What's the plan?"

"Did I say I had a plan?" Windley hacked through one vine, ducked a second. "Bloody hell—I'm half useless with my other hatchet buried in that thing!"

"Vita says Exitium left it behind—it's blight. Do you know what that means?"

Windley bounced on the balls of his feet, tracking each twitch of the ooze. "Rot-magic—same stuff blood stags drip after they gore a tree."

"Blight?" Edius's voice shot up an octave. "Brilliant. Farewell, arm!"

"Quit flapping." Windley slashed a feeler in half. "It's treatable."

"Oh, sure. And the antidote just grows on trees up here?"

Their jargon might as well have been moon runes to me.

Hatchet extended defensively, Windley glanced toward our tent and belongings. "Leaving our supplies behind would make for a tough journey home, Merr, but we might not have a choice. Ed's right—a blight curse can only be cured by a Seelie, and I haven't seen one of those in...phoo. Let's just avoid letting that thing touch us."

Windley was right. We *didn't* have a choice.

A second creature slid silently from the darkness behind

Edius. "There's more!" I shouted, panic rising as the woods seemed to close in, cornering us against the campfire that licked our backs like a hungry chimera.

The new attacker flung a vine at Edius, who instinctively blocked with his already-blighted arm, screaming through clenched teeth as his skin sizzled again.

"Maybe try a weapon other than your own flesh, mate!" Windley pushed me protectively behind him, frantically eyeing the forest for an escape route.

In the chaos, I desperately wished I could summon the one word that had rescued us time and again—a word that could obliterate these creatures with shadowy force. The name of the very being who'd left these monstrosities behind.

"Place your faith in ME, Merrin! Destruction is merely the easiest answer! There are always others! Speak to the mud beneath the moss! Tell it to aid you! Do so NOW."

Compelled by Vita's influence, I dropped to my knees and plunged my hands into the thick, damp carpet of moss and soil.

"No pressure, darling," Windley called over his shoulder, "but I hope you've got a trick in that glow of yours!"

No promises. After all, what could I possibly do with mud?

Golems. That was what.

My inspiration came from the blighted creatures themselves—sentient entities born of nature's refuse. Rubbing the cool earth between my fingertips, I pictured a new beast to challenge the blighted ones, equal in form and large enough to protect us.

Acting on instinct, empowered by the divinity flowing in my veins, I imagined the mud-creature's shape forming from the clay of the earth—its size, its limbs, its strength.

The ground beneath us began to rumble.

"Merr?"

In the next instant, our tent exploded skyward as a muddy beast rose up, splitting the mossy ground below.

"For rot's sake," Edius snarled, ducking a slop-tongue. "Spend five minutes with you two and the world falls apart twice."

"It's okay!" I reassured him. "This one's mine!"

A broad, hulking figure of mud stood ready, a tent pole speared through its side, its bulk matching the blighted creatures' own. I felt no creator's love for this being as I had with Flora—it held no soul—but I admired it nonetheless, the way one might admire a painting they'd crafted or a home they'd built by hand.

"Golem! Lend us your strength!" My command boomed, every bit the queen I'd become, and I flung my hand toward the attackers. "Defeat those who stand to harm us!"

Immediately, the golem charged toward the nearest blighted beast. Bracing myself for a messy clash of mud and vine, I watched in surprise as the enemy ignored my creation completely, focused only on living, breathing targets—of which the golem was neither. Unhindered, my muddy guardian slammed into the blight beast, engulfing it beneath its earthy surface and absorbing the curse as easily as clay drawing poison from a wound.

Both Spirites straightened and watched as the golem turned its attention to the second blighted beast still whipping out bits of decay in our direction.

The attacker was absorbed within seconds, after which the mud-man spat Windley's lost hatchet onto the ground before stiffening, awaiting further instructions.

"Patrol the area until dawn," I commanded, "and swallow any others that come for us!"

At once, the creature lumbered into a wide, obedient circle around the campsite.

Vita's power was incredible.

Windley, Edius, and I were only three small souls in a wide, wild world filled with powerful enemies—but that world felt much smaller when allies could rise straight from the earth itself. When life could be given as swiftly as it could be taken. When one could will things to grow.

Edius slumped against a moss-slick trunk, cradling his ruined arm. "Tell me this isn't a typical evening in your company."

Windley wheeled on me, eyes alight. "Goddess, Merr—look at you." Whatever else he meant to say tangled on his tongue; he just shook his head, a breathless laugh escaping. "Come here," he murmured, and hauled me against his chest.

I would never harm you, Merr.

The heavy thud of his heart couldn't lie, pounding deep with desire, admiration, devotion, and longing. Was it enough, I wondered, to hold back his primal nature?

A low, pained groan sounded behind us.

"Edius!" I broke free of Windley's arms, rushing closer to inspect the skin of Edius's arm, which now appeared blackened and festering, decaying from the outside in.

"Don't touch it." Edius wrenched away quickly. "We can't have you catching it, highness."

"The only cure is a Seelie?" My mind raced through every curative in my queendom as I studied the blight. "You mentioned them before, Wind. I think you said they have light in their veins?"

"Yeah." Windley frowned thoughtfully, rubbing his chin. "They can heal magical ailments, but they live in the far south, and we're smack in the middle of nowhere."

"Maybe Vita can do something," I suggested.

Windley shot me a teasing grin. "You've got a closer relationship with this one, huh?"

"It's different. I can tell she cares about us. We aren't just pawns to her." I felt Vita's warmth glitter in my chest. "I...like her."

Windley leaned toward Edius with exaggerated seriousness. "My girlfriend's friends with a goddess—no biggie."

But Edius was beyond caring about our banter. The blight was rapidly creeping up his shoulder, veins of purple threading beneath his skin. Heart racing, I hurried into the other realm.

"Yes, little royal. Though you cannot heal the blight, you can transfer it. Choose what will suffer the curse in the beastling's place."

"Another living thing?"

"That is correct."

"Oh dear. Does it need to be an animal?"

"It does not, so long as it is mighty enough to bear the blight."

Meaning no mere weed would suffice.

"One of the mammoth trees?" I suggested.

"If that is what you choose."

But it was heartbreaking to think of sacrificing such an ancient, noble being.

More heartbreaking still to watch Edius be devoured by rot.

"Come here." I took his oversized hand with deliberate care and guided him toward a mighty tree already stripped of half its branches by some past trauma—perhaps a lightning strike or windstorm.

"What're you about to do?" Edius asked, wary and suspicious as an injured animal. "You aren't half Seelie, are you? Nah, I'd know that smell like my own."

He would recognize a *Seelie's* scent?

"No, I can't heal your ailment, but I can transfer it to another living creature. I choose this one. Its pulse is weaker than the rest. I suspect it's already nearing the end of its days."

Windley observed casually, leaning back as if patiently awaiting the conclusion of one of my market transactions.

"You're gonna suck the blight out of me?" Edius eyed the tree as though expecting it to retaliate. "Is that even possible?"

"Have faith, Edius." It had taken me long enough to learn the value of it myself.

Vita's gentle laugh glittered inside me.

I coaxed Edius's fingers open against mine, pressing my other palm to the tree's rough, dying bark. Closing my eyes, I listened to its faint heartbeat, catching the slow, labored breath of Vita moving through it.

Exhaling steadily, my glow flared brighter as I drew the blight from Edius's body, channeling the rot through myself and into the tree. The ancient being shuddered as the curse flowed into its veins—unfair, undeserved, but necessary.

When it was done, I dropped Edius's healed hand but kept my other pressed mournfully against the trunk.

"Easy there. What's wrong, lion queen?" Windley's concern spiked, seeing tears rolling freely down my cheeks.

"I feel bad," I sniffled. "It's only a tree, but it had a pulse. And now it suffers for us."

The bark, once sturdy and gray, now bore streaks of sickly purple, spreading through cracks like infected veins. Nearby, Edius marveled quietly, flexing fingers now cleansed of rot.

"Do not lament, little royal. It is glad to be of use in its last days."

"Really?" I whispered. "That's...so kind."

Without thinking, I threw my arms around the weathered trunk, pressing my cheek against its rough ridges—drawing confused looks from both men who couldn't hear Vita's comforting voice.

No, I had never before felt love for a tree. But it was real.

Love and life were everywhere in creation, if one had ears to hear it.

I was lucky enough to hear it.

"You did well, Merrin. You are learning."

Finally, Vita's power was beginning to feel natural.

Thank goddess.

Yes, that goddess.

"There, there," Windley comforted, rubbing my back long after my tears had dried. "I'm sure it lived a long and happy life standing right here, never moving or seeing the world, or experiencing love, or tasting dessert..."

I elbowed him. "Scoundrel."

But I was smiling, and so was he, and that was one of Windley's greatest gifts—his uncanny ability to brighten even the darkest moments.

I would never harm you, Merr.

I believed him. Believed he would fight anyone to protect me—even himself.

He had shown restraint time and again. For eight long years, he had shown restraint.

He had fought for me, encouraged me, praised me. He was the one who warmed my heart enough to alter fate itself.

Wrapped in his arms, I wasn't afraid.

I would never be afraid of his embrace.

Once our tent was repaired, we set our sights on sleep, comforted by the thought of a giant mud guardian circling our campsite. It was with eyes fixed appreciatively on that very guardian that Edius stopped me at the mouth of the tent.

"Heya. Thanks for that. All of it." He paused awkwardly. "Sorry I considered running before. Won't happen again. I mean to be a proper guard to you until this is over, alright?" He glanced away stubbornly. "But I'm still not bowing."

"I understand. I have my own doubts from time to time.

The important thing is working through them to arrive where we're meant to be. It makes us stronger."

I would never harm you...

Edius's piercing gaze lost some of its edge, lingering on me in thoughtful appraisal.

"You sacrificed your flesh for us," I added gently. "That's commendable. Very guard-like, in fact. But don't worry, I'll never make you bow for me...Edi."

Like an instinct, Edius reached out, poking me lightly in the forehead.

It wasn't the only thing in motion.

Inside his chest, something squirmed.

II

THE WAY HOME

I paid close attention to Edius's heart the next day, listening carefully for any signs of growth. I wasn't entirely sure what that squirm had meant, but I had a strong suspicion—and if my suspicion was correct, it came with multiple reasons for concern.

One: Edius was already promised to someone named Gwen, and I had no intention of drawing his affections away from her.

Two: Windley held my heart—and he held it tightly.

Three: A Spirite could only fall in love once. If Edius wasted his on me, he'd be forever unrequited.

I had to ensure that squirm remained dormant.

But Edius's heart stayed closed the next day, and the next—pit-like, exactly as it should be. Even when I renewed the dressings, working vera into the wounds he couldn't reach, his heart remained stubbornly small.

Besides, surely I wasn't so arrogant as to think my mere presence could ensnare someone's heart, was I? In fact, I doubted I'd ensnared anyone's heart in all my life, save Windley's.

I tucked that worry away as we traveled through the Emerald Wood, golem lumbering dutifully behind, practicing Vita's powers by coaxing ferns to unfurl and slyly sending vines to trip Windley whenever we broke camp—also by withering great patches of moss before refueling them with Vita's breath, returning them to the emeraldest of greens. Vita's power felt increasingly natural the more I used it. I could stamp it into existence through my feet, gesture it to life with my hands, or simply blow it into being. Flowers sprouted wherever I stepped.

"She's like some gods-damned wood nymph," I overheard Edius mutter to Windley.

"*Showoff*," Windley coughed theatrically into his sleeve, prompting me to lift a subtle hill of moss beneath him, sending him stumbling sideways.

"Defend me, Edmond! What the nymph does to one of us, she does to both of us!"

"You're on your own," Edius smirked.

I loved this—the ease of their growing camaraderie, Windley's guard steadily lowering, Edius softening. The nights spent in our little tent began to feel as natural as any night spent alongside Rafe or Albie. The conversation I'd overheard—though uncomfortable at the time—had unburdened Windley, and I was grateful. He deserved a friend who understood his struggles.

Progress was slower than we'd hoped through this stretch, the scattered trees preventing the prancelopes from reaching full speed—not that they weren't determined to try. Edius and Windley had their hands full, wrestling the beasts away from sudden obstacles appearing at the last possible moment.

"Ugh. Reminds me of that naughty stag of yours, queenie."

We emerged from the woods with mingled relief and frustration, spilling into the open expanse of northern fields, where our beasts could run freely through clover meadows swept by autumn breezes.

Perhaps it was imagination, but the air tasted different on this side—flavored with northern flora, peppered with memories, salted with a sense of home.

This was the air I'd breathed in my first decades of life. This was the air in which Windley had first revealed his heart to me. Maybe it simply felt good to return to familiar greens.

But it wasn't long before those greens became distinctly unfamiliar.

"Hey, lion queen. Are you seeing this?"

Peeking out from behind Windley's warm back, I surveyed the grass stretching before us. "Is that paint?" I asked, squinting at the patches of ground periodically splashed with something silver—the largest patches stretching yards wide.

"Oi, Ed! Time out!"

Windley slipped us both down from Dandelion, crouching to examine the strange substance.

"It's dry, though," I mused, running my fingers over the peculiar markings. They had a metallic sheen, smooth as mercury, stretching far across the field. Whatever this was, it would've taken an army to spread it all.

"What is that stuff?" Edius asked. "Someone murder a star stag?"

I clutched my chest in horror. "Oh my goddess—"

"No, star stags aren't even real," Edius scoffed before I could fully panic.

I squinted pointedly at him. "Right. Because *star stags* would be ridiculous. Unlike, say...mirefoxes."

Windley hummed thoughtfully, rubbing his chin. "Not to alarm you, queenie, but this paint smells familiar."

To him, perhaps, but my human nose wasn't sensitive

enough to define the scent. I plucked a silver-stained clover and held it up to the sunlight, admiring the way tiny specks of glitter danced upon its surface.

"It smells just like those creatures Luna sent after us at the southern mountain," Windley clarified.

Instantly, I tossed the clover away.

"Ah! Not at me, Merr!"

By creatures, Windley meant Luna's moonbeams. We'd assumed she could no longer summon them since being exiled to the skies—but, in truth, we had no proof aside from the fact she hadn't sent any since the destruction of her body. Since I had destroyed her body. It was troubling, though, that the thick canopy of trees had hidden her from our view the past few nights.

"*Your companion is correct, little royal. These streaks are lunar residue—the essence the moon-goddess sloughed off while forcing herself toward the mortal plane.*"

"She didn't actually break through, did she?"

"*She did not, and she cannot. This is merely evidence of the wound she gave herself in the attempt. Perhaps the pain will teach her caution.*"

Good. For Rafe's sake—and Beau's.

Windley wrinkled his nose, scraping the silver smear off his boot heel.

"'Lunar residue,' huh? Any clarification on *what* part of Lady Moon we're wading through?"

I grimaced. "Since we shattered her giantess form she's nothing but an orb of raw magic, so...call it moon-run-off?"

"Giantess? Moon run-off?" Edius arched a brow at his prancelope, as though the animal might confirm we'd all gone mad. The beast only nickered for a scratch, and Edius obliged with a dry, *well-this-is-my-life* sigh.

He often did that—smiled with parts of his face that

weren't his mouth, humor flickering briefly in his eyes. It differed from Rafe, who typically showed no amusement whatsoever, and far different from Windley, who tossed smirks around like candy at a festival.

"What are you thinking about?" purred a devil in my ear.

I'd been staring...at the *wrong* Spirite.

"Edius," I admitted, turning to the right Spirite.

Windley lifted his palms dramatically. "Not even going to attempt a cover-up?"

"There's little point. You know me too well."

"Right you are. Well then—" He spun me gently, placing his chin on my shoulder to see exactly what had captured my attention. "What about him? Those rippling abs? That monochrome hair tied back like a maiden's? Or maybe that unreadable stare—never quite sure if he wants to murder or undress you?"

"The way he smiles without smiling," I mused softly.

Windley squeezed my arms lightly. "You're thinking about another predator's smile. *Wonderful.*"

"Lack of smile." I nudged him playfully. "And you aren't worried."

"You're right." He released me with an exaggerated sigh. "I'm not. The way I see it, I have about eight years before I need to start worrying. After all, that's how long it took you to realize you had a thing for me—and I'm infinitely more charming."

"Less so every time you proclaim it."

"I mean, you created an entire person and rewrote time just to court me. Thoroughly enamored, Merr. How will I ever escape?"

Unbearable. Just the way I liked him.

Windley's smirk deepened as if hearing that exact thought. His confidence radiated from him like sun-warmed stone. He knew precisely how to push my buttons, how to tease just enough to keep me engaged—to keep me sparring. A game we'd played for years, one I'd never tire of, and one that had changed in ways neither of us could've imagined since that first kiss.

"We should give the beasts some rest before dark," Edius called, nodding toward the prancelopes. "Still planning to ride through the night?"

"Good thinking, Edmond. But watch out for the moon splooge."

Edius halted mid-step. "That's what this is?"

Windley shrugged innocently.

"Don't listen to him, Edi," I assured. "It sounds more like it's closer to blood than to..." I frowned, searching for a more queenly term than *splooge*.

"Blood's not much better," Edius muttered, eyeing the silver streaks with undisguised disgust. He carefully guided his prancelope around the largest splotches.

Windley, being Windley, promptly stepped directly into the thickest patch, turning back with a jester's grin as if awaiting applause.

Schemer.

I rolled my eyes, preparing a proper scolding, but before I could speak, Windley patted his thigh with an inviting gesture. "Come on, darling."

I barely had a moment to brace myself before he dipped low, inviting me to hop onto his back like a child. He hoisted me effortlessly, spun us once purely for drama, then trotted forward through the clover.

Sigh. Goddess, I could've squeezed him senseless.

Come to think of it, perhaps that's exactly how he felt about me.

He carried me across the fields, purposefully stepping into

more moon-drippings and laughing while Edius hopped about, irritated, like a finicky cat avoiding puddles.

Schemer and menace.

I tightened my arms around Windley, pressing my cheek against his strong back, inhaling the warm, familiar scent of him. His body was solid beneath me, his shoulders broad under my palms. The fabric of his shirt was worn-in and buttery, yet his heat still bled through, seeping into me like kindling eager to ignite.

"Wind."

"Hm?"

I nestled closer, lips brushing the curve of his ear. "I think you might be onto something."

"Oh?"

"I fear I might actually be enamored with you."

His breath hitched, but he said nothing.

I allowed the moment to stretch, leaving him in sweet suspense—then, with all the gravity of a queen delivering prophecy, murmured: "My crush on you is growing at an alarming rate."

And then I took his pointed ear between my teeth.

"Also, you're kind of hot."

Perhaps I'd said it just to feel his heartbeat surge beneath my chest.

"You're trying to torture me, aren't you?" His voice was controlled, but I felt the shift in his grip, fingers tightening around my thighs. A careful breath, his touch curling slightly into my skin. "Keep it up. Your punishments continue to grow."

The breeze seemed to delight in our exchange, swirling around us, stirring Windley's dark hair against my cheek, mingling his scent into the air.

Goddess, I wanted nothing more than to sink into him.

"Plenty of open space out here, queenie. If I run off with you, you'll never be heard from again."

"Is that meant to be a threat or a promise?"

"You won't know until we get there," he replied lowly.

Instincts—I had a few of my own. It was probably for the best that they were interrupted by Edius.

The Spirite had moved a bit ahead, gesturing toward an especially large silver patch. "Hey! Something you two might wanna see up here."

Windley blew a bull's breath from his nose—"Behave."—before trotting toward Edius and sliding me carefully from his back so he could examine the ground. "Wait, these are—"

"Hoofprints?" I finished. We were deep in the wilds, yet here were north-facing hoofprints cutting through Luna's strange discharge—the remnants of her fallen moonbeams. "Rafe!" I gasped. "He rode through these while they were still wet!"

"Looks that way." Windley's eyes settled on the northern horizon. "At least we know he made it this far. And if he was riding alone, it must mean Queen Beau and the others returned north when you sent them back."

Both good news and bad—for while it meant Rafe was safe, it also meant the queendoms were that much closer to Exitium's reach.

"Rafe's the magician you were traveling with?" Edius clarified.

"The one you impersonated," I reminded.

"Riiight," Edius drawled.

"Chap's caught up in some goddess drama. Sneaking around with another queen. Whole thing," Windley summarized lazily.

Edius glanced at me pointedly. "Seems to be a lot of that going on up north."

"Alright, beacon of purity," Windley scoffed, folding his arms.

But Edius was right. Aside from my affair and Beau's, Windley claimed Queen Esma had invited him to bed, and I'd witnessed Sestilia make a similar offer. Perhaps we were all destined to desire someone beyond our blood. Maybe none of us truly loved those we were promised to.

...Even my mother?

"Heya, Merrín? You've got a leaf or something in your hair."

"Ignore it," Windley advised. "There's usually debris hiding in that mane of hers. Though she does go weak in the knees if you pluck it out for her." He leaned in, deftly removing the leaf and releasing it into the wind.

Impossible to argue how good it felt to have someone tug at your hair.

I was busy proving Windley's point, Edius watching my reaction with concealed amusement, when both Spirites suddenly jolted—as if shot through their chests with arrows.

"What is it?" I lurched forward, recognizing their reactions. "You feel something?"

They had turned their heads simultaneously in the same direction, expressions darkening. Windley seemed reluctant to speak, but finally admitted, "It's Ascian. Stronger this time." Something else went unspoken.

"Tell me," I demanded.

The Spirites traded a look.

"Bad news, Merr," Windley said, voice gone flinty. "Whatever's rippling, it's coming from the next bend of coast."

That curve hid two crowns:

The Cove—Sestilia's serpent-pit.

The Crag—mine.

I'd left the Crag trusting it would hold: Lekhana on the

dais, Mother Poppy guiding council, Saxon drilling what few lancers I'd allowed to stay while the veterans rode at my command.

But weeks had stretched the realm thin. Ascian's ring had landed on a venomous cupcake's finger, her pet boy brimming with spider-spawned power—and every fresh ripple of that magic seemed to be homing for my coast.

I hadn't acted queenly of late, yet the title still clung to me; if those waves reached the cliffs before I did, *Queen Merrin of the Crag* might be all that was left of either.

12

GROUND RULES

We rode on faster than ever before, urging the prancelopes' hooves into a thundering gallop, cutting through barren countryside until the first sparse signs of civilization began to dot the landscape. Part of me wished the ripples came from the Cove, to spare my own queendom from Charmagne's wrath. Yet another part feared encountering Pip and his "creature" within the domain of an Exitium-possessed Sestilia.

Could our enemies truly be converging? Was it mere coincidence?

Either way, setting the Cove as our destination made sense.

But the coast wouldn't bend to our urgency; every gallop felt tar-thick, every pause a theft of time.

Ascian was ashes—I'd seen to that—yet Edius and Windley twitched whenever a fresh ripple of his power rolled across the air. It was Charmagne, lashing his ring and spilling his curses northward. She knew nothing of my bloodline, no reason at all to strike the Crag—yet dread whispered she would.

Lekhana—barely twenty-one—held my throne with

polished council poise but no taste of war. I had kept only Albie and Rafe beside me; the rest of our steel I'd scattered—wings south to hunt for Beau, wings west to shore up the Clearing—leaving Saxon home with green recruits and the Crag's reputation for curatives to keep neighbors polite.

I had thinned the hive to chase fires on three fronts. Had my crown's absence already doomed the very people it had been forged to shield?

I withdrew into reflective silence, revisiting every step that had brought me here—doubting, questioning, replaying each choice. All the while the devil before me struggled not to deepen my burden, tucking his own worry behind a practiced grin—yet I sensed it plainly, now that his pulse and heart were bound to mine. Edius, too, fell unusually still; after our talks in the Emerald Wood he knew why Windley and I had grown so solemn, and he kept his distance—whether out of respect or simply uncertainty, I could not tell.

We took a different path back north, staying close to the coast without care for who saw us—no one could catch us anyway. The night soon shimmered with ruby-red firebugs, signaling we were drawing closer.

It was amid their glowing dance that we stopped for dinner on a cliff overlooking the sea, Luna's oblong weight gently tugging waves ashore. Sitting at the edge, watching her silver reflection ripple across the water, I was relieved to see she wasn't leaking. Relieved to find the world seemingly unchanged despite my fears.

"Heya."

With knees hugged to my chest and hair tousled by the chill night air, I turned to see Edius.

"Windley wanted me to see if you're in the mood for turnips. Said you only like them forty percent of the time."

"I notice you've stopped calling him Windalloy. I'm sure he

appreciates that." I smiled softly. "Though I doubt he'll return the favor anytime soon."

Edius's mouth curved, betraying subtle amusement as he folded his arms. "Turnips or no?"

"Turnips are fine. Can't exactly afford to be choosy out here. We were lucky to find a farmer willing to trade."

He studied me for a moment, eyes unreadable. "I'll tell him you don't want any."

True, I didn't.

I turned back to the sea, but Edius lingered, crouching beside me. "Everything okay?"

A heavy question.

"I'm fine. Just tired."

Yet Edius didn't move. "No, you're not."

He was right, of course.

I gazed into the sprawling beauty of night, fighting to keep my feelings from rising to the surface. "I'm worried about my queendom."

"I bet." Edius's presence felt solid beside me, like a steady rock. He rested his wrists loosely over his thighs, patiently waiting for my confession.

"The northlands are peaceful, and my queendom is protected due to the curatives it produces. I didn't fear leaving them when all this started, but..." Moisture blurred my vision despite my efforts, and I blinked it away, focusing instead on Luna's deceptive beauty. "I don't understand why Charmagne would set the coast as her destination. She knows nothing about my origins, so it can't be personal—but she knows my name, and if she starts asking around..." I wiped my cheek against my shoulder. "I basically abandoned my rule to follow Windley, and while I'm more than willing to fight the ghosts of his past, I never meant for my subjects to get dragged into it."

After quietly absorbing my words, Edius shifted his gaze out to sea. "So you really are a queen, after all."

"Though I hardly feel I have the right to call myself one. What have I done for my people lately, other than abandon them and send danger their way?"

"Well, for starters, you stopped yourself from blowing up the world."

True.

"And you rescued your friend—that other queen?"

Also true.

"And you put an end to Ascian, who would've eventually set his sights north anyway."

Speculative, perhaps, but comforting nonetheless.

"Look, we don't even know Charm's headed to your kingdom for sure—"

"Queendom," I corrected gently.

"Right. We don't know that's her destination. Like you said before, she probably headed straight north from the beach. Won't know for certain until we get closer. And didn't you say there's another queendom before yours anyway?"

I nodded. "The Cove."

"Way I see it, she can't be that far ahead of us. Sure, we spent time at that Flora chick's place and detoured back to the house, but Pip would've needed more breaks than we did, and there's no chance she'd leave the kid behind, knowing how powerful he is. If they're passing through your queendom to reach wherever they're headed, we'll catch them. Those ripples are getting stronger every time we feel them."

"They are?" I turned sharply to search his face for signs of pandering, catching Luna's reflection glimmering in the moisture at the corners of my eyes.

Edius met my gaze and gave a single, confident nod. "Not one to blow smoke, Merrín."

That was a relief—and grounding. Wherever Charmagne had suffered as a child, it hadn't been within my queendom. Edius was right; we were swiftly closing the gap on Ascian's rippling power. The coast probably wasn't Charmagne's destination, just convenient terrain.

"Oh." A deep sigh of relief rushed from me. "Thank you, Edi. That makes me feel much, much better. To be honest, I've been stewing."

"Yeah? Couldn't tell at all."

A joke. Because I was awful at hiding my emotions, even from someone new.

"Your boyfriend's been stewing too," he added, nodding back toward camp.

"I know." Another thing to feel awful about. "We've been playing this game, neither of us mentioning it, afraid of hurting each other. I suspect he feels guilty Charmagne is here in the north, and normally, I'd reassure him, but I can't do it without getting emotional myself, and I don't want to add to his pain."

"You're too nice for your own good, Merrín."

"I'm not that nice. I've beheaded plenty of ne'er-do-wells in my court. They call me Merrin the Cruel."

"Hah! Now that's a load of wallop-shit." Edius flashed a rare, full smile. "Well, if you need to get something off your chest, I don't mind listening. I owe you that much. Better than holding all that crap in."

I sensed he was holding things in too.

"Thank you, Edi."

He stood, ready to leave, but I caught his sleeve.

"And thank you for comforting my fears even though you're worried, too. Gwen must be extraordinary for you to trade your freedom for hers. I swear I'll do everything in my power to break the hex Charmagne holds over her." Hesitating, I added, my words tinged with stark empathy, "No one should have to lose themselves for the one they love."

His gaze snapped to mine—ancient, piercing—and I hurriedly released his sleeve. But it was too late. I'd already felt it. For certain this time.

Edius's heart gave one heavy, undeniable throb—and from the intensity of his stare, it wasn't for Gwen.

His focus narrowed, expression unreadable, movements measured as he eased down to a crouch beside me again.

"Edius?" I leaned back, sensing danger in the predatory way his attention had latched onto me, instincts swelling unchecked. "*Don't.*"

He didn't move. Didn't speak. He simply swallowed thickly, hand lifting toward me—hesitantly, as if even he wasn't sure what he was reaching for. More troubling still was the frantic flutter of his heart, like a butterfly fighting free of its cocoon.

"Stop." I pushed his hand away firmly. "If you open your heart to me, I'll never be able to reciprocate."

Magic words. His heart snapped shut like an oyster.

Unfortunately, his instincts weren't so easily restrained.

"Got nothing to worry about there, highness," he muttered, his words slipping into a smoke-rough midnight thrum. His temple flexed; his gaze dragged to my throat. "Become my pet, and it won't be for loving. It'll be for feasting and fucking."

My hand lifted instinctively, ready to strike—but I froze. Edius had already endured far worse treatment than any soul deserved, and while my instinct was to slap him to protect my honor, my mind flashed to the scars still fresh upon his back. Instead, I closed my fingers around his shoulder.

"Edi." My voice stayed level, rock-steady. "Control yourself."

His whole frame tensed. A knife-edge breath flared his

nostrils, and something raw flickered across his face—unmasked, hungry—only to vanish behind clenched teeth.

"Huh?—Fuck."

Two fingers tapped my forehead before he rocked back on his heels, dragging both hands over his face. "Gods." A ragged groan slipped out. "It's that martyr streak of yours—so damned selfless. Swore I wouldn't let it worm under my skin, but your soul's just—" A low snarl and a handful of muttered curses. "I'm sorry, your highness. I mean it."

He looked ready to punch through stone to erase the moment.

"There's nothing to forgive."

His gaze fixed on the ground. "If you say so."

"I'm also not one to blow smoke."

He didn't know me well enough yet to believe that—so I offered the truth of it straight on:

"Edius, I can't pretend to fathom predatory blood any more than you can live inside a human queen's skin. Our natures sing different songs. But leniency has *always* been the first law of my court, and I extend it to you. Learn my truths, and I'll learn yours. Keep wrestling those instincts, and I'll never withdraw my trust over growing pains."

Silence.

Pensive? Not exactly.

"Stars above," he muttered at last, and my confidence wobbled.

"What?"

"That blaze of righteousness—is that how you won the crown?"

"I didn't win it. I was *born* to it."

"Kidding." A crooked grin softened his blunt features. "Persuasive, though. I see why they call you queen. And yes, I'll play along if it means I keep my head. Behaving was the plan anyway." He folded his arms. "Lesson one?"

"Lesson one," I echoed. "Telling someone you want to bed them when they're already involved is generally frowned upon. Humans tend to braid sex and love together."

"Mmm. Some do."

"I do," I said.

"That much is obvious. Never met anyone so...unflinchingly proper."

I answered with a flat stare.

A dry laugh slipped past his lips, eyes warming for a heartbeat.

"Relax, it was a joke." A pause, softer. "Mostly. Truth is, I start rattling off nonsense when I don't know what else to do—when the real storm's pounding in my chest." He raked a hand over his jaw and blew out a breath. "Point is, I'm grateful you're putting up with me, and for what you're doing for Gwen. She doesn't deserve any of what's happened to her. So I'll shut my damned mouth, behave, and do whatever it takes to earn your help."

Edius might be jagged around the edges, but beneath that he wasn't so bad. His blunt honesty was almost refreshing.

"But I may not be so nice next time," I warned, amused by the echo of his earlier threats.

"Was that supposed to be me? That what you think my voice sounds like? A gods-damned bear?" He dismissed himself with a laugh and a scoff. "Extra turnips, coming right up."

"Don't listen to him, Windley!" I called toward the flickering firelight of camp. "He's trying to poison me!"

Unwise, shouting into the dark.

You never know who might be listening...

13

HELLO, OLD FRIEND

"**W**ill you be deciding to share it with me, this strengthening of bonds you and *Edmond* have undergone?"

Of course, Windley—abnormally attuned to my every movement—had noticed my interaction with Edius took far longer than necessary for mere turnip discourse. Of course, his pointed ears had perked to ensure my safety.

"Well, he did comfort me," I admitted softly, "because I was worrying."

"Yes, I've been waiting for you to bring it up."

I was unwilling to add to his burdens for the sake of easing my own.

"Honestly, we're fine," I said, flicking a hand. "I thanked him a little *too* sincerely, his instincts flared, but he muzzled them. Then he looked...well, mortified."

"And I assume you gave him a hearty speech to lift him up?"

"Obviously. And he mocked me for it."

"Of course he did." Windley offered a roguish grin. "Well

done, queenie. Though I must admit I'm jealous. If you want to gaze romantically at the sea alongside a mysterious southerner, I'm entirely at your disposal."

His fingers drummed lightly at the small of my back while turnips roasted steadily over the campfire.

He wasn't jealous, not truly. He knew exactly where my heart lay. I had proven that beyond doubt when he'd unburdened himself of his past.

Yet, the more understanding he showed, the guiltier I felt over my reaction upon first meeting Flora.

"What's that look for?" he teased.

"Ugh. Sometimes I fear my affections dull my wits."

"Excellent. I could use a level playing field. Come here, let me dull them further."

Hard to resist such an invitation. Not with such devilry glinting in his smile. Not with his heart opening fully to embrace mine. Not with his fingers artfully coaxing beneath my chin, drawing me closer—

But he hesitated, eyes tracing my features with reverent caution.

"Though it would be a shame to dull something so bright."

If anyone sparkles, it's you, my queen....

Perhaps he'd hinted at his fears all along. Perhaps I'd been ignorant to assume someone like Windley harbored no reservations toward physical love.

"I'm not afraid of you dulling me, Wind." I leaned into the space he hesitated to bridge, pouring all the love in my heart into my eyes. "I know you would never harm me." *Never.* "Your arms have never been a place of fear. And if it means being close to you, I'd gladly share my shine."

He swallowed, looking at me in countless unspoken ways. "You, Queen Merrin, are—"

"Look what I found!"

A deep voice shattered what would've been a fireside kiss.

Edius had returned from scouting sooner than promised—clearly for good reason.

Windley sprang up, hatchet unsheathed, as the brawny Spirite pushed a figure into the flickering firelight.

"He was skulking around over there," Edius explained gruffly. "Not calling him a spy, but he sure looked like he was spying."

I recognized the newcomer's cloak just as Windley recognized his face.

"Beau's cavalry!"

"Phylo?"

What I knew of Phylo: he was a "terrible flirt," Windley had little patience for his "fuckery," and he appeared painfully plain next to two Spirites of predatory descent.

Oh—and last we'd seen him, Windley had mischievously sent him and another guard spiraling into mutual ecstasy.

Phylo looked up sheepishly, then shrank further. "Sir Windley? And Queen Merrin? But you two were about to…"

We were back in the north, and thus, the old rules applied.

"I was cleaning her face."

"He was cleaning my face."

A dreadfully awkward silence followed, seeing as no rags were anywhere in sight and our canteen lay well beyond reach. Phylo was quickly noticing both discrepancies.

"What exactly are you implying, *Phylo?*" Windley leaned forward menacingly, flames reflecting ominously in his eyes. "You aren't spreading stories about the queen, are you? Because if so, I'll have to defend her honor."

"N-no! Of course not!" The poor man dropped immediately to a knee in a knight's humble bow. "Forgive me, Your Grace."

Edius arched a brow, bemusement flickering in his eyes.

Windley, meanwhile, slid a subtle glance my way and nodded encouragingly.

"Forgive me—*Phylo*, is it?—for what this must have looked like," I said regally. "You see, Sir Windley has been accompanying me on a royal tour of the southern outlands to collect rare flora."

Windley flashed me an approving thumbs-up behind Phylo's back.

"My queendom had scheduled this journey for later in the fall with proper guard detail, but after Queen Beau's rescue, I saw an opportunity. Sir Albie appointed Sir Windley as my personal guard due to his knowledge of the region. But, as you can see by my attire, we've faced unexpected hardship, and he has graciously stepped in as handmaid in the absence of a proper one."

"Of course, Your Grace." Phylo hesitated, quietly mustering courage before venturing, "But, er, who's that fellow?"

Ah, yes. Edius would be a trickier lie to spin.

"My cousin," Windley declared easily. "Guiding us through this terrain. A country boy, as you can plainly see."

Edius, with his tight jacket and city attire, looked distinctly un-country. "I milk the wallops," he said, matter-of-factly.

Windley shook his head slightly, for wallops didn't live north of the wood.

"Er, goats?" Edius amended.

Windley shrugged a silent, "That'll have to do."

Phylo frowned, clearly unsettled by their exchange. "Are you certain, Your Grace? You aren't"—he cast a wary glance at Windley—"in any danger?"

"In danger? Heavens, no!"

Phylo scrutinized us skeptically—the Queen of the Crag looking ragged, flanked by two men of dubious appearance. He lowered his voice, addressing me directly. "It's just...the last time I saw Sir Windley..."

"You saw him at the campfire after rescuing Queen Beau, yes?" I encouraged.

"B-before that."

Windley lifted a single sardonic brow, inspecting his nails. "You finally hooked up with that girl of yours?"

Phylo scrambled upright. "I knew you did something to us! What was it?"

"The magic of the Emerald Wood, perhaps." Windley lovingly stroked the handle of his hatchet, his voice casual but edged. "Unless you've a different theory?"

Phylo gulped audibly. "No."

These lies were terrible—entirely unbelievable and poorly delivered—but Phylo was wise enough not to openly question a queen, no matter how suspicious the situation.

"Thank you for your discretion, SIR Phylo," I said, spreading a thick layer of royal icing over the awkwardness.

"Ah, well...not actually a 'sir' yet, Your Grace," he mumbled, blushing furiously.

"Well, I'm sure you will be soon enough!"

Windley caught my eye, shook his head slightly, and pulled a face that all but screamed, *Nah.*

Edius exhaled, patience worn thin. "So...why don't we just drain him?"

"Ha! Your cousin, Sir Windley, ever the jester!" But Edius looked decidedly unamused—indeed, rather frightening. "A-anyway, what are you doing out here, Phylo? Where's the rest of the cavalry? And Queen Beau?"

"Back at the Queendom of the Cove. Sir Albie only sent a few of us to scout ahead."

"Beau's at the Cove?" My voice rose in panic. "But why?"

"One of your guards—the magician fellow—caught up with

us while we were heading home. After that, we changed course for the Cove. Queen Beau wished to speak with their queen."

To warn her about the echoes, undoubtedly—unknowingly drawing Exitium straight to her target.

Why would Albie have allowed this, knowing Sestilia's nature?

Windley sensed my rising panic. "Hold on—" He quickly calculated something in his head. "When exactly did you all arrive at the Cove?"

"Only last night."

Meaning the echoes had likely already begun to seize Sestilia. But according to Vita, possession needed a triggering event—betrayal or despair strong enough to tip the scale.

Sestilia held an abnormal fondness for me. Perhaps I could still convince her to dispel the echoes before they fully rooted.

"How far from the Cove are we, Phylo?" I pressed urgently.

"Just a couple of hours, Your Grace. Keep on this road and it's a straight shot."

"Then ride ahead of us. Tell Sir Albie to meet us at the city's entrance, but don't inform anyone else you've seen us. Can you manage that?"

"Of course, but is something wrong?" Again, he glanced nervously at Windley and Edius, as if waiting for a secret cue.

"No, no. Simply eager to reunite with our friends. Ride swiftly—we'll be right behind you."

Phylo departed looking equally relieved to leave Windley's intimidating presence and worried about leaving me in it. We waited until his stag's hoofbeats faded completely into the darkness before exhaling deeply.

"Well, that was..." I began hesitantly.

"Not bad," Windley offered.

"I was going to say 'a complete mess,' but I'm glad one of us is confident."

"You aren't?" Windley challenged. "Look—first off, we're right behind them. Sestilia has no idea what she's dealing with, and meanwhile, you've been honing your powers for days. You'll run circles around that fruitcake."

"Ohhh," Edius remarked knowingly. "*She's* the fruitcake."

Windley ignored him. "Secondly—Phylo won't say a word. I'll make sure of that. Very few of them realize my hearing is sharper than a human's..."

"You've got blackmail material?" I asked.

"He's definitely got blackmail material," Edius confirmed dryly.

"Don't fret about that," Windley assured me, his energy full of mischief. "I'll handle as many guards as necessary. You just handle Sir Albie."

Yes, that would undoubtedly be another tangled mess.

"Good grief," Edius grumbled. "You're a queen. Thought you made the rules."

"It wouldn't be fair if I simply made up rules. Plenty of people hold me accountable."

"In some ways, she has less freedom than the rest of us," Windley said, almost tenderly. "Though she's rebelled against it her entire life."

"This one?" Edius feigned astonishment. "Nah."

"Oh-ho, speaking of rebellious acts, Ed hasn't even heard half the good stories about our fearless leader yet!"

"No—"

"Remember that time you sleepwalked straight into the guards' chambers?"

"NO—"

"Or that time you stole the captains' desserts and handed them out to street children?" He paused, a spark of admiration lighting his gaze. "Though you eventually solved the problem by founding that orphanage." An unguarded tenderness surfaced in his expression—both of us orphans, both knowing what it meant to be alone. "You know, Merr, for a rantipole, you make a remarkably good queen. I don't think I've ever explicitly said so, but I truly mean it."

I was a good queen—or at least, I tried to be.

Yet not so long ago, I'd decided Windley and I could never go back to life as we knew it. Now that we were returning home, guilt and uncertainty tangled painfully within my chest.

I hadn't chosen to rule, but I had done my best, speaking for those without voices, fighting for safety and well-being. Yet gowns and formalities never suited me; I preferred hiding beneath willows, racing barefoot through open fields. Having tasted the untamed freedom of the world, could I ever return to the cage?

And there was...

I want you, and I would give up everything to have you...

I watched Windley quietly pack up the campsite, feeling his heart tug at mine every time our eyes met.

It was my royal duty to bear an heir for the Crag, yet with my heart as it was, I could imagine no other man but Windley at my side.

"Something happen?"

That was Edius, noticing my unease.

"Even without the echoes, the Queen of the Cove is terrifying. I worry Beau might be in danger." Not exactly a lie, though only part of the truth.

He studied me carefully, sensing more beneath the surface. Then—"We'll hurry"—he stepped forward to help Windley extinguish the fire.

"If you will not share your concerns with the beastlings, Merrin, will you share them with me?" Vita's voice shimmered within my chest.

No sense trying to hide from a goddess.

Letting the deep night wrap around me, I stared toward the far-off fields. "I'm good at what I do. It's a privilege, and there are pieces of it I even love, but..."

The horizon felt broader now—my world so much wider than a single throne.

"A heart may change in weeks, days, hours, even minutes. To worry now is a waste. Focus instead on how you may exile the destroyer; your heart can rest until after."

Meaning I should only worry about my mortal woes once the Nemophile's task was finished.

Easier, anyway, to push it aside for now.

We rode at a furious pace toward the Cove, passing sleeping villages and isolated dwellings warmed from within by cozy fires. On we blurred through the deepening night, until—

"Ed! You feel that?" Windley called.

"Sure did."

"Ascian's ring?" I asked anxiously.

"Yeah, and it was strong," Windley confirmed, glancing over his shoulder. "We're on the right path, queenie. Your queendom is safe—for now. They aren't at the Crag, at least not yet."

He was right. As we rounded the bend of the coast, the Cove came into view, luminous against the darkness like a beacon.

There, my dearest friend awaited.

There, we would confront Exitium and reclaim Ascian's ring.

And there, unbeknownst to me, my heart would shatter in ways I had never imagined possible.

14

RETURN TO THE COVE

The dawn found us drifting in the liminal space between waking and dreams, painting hues of sherbet orange and blush pink across the coastal sky. Salt-stirred air beckoned us toward the sleepy queendom as gulls pecked at shells dotting the shore.

It was there, as we neared the deceptively pleasant hamlet, that I spotted him—a figure as weathered as the stones of the Cove's outermost walls, as creased as the ragged banners bearing its crescent symbols. A man dutifully awaiting his queen's return.

Windley called after me as I slid from the prancelope and ran toward the wizened knight. My feet were more calloused than the last time I'd seen him; my muscles harder; my cheeks far dirtier than Albie would ever permit.

And Albie was jogging to meet me, as quickly as his weary frame allowed, gripping Faylebane's hilt and casting wary glances at the Spirites, who'd wisely halted their steeds at a safe distance from the Crag's most devoted knight.

"Queen Merrin!"

His grizzled voice broke as his arms closed around me. It was more than a knight's reverence; he was family—just less sticky—and he trembled with conflicting emotions, anger battling relief.

"Albie." I clutched the back of his cloak, breathing in the familiar scent of barrel wood and tobacco. "I missed you."

"My Queen," he murmured again, pressing a fatherly kiss to my forehead. "My heart nearly gave way."

"I know, my knight, and for that, I'm sorry. But I've been swept into something far greater than myself. What happened at the southern mountain—it was only the beginning."

Albie barely seemed to hear me, lost in his own relief and worry. He pulled back, his gaze roaming over me. "Are you all right?"

A weighted question, but physically—"Yes."

He nodded, as if forcing himself to believe it. Then: "I am profoundly disappointed in you, Queen Merrin."

It stung.

"Whatever you've gotten tangled in, you should've known better than to go venturing into the wilds without a proper guard."

"I did...have guards," I protested.

"The hounds hardly count!" he barked, shooting daggers over my shoulder. "Yeah, I see you there, lad. No use hiding— you'll get your turn."

For Windley, Albie's disapproval was likely more terrifying than Luna's wrath, the blood stags, or the blighted beasts. Albie's scowl alone could bring a battalion to heel.

My gaze drifted—unbidden—toward the Spirite, and the soft edge in my eyes told Albie everything.

He exhaled like a man grinding steel. "So the lad's pinched your heart, has he? Call it a tryst, My Queen. Easier mended than you think."

"It isn't a tryst," I said, voice even. "I love him, Albie—and you knew it long before I did. The kin of the Cacti will have to court elsewhere."

"I don't want to hear any of that now," he grunted, waving off the notion. "You're tired and filthy. First things first: get you fed and looking proper. Then we can discuss what needs doing about him."

"Nothing will be done about him," I said firmly. "And it hardly matters now. We're dealing with threats beyond the mortal realm. We need to reach the castle without delay. Something dark is coming."

Albie studied me through tired, wary eyes. "So it's true, then? What Rafe said? The lad found us a couple days back, babbling about danger coming for the royals. Didn't make a lick of sense, but Queen Beau insisted on riding out. Never seen the lady so determined."

"It's all true. More than you know. Please—I beg you to trust me. I wouldn't have left without good reason. You raised me to have sense."

He let his hands fall from my shoulders. "Sense, yes—but recklessness, too. You got that from your mother." He sighed, rubbing his weathered palms—hands that held countless stories —over his lined face. "The big fella's with you, then?"

"Mm," I confirmed. "His name is Edius. He and Windley share similar wounds. It's one of the reasons we've returned."

Albie's tension finally eased, just a fraction. "Then let's not waste another minute, My Queen."

"Oh, My Queen. I knew he'd be trouble for you the moment I saw you two together. Should've never let him get so close."

We had no time to waste soothing Albie's anxieties over my

relationship with Windley, but I suspected his initial response was just the simplest reaction. After all, I'd just given him everything—Exitium, Luna, Ascian—the quickened version, anyway, adding at least four more wrinkles to his face in the process.

"Please tell me Beau isn't really meeting with Sestilia," I entreated.

"Aye. She'd have it no other way."

"You have to get me in there! Sestilia's dangerous enough on her own. Add a goddess of destruction trying to awaken her bloodlust, plus Edius and Windley sensing their former master's power somewhere in the city—this is no time for Beau to be caught in that spider's web!"

"And what good will getting you caught in that web do?" Albie countered. "Rafe's with her, along with half a dozen cavalrymen. Doubt even the Queen of the Cove will try anything with that many guards around."

"Albie, she's crazy."

He couldn't argue with that.

"Argh." He rubbed his temples, frustration etched across his face. "Give me time to sort through this mess, My Queen. Vengeful southerners, fallen goddesses... Let's head back to the inn. Keep your presence quiet for now. I'll send someone to retrieve Queen Beau. I'm sure she'll come the moment she hears you're back. Then we'll figure out what to do about all this."

A fair enough plan. It was probably wisest not to announce my arrival to Sestilia until we learned about her current temperament from Beau. After my escape last time, there was no telling if I'd be the spark that ignited her fury.

"But first, we need a task force to search the city for signs of Charmagne and Pip," I insisted.

"A teenage youth and a woman, you said? Pair like that

would've caused a stir. Spirites aren't common, even down here
—but I've heard no mention of anyone fitting that description.
I'll see if Delagos can lend us some scouts. He's already sent a
few north at Queen Beau's behest—checking for signs of upset
or possession, I suppose."

Marvelous, brilliant, ever-clever Beau! She had taken Rafe's
warning seriously and had already begun preparations to safe-
guard our queendoms.

...Even if she had inadvertently brought the danger straight
here.

A sense of foreboding filled me as I instructed Windley and
Edius to release their prancelopes, pull up their hoods, and
follow us into the sea-sprayed city, offering only half-hearted
introductions given the circumstances.

"Edius, Sir Albie. Albie, Edius. Edius has temporarily
taken on the role of bodyguard."

Albie eyed him skeptically from head to toe. "You look a
crafty one. You crafty, boy?"

"Not...particularly?" Edius replied flatly.

Albie's keen eyes flicked from Edius to me. "Our kind-
hearted Queen, always collecting strays. Long as he knows
what happens to strays that bite."

Edius raised his hands in surrender. "I don't want any trouble. I'm at your queen's mercy."

"I trust him, Albie."

Edius wasn't a bad guy—and after everything we'd faced
these past days, I'd come to truly believe it.

Albie's scrutiny lingered, heavy and appraising, but he gave
Edius a curt nod—neither warm nor hostile, simply acknowl-
edging the new presence by my side.

Then his gaze swung sharply to Windley. "Lad." He
grabbed the Spirite roughly by the collar. "We're going to have
a chat."

Windley, ever the irrepressible charmer, tossed me a playful two-finger salute as though marching bravely to his execution.

"A-Albie! I forbid you to scold or deter him!"

"Aye, My Queen." But Albie's agreement was half-hearted at best as he dragged Windley ahead, clearly determined to say whatever he pleased.

"Your Majesty!" Windley used my proper title in an attempt to win back favor. "You left out 'maim!' Don't forget 'maim!'"

Albie cuffed him upside the head. "Think it's funny, do ya?"

Windley straightened. "I don't think it's funny at all, Sir Albie. I'm in love with her. I'd do anything for her."

"I know that, you nitwit. Seen it in your eyes a thousand times. But you weren't supposed to tell her that! Only made it harder on yourself—and her—by saying so. Trust me, I've watched this story play out more times than I care to count. Never ends well. Even the long-term ones."

Did he mean affairs between queens and their paramours?

Windley's face was unreadable as he walked alongside Albie, their voices dropping to tones I could no longer make out.

I sighed and fell into step beside Edius, who'd been observing the exchange with arms folded across his chest.

"A-are you doing okay?" I asked, realizing belatedly how absurd it was to check on him when I was the one under scrutiny.

Edius smirked faintly. "Just enjoying the show."

Spectacular.

"And you, Vita?" I asked, desperate for comfort in the goddess's presence.

"Do you seek distraction? I will offer it. You may pretend you are convening with me."

I accepted the offer gratefully. "Sorry, Edius. Goddess stuff," I explained, tapping my temple.

"Sure?" He arched a dubious eyebrow.

"You are terrible at deceit, Merrin." Vita's tinkling laughter filled my mind.

I knew that.

The city felt unchanged since my last visit—the briny scent of the markets, salt in the breeze. But this time, it was as though we walked upon the silk threads of an immense spider's web—deceptively welcoming, easy to enter, difficult to escape.

It was with mounting relief that we reached the tavern where Albie and a skeletal troop of cavalry had holed up. The common room was chaos—maps still stabbed to the walls with daggers, half-laced saddlebags strewn about, ration packs stacked by the door—proof they'd been minutes from riding out to hunt for a missing queen—*me*, presumably.

Guilt hit me.

Albie made no comment, just guided us past the disarray and into a snug chamber decked with paper umbrellas and watercolor blossoms.

"The decor!" I gasped. "It's like the Queendom of the Cloudfall!"

"Aye, owned by immigrants from the northwest. But how do you know that, My Queen? You've never been to that region."

"I saw it in one of Mother Poppy's books."

I'd pored over that book—my father came from the Cloudfall, another foreigner like Albie, and his pale western skin mingled with Mother's warm umber, leaving me lightly in between. Among royals, such braiding of bloodlines was nothing unusual.

"Ah," was all Albie said. "Lads, draw the queen a bath. She can't meet either queen looking like she crawled out of the wilds. I'll fetch her things."

He meant the belongings I'd left behind when I ventured away from camp with Windley. Realizing this, Albie paused at the door.

"Think about running off with her again, son, and there'll be far worse than maiming in store for you."

The door slammed shut behind him.

Edius let out a low chuckle while Windley sagged, looking like a pillow stripped of feathers.

"Well, that went about as expected," Windley muttered with a sigh.

I pretended to scrutinize him closely. "You appear unscathed. Was it horrible?"

"Eh, could've been worse. He didn't say anything that wasn't true. But it doesn't matter. They could ship me off to the Queendom of the Cloudfall tomorrow, and I'd be back at your side in a week."

There was something deeply endearing about being pursued by the Clearing's naughtiest guard.

"Are you saying there's no way to rid myself of you?" I teased.

He placed a gentle hand atop my head. "I'm annoyingly persistent." He slid his hand to the nape of my neck, drawing me close and murmuring warmly, "As I've said before—even if your feelings change, mine never will."

"Should I have, like, shaken his hand or something?" Edius asked, still staring at the door.

"No," I replied, turning from the intoxication of Windley's aura. "Give him time. He's a bit...overprotective. And I've never disobeyed him as thoroughly as I have these past weeks. Sorry you weren't given a kinder greeting."

"So long as they let me stick around." Edius nodded toward the washroom, already investigating the bath situation. "This place have a Naiad, or—?"

"Naiad?" I repeated, unfamiliar.

"Water folk," Windley clarified. "Not up here, Ed. You'll have to pump water the old-fashioned way." To me, he added, "In the south, most cities have a Naiad managing water—conjuring, purifying, heating it."

"Handy. We should employ them in the north."

"We'll get right on that initiative—*after* we save the world." Windley kissed my forehead softly.

He was forced to release me when the doorknob rattled, signaling Albie's return. The wizened knight shook his head, exhaling slowly at the sight of us suspiciously standing stiffly apart.

"You'll come with me, Windley. Let the queen get some rest."

"I can hardly rest at a time like this," I protested.

"He's right, Merr—er, Queen Merrin," Windley corrected quickly. "We need your life force at peak strength before letting you anywhere near that gaudy castle."

"But surely you need rest too! We've been riding for—"

Windley held up his hand. "I'm fine, darling. Not that tired, and I'm still a knight."

Albie cleared his throat pointedly.

"Er, Your Majesty," Windley amended.

"Better," Albie grunted approvingly. "We'll see Captain Delagos. You can describe these Spirites yourself. Borrow a few more men if needed."

Windley nodded. "Ed, your instincts sharp?"

Edius poked his head out from the washroom, pumping water manually. "Yup."

"You stay here with the queen, yeah?"

Albie scowled again at Edius—at his flat mouth, crafty eyes, the muscular frame beneath his shirt.

"We trust him," I reiterated. "And even if you don't, trust I can defend myself." Indeed, a potted tree sat in the corner, earth just beyond the window.

For emphasis, I guided Vita's breath through the room, coaxing a bloom from the tree with a fingertip. "See? I'm not defenseless, my knight."

Albie paled, quickly plucking the flower and pocketing it. "Best keep that quiet, My Queen. You never know who's watching." He swiveled on his heel toward Edius. "Break my trust, lad, you won't get another chance."

Edius gave me a sidelong glance. "Where've I heard that before?"

Albie ignored him. "Rest, My Queen. We'll handle things for now."

No, I wouldn't let them handle everything alone—but Albie needed control, at least for now. Not to mention—

"Your vitality wanes, little royal," Vita warned gently. *"Rest now."*

"Ugh, be careful, Wind. Exitium's bound to know you were the spark that swayed my heart and flipped her scheme—now she and Charmagne both have you in their sights."

"Psh. Me? I'm always careful."

If caution were coin, he'd still be broke.

Windley clapped Edius's shoulder. "Don't let her out of your sight, mate. Counting on you."

With a flash of forced optimism, he waved and followed Albie down the corridor, leaving me alone in the kaleidoscope-bright chamber with Edius. A perfectly safe situation.

Perfectly.

Safe.

Situation.

15

GHOST OF A NUZZLE

"Hey, your bath is ready, I think."

Edius was no trained knight. Where the others spent their days tending to queens, the thought of someone so dour-looking waiting upon me felt completely out of place.

I dropped my head into my hands. "I'm sorry, Edius. When I took you on as a guard, I didn't mean, you know, drawing baths for me."

"I don't mind. I've drawn lots of baths."

He had? I lifted my head to study him. "Really?"

"For Gwen." He didn't appear to be jesting.

"Oh." I studied him quietly for a moment before shuffling through the bag Albie had brought, stopping abruptly when I saw its contents. "I'm not ready for this."

"For your bath?"

"No—for all *this*. Albie, being protected, formality. And look what he brought me to change into! Gowns. He didn't pack any of my extra britches." Frustrated, I tossed the crown of silver ivy onto the bed. "Do you have any idea how hard it is to run and climb in dresses?"

Edius chuckled softly, leaning against the wall. "Don't blame you there. Looks suffocating."

An apt description if I'd ever heard one.

"Thanks for the bath, Edi. Albie left food—help yourself. They're famous here for smoked fish and aged cheese."

With that, I retreated into the washroom, soaking away the scent of wild earth and uncaged air, and felt unexpectedly melancholy. In some way, it seemed I was washing away the fantasy itself—the traveling, the magic, the freedom. All things I had grown deeply attached to.

"What is wrong, Merrin? Though your body is clean, you remain sitting like a sad carrot in stew."

A carrot in stew? That wasn't a very Vita-like thing to say.

"I have heard you comment on the conjurer's cooking," she explained.

The goddess was trying to be relatable? A divine entity residing within my soul was attempting casual conversation?

But it was only a brief distraction from my true worries. "Coming back here—it's like returning to reality. I'm not sure I'm ready."

"The same worry you carried last night? My answer remains unchanged. You have much left to accomplish, Merrin. Worrying will not help you send the destroyer to the end of days."

Yes, I was meant to focus on using the Crown for its true purpose—though I still had no idea how.

Vita read my thoughts effortlessly. *"The Crown of the Wood remains severed. You must repair it and don it fully. Only then can you carry the destroyer to the end of days."*

"Even when I wore both halves before, it was still broken?"

"That is correct."

"How do I repair it?"

"*That should come easily to you now that you understand what it means to be a creator. Once you again wear both halves of the Crown—*"

"Wait, I have to wear both halves again? You mean I must take Exitium into myself again?" The bathwater sloshed violently.

"*It is as you say.*"

"But my bloodlust—!"

"*Your mistake last time was speaking the destroyer's name. Do not speak it again, and your bloodlust will not swell.*"

Yet the thought of those disembodied hands and haunting whispers at the edge of perception unsettled me deeply. "But if I take the echoes into myself again, I won't hear your voice anymore."

"*When you take the destroyer within, you must do so without her followers.*"

"You mean the echoes were blocking your voice before? How do I separate them from Exitium?"

"*Those you call 'echoes' are not tethered to her; rather, she has collected them during her time as a fallen one. Most have forgotten how to live. You must dispel them when you feel most inspired to create.*"

Vague. Vague, vague, vague.

"*When are you most inspired?*" Vita pressed.

"When?" The answer came naturally. "At dawn, when life stirs and earth is painted with morning's first colors. In those fleeting moments when night fades into day."

"*That is when you must do it. I will aid you when the time comes.*"

But that was hardly enough for a concrete plan.

"*This fight is not yours alone, Merrin. Trust the force of my will and the truth of my vow.*"

Regardless of my reservations, Vita's warmth spread through my limbs, calming my pulse and sinking my fears beneath the bathwater.

Faith wasn't always easy. But it grew easier with practice.

When I was suitably clean and feeling more myself—save for the billowy white nightgown, perfectly befitting a virgin queen and clearly forced upon me by a certain mustached knight—I darted across the room to the bed, hurrying to hide my frilly appearance beneath the covers before Edius could see.

"What?" Edius glanced toward the washroom. "Somethin' in there?"

"No, it's—" I gestured helplessly at myself.

"Too girly for you?"

"Girly has nothing to do with it. I like wearing things that make me feel capable, not delicate. How would you feel in something like this?"

Edius stared blankly for a long moment before succumbing to a snort.

"See?" I laughed, picturing his muscles straining against needlepoint lace. "You'd never wear this either!"

"Get rid of the lacy bits, then we'll see."

Amusement crept across his face, slow as sunrise, and actually stayed—for a breath or two—before he schooled it away.

"Get some sleep," he said once the grin slipped back into hiding. "I'll keep watch till your boyfriend returns. Make sure no one else sees what you don't want them to see."

"Thanks, Edi." I settled deeper into the bed. "But you should rest too. There's no telling when we'll need to fight again. There are extra blankets in the closet if you don't mind the floor."

"You aren't planning to sneak off and steal a cavalry

uniform, are you? Your grandpa's trusting me to keep you in line."

"My grandpa?" Albie would've keeled over had he heard that. "No," I laughed. "I'll stay put. Queen's honor."

Edius eyed the floor. "Then sure, thanks."

My feelings for Windley were sound. I didn't fear Edius's instincts or his heart. If I had, I never would have suggested it.

Perhaps I was naïve.

"Heya, Merrín?"

"Yes, Edi?"

"You're awake."

Unfortunately, yes. Not for lack of trying. We'd been lying there twenty minutes at least—he on the floor, me in bed facing a window whose wooden shutters did nothing to keep out the morning light.

"You wanna talk about it?" he offered.

Undecided.

Birdsong filtered gently through the shutters. What I was feeling—it was anxiety. And if I'd learned anything, it was that anxiety disliked being ignored. The surest way to quiet it was to give it voice, especially when someone was listening.

"I'm thinking of Beau, trapped in that castle with Sestilia— who's about three shades past sane. And Windley, half-dead on his feet, being paraded around by Albie. And Exitium, surely already inside the castle, maybe even inside Sestilia, trying to trick her into speaking her name. And Charmagne and Pip, somewhere in this city, capable of horrors I can't even imagine."

"...That all?"

I rolled over to find him lying on his back, hands behind his head, in the same tank top undershirt he always slept in. "I'm sure there's more," I admitted. "Your turn."

"Heh. I'm good."

"Edius, you deserve to unburden yourself too."

The birds outside persisted.

"Fine," he sighed. "Yeah, I'm worried. Worried that I haven't sensed Charm and Pip at all—only Ascian. Worried he might somehow still be alive. Worried about what state Gwen's in now."

I didn't know what to say; all were valid concerns. "Feel better?" I ventured instead.

"No."

"Me neither. But at least now we don't have to waste energy pretending."

"Pft. Fair."

The birds meddled onward.

Edius's gaze slid to the potted tree I'd inched closer to the bed while he was in the washroom.

"That for me?"

I hesitated.

He blew a slow breath through his nose. "Can't say I blame you." His voice dipped, unreadable. "After last night's... moment." A beat. "But what I told you stands—I'm in control."

His fingers flexed once, testing the leash. "Gets easier the longer I stay close. Your scent's already duller. Happens over time—had to relearn the trick after years with Ascian."

"I'm not afraid of you, Edius. First, I believe your motives. Second, you know I can do this." I stroked a leaf; it withered to gray dust. "Third, I see the good in you. Saw it even before you joined us. Honestly, I'd have brought the tree over anyway—same reason Windley sleeps with his hatchets."

"Ha. Swear I saw him cuddling one the other night."

"Be glad he wasn't cuddling you," I teased.

"Not like he hasn't tried."

I let out a quiet laugh at the thought. "Come to think of it," I continued, "I've been meaning to give you something. You don't have a weapon, so—" I rifled through the bag at my bedside, pulling out the ornate-handled knife Windley had gifted me days ago. "Here." I slid it across the floor to him. "Now you have something to cuddle too."

"Thanks." Edius's shoulders eased a notch; he ran a thumb along the knife's hilt before tucking it away. Then he sat up from his blankets, elbows braced on his knees. "Can I give you something in return? Uh, less of a thing, more of a service."

"What do you mean?"

"First off, that light's killing me." He grabbed a spare blanket and moved to the bedside. "Er, excuse me." Leaning over, he draped the blanket across the window, blocking the harsh daylight. "Better?"

"Yes," I said.

"Also—" He crouched beside the bed, stretching his hand toward me cautiously, as one might approach a wary animal. "Not smart to use my power and let them know exactly where we are. But I can do a couple of small bursts—they'll only sense direction, not proximity. What I'm saying is, I can help you sleep, highness. Knock the worry outta you." His hand flexed carefully. "But I get it if you don't want me touching you. Don't wanna overstep."

"No...that's nice of you, Edi."

There was more he wanted to say. I waited.

"You don't know it, but agreeing to help Gwen... It's something I can't ever repay. So, if I can help you, I want to. I know you're worried about Windley, and about your queen friend... Let me dull it?"

His fingers hovered near my cheek, seeking permission

rather than taking it. Resolve—not desire—anchored his gaze, his breaths slow beneath the tumble of dark hair.

I nodded once. He closed the space between us, one broad palm settling against my jaw—warm, deliberate, almost weightless.

"That okay?" His voice had shed its usual harsh edge. He regarded me as though I were a puzzle worth solving; weeks ago in those woods, I'd never have guessed he possessed such gentleness.

I nodded.

"Might feel a little strange, highness. Means nothing more, I promise."

His thumb swept once over my brow, unhurried, deliberate. Warmth drifted down my spine. "Feel that?"

"Yes," I breathed. "It's...nice."

"I'll send another. You'll start drifting."

His voice softened to a murmur as his thumb traced the same path, a second pulse of calming magic sinking through muscle and bone.

Weight lifted from every limb; the mattress seemed to rise and cradle me. His hand stayed where it was—steady, anchoring.

A third, slower wave.

Drowsiness gathered, and—without thinking—I tilted into his palm. My lips brushed the heel of his hand, more instinct than affection.

The ghost of a nuzzle.

Edius went perfectly still—no breath, no blink. "That wasn't supposed to happen." His voice slipped an octave, rough around the edges. Eyes half-lidded, he studied me with unnerving focus.

I barely noticed; my lashes were heavy, my skin buzzing with lazy warmth.

"I haven't done this in a long time," he murmured, gaze never leaving mine. "Not for someone else's sake... Forgot what fondness feels like."

His thumb drifted down, tracing the curve of my bottom lip and catching lightly at the corner before retreating.

For the space of a single breath I wondered how his wild hair might feel between my fingers.

"Too much." He jerked his hand back as if scalded. "I'll, uh, be spending the rest of the night in the hall."

Though it wasn't night. And he didn't leave immediately. Instead he lingered, watching me once more—expression unreadable—then pressed a quick kiss to his fingertip and tapped it gently against my forehead.

The last thing I heard was the door closing behind him.

And then—nothing.

"Lion queen? You awake?"

"Windley!" I shot upright, blankets pooling at my waist.

No. No, no, nonono. That moment with Edius had been a little bit...hm.

"Edius, he—and I—I didn't mean to—"

"Shh. It's okay." Windley leaned casually against the bedside, watching me with those keen, knowing eyes. "He already told me."

Which raised one very pressing question: exactly what had Edius told him?

Windley leaned against the doorjamb, arms folded. "Bloke said you conked out, things got...instinctual, so he bailed. Sounded harmless enough. You all right? You didn't feel—violated?"

"Not violated. Just...wrong." My cheeks were still too warm. "You're not angry?"

He huffed a low laugh. "Angry? Side-effect of his mojo, that's all. Though"—he flicked me a sideways look—"I'd be lying if I said I adore the image. At least you got some sleep."

A tiny, traitorous part of me had wanted more than understanding; I wanted a spark of jealousy.

"I'm almost afraid to tell you what I did to fetch that wine," he mused, tapping his chin.

I frowned. "Please don't."

"Kidding." A crooked smile surfaced. "Far less intimate than a *nuzzle*."

Oh goddess, it *was* a nuzzle. I groaned into my palms. "I am never nuzzling anyone again."

"You may nuzzle whomever you please," he purred, "so long as you nuzzle me most."

Peeking through my fingers, I caught the wicked tilt of his mouth—clearly delighted with himself. The grin vanished in a blink, shoulders squaring.

"But not right now, lion queen. We've got word—some of it welcome, some of it grim."

16

BEFORE THE FALL

"**C**an this part be tightened, lass?"

There was welcome news and grim news, and the grim news was precisely why I now found myself being fitted for a gown far more extravagant than circumstances warranted. The dress was admittedly gorgeous, but I was still bitter about how things had turned out.

Here's what happened:

Cheerful Captain Delagos had heard Albie and Windley's plea and agreed to lend the Cove's royal guard to our cause, dispatching scouts throughout the city to search for Pip and Charmagne. That was the welcome news.

The grim news involved Beau—lovely, diplomatic, and pregnant—who had declined to leave Sestilia's castle, sending only a coded message in her stead.

My darling, how I've missed you. Alas, I cannot see the gemstone until tonight. Timber and I will find you over the first hill. Wait for me.

Timber was Rafe. *Gemstone* was our codeword for queen. And over the first hill? That meant tomorrow. Beau and Rafe planned to stay overnight at the castle because Sestilia refused to see her.

Delagos had even shed some light on why.

"Sestilia's birthday?" I laughed in open disbelief in Windley's face when he relayed it.

"A birthday ball, to be exact," Windley clarified. "How come you've never had a birthday ball?"

Because I preferred to spend my birthdays drinking ale with Beau at the forest fortress, devouring sweets from Beau's finest pastry maid, and playing cards by candlelight.

"By refusing to see Beau, she's essentially holding her hostage and forcing her to attend the party!"

"Oh, that's exactly what she's doing," Windley said with sardonic amusement. "Doubt she could get foreign royalty to attend any other way."

"Well, it won't work! We aren't leaving Beau there overnight. We'll depart for the castle at once."

"No, My Queen," Albie interjected firmly. "We'll go. You stay here—"

"Absolutely not! I shall go, and that's a command!" Anger flared acutely within me before subsiding. "You forget, my knight, I hold power equal to that of Exitium. Of anyone, I should go."

Beau knew the danger of the echoes better than anyone; her family had carried their burden for generations. Now she remained Sestilia's guest out of duty, refusing to leave until she warned the first of several queens of what was coming.

But Beau didn't know the truth. She didn't realize that by seeking to warn the mad queen of approaching darkness, she'd delivered the darkness directly to its perfect host.

The one in need of warning was Beau herself.

It took no small amount of arguing to make Albie relent.

"Very well, My Queen. But if you're attending a royal event, you must present yourself accordingly."

Our old friend, *decorum.*

Something for which I had neither time nor patience—not with Exitium poised to strike, not with Charm and Pip lurking somewhere in the city.

But Albie was stubborn. "There are rumors floating among the Clearing's cavalry about where you've been and who you've been with. You're still a queen—and one born to a privileged reign. Loyalty isn't freely given; it's earned. The reputation you defend isn't yours alone—it's your queendom's. I'll allow you into that castle only if you enter as the Queen of the Crag. Those are my terms."

Albie was hardly in a position to demand terms from me with so great a threat looming, yet he was right. I'd been selfish these past weeks, guilty of abandoning my court and everything I'd pledged as their leader—everything my mother had entrusted me with. I was Beau's friend, Vita's vessel, and Windley's partner, yes—but I was also a queen, and my life was not mine alone.

I'd trade a guard's cloak for a gown if it meant stability for my people. I owed them at least that much.

Thus, Albie and I found ourselves at the Cove's fanciest boutique, fussed over by a seamster and seamstress thirsty for coin, while a third attendant flashed strings of pearls and gems around my neck.

"I have a pendant, thank you." I clutched my mother's necklace tightly, hoping it might lend me patience. "And a ring," I added as he moved toward my hands, speaking of my emerald namesake ring, which I'd left off for several days now.

"This side cinched in, lass," Albie instructed, overseeing

the alterations. "And shorter here. You there—enough with the rings. Start on the duchess's hair."

Duchess. That was the role we'd settled on, to avoid tipping off Sestilia and giving her any opportunity to sabotage us. Captain Delagos had even secured an invitation under the guise of a distant duchess and her personal detail passing through on a tour of the queendoms.

I suspected the Cove had never seen such excitement from foreign royals—first Queen Merrin of the Crag, then Queen Beau of the Clearing, and now a duchess from the far north, all supposedly on unrelated business.

I only hoped Sestilia wasn't as shrewd as she was beautiful.

"Glad to see you've still got it, my duchess," Albie noted, nodding toward my neck. "Feared you might've lost it during your southern exploits."

By the angle of his gaze, he meant my mother's necklace, which I never, ever would've lost. "It's one of my most prized possessions," I assured him.

"She'd be pleased to hear that." A quietness settled over him as he regarded the keepsake around my neck. "You know, your mother's heart was much like yours—always torn between what should and shouldn't be."

It was rare for him to speak of her so openly.

"What do you mean, Albie? Did she...?" I struggled to phrase it delicately in front of the busy seamsters. "Could it be that she—?"

"She chose right, my duchess. I hope you will too."

Had she also taken lovers beyond royal lineage? "Albie—"

"By the way," he cut in mildly, "that necklace was a gift from your father. The pendant's genuine crystal coral. He had a matching one—brought them for your mother all the way from the Crystal Sea."

It was also rare for him to mention my father so freely.

"You've never been there," Albie continued in quiet reflection, "but it's a sight. Pieces of the crystal reef wash ashore, sparkling like jewels beneath the sun. Beautiful place. I always hoped to take you someday, so you could see where you came from."

"But Albie, wasn't my father kin of the Cloudfall? The Crystal Sea is nowhere near that queendom."

"Aye, consider it your father's second home."

Though I waited, he offered nothing further. His grayed eyes were tender, almost sad, watching me with a love entirely unlike Windley's.

"This hume holds considerable adoration for you, little royal," Vita chimed softly.

Yes, and I for him.

"If anyone has been a father to me, Albie, it's you."

"Don't go saying things like that now, My Qu—duchess."

Certainly improper for a queen to say such to her guard, but I didn't care. Tending scraped knees, reading poems to chase away the dark, fixing midnight cocoa after finding me out of bed in places I shouldn't be—it was because of Albie I had never truly felt motherless.

"I have incomparable fondness for you, my knight, and that's why I feel such guilt for leaving you the way I did, knowing what you must have endured in my absence." Gently, I cupped his wrinkled cheek. "Though I'm not sorry I left, I am sorry for the pain my actions brought you." For every new line of worry etched into his face. "I left for selfish reasons, reasons driven by affection, but know this: what I fight for now—this quest—it's no longer about me. It's for us all."

Albie placed his rough hand over mine. "Wish you'd leave it all behind."

"It's not my destiny," I said softly. "I'm capable of far more now. I've changed."

He studied me for a long moment, as though making up for lost time—searching my face for whatever wisdom it might hold.

"And I'll be by your side whether I agree or not," he said finally.

"Thank you, my knight. The choices I make today are guided by lessons you taught me yesterday. If you have faith in nothing else, have faith in that."

He nodded solemnly, then turned to the attendant working on my hair—which felt *divine*—and ordered, "Keep room atop for this." He meant the crown of silver ivy, brought carefully along with us. Once all was complete—gown, hair, rouge—Albie looked me over.

"The hounds will be out for sure this time."

The hounds, currently back at the inn resting off our travels as Soleil crept ever higher.

"I won't wear this through the city, though," I said. "I'll put guard attire back on and send the dress ahead. You said Delagos secured rooms at the castle, yes? I'll change there."

"Aye, wouldn't want it dirtied."

That was the least of my concerns.

It took forever to get gussied up—especially when your hair was as unruly as mine, especially when your keeper had standards as exacting as Albie's—and every minute increased my anxiety: anxious to reunite with the others, anxious to step outside, anxious to see Beau again.

One final spritz of perfume—far too flowery for my tastes—and Albie and I stepped into the orange-drenched city, adorned with seashells and driftwood. A wide-mouthed hood shadowed my face, Albie walked ahead, and Beau's two cavalrywomen brought up the rear.

"Albie, why that way? Aren't we going back to the inn first?"

"Nae, the hounds'll meet us at the castle. Already sent word. We'll find the captain at the courtyard gate and sneak you in through the side."

Whatever Albie thought of our broader quest, his aged eyes sparked brightly at the chance to lead this infiltration—sending guards here and there, arranging secret meetings, ordering "lads" about to do his bidding.

Above the cityscape rose the castle's crescent towers, where untold horrors waited behind deceptively warm and inviting doors, coaxing unsuspecting flies into the spider's web. The sound of my new shoes tapping over cobbles was nothing compared to how they'd echo across glassy castle floors, reflecting dim lights held captive in vampiric fixtures. With luck, we'd be offered rooms in the wing yet untouched by Sestilia's "distinct" influence.

I heard it before I saw it—the pebbled walkway leading to stone steps, crowded with visitors arriving to pay respects to Queen Sestilia. More than I'd anticipated. Perhaps she had friends after all.

"Who are all these people?" I whispered to Albie.

"Kin of the Cove, I expect," he answered quietly as we slipped around the side.

"All of them? Surely the Cove doesn't have that many royals. Last I was here, the castle was nearly deserted, save a few frightened stewards."

"Mm. Seems many moved out after the, er, tragedy."

He meant after Sestilia's sister had "fallen" to her death.

"And yet they've returned to make merry for the one most likely responsible?"

"Doubt they've much choice. Not with the queen hiring out that assassin clan. Speaking of which—" He nodded behind us, where a hooded figure quickly ducked into an alleyway.

"You don't think that's them!"

"Aye, been tailing us since that boutique. You're not to wander off once we're inside, understood? Delagos knows what happened last time and assures me his men are loyal, but I hear the queen's private network runs deep."

An unsettling dynamic. A court holding no fealty to their monarch, guards merely going through motions, and a queen ruling by shadows and fear.

"We should send Rebella and Lekhana down here as an example of how not to rule," I murmured, glancing back to ensure the figure hadn't reemerged.

"They'll never need to rule now you're back," Albie said quietly, clearly expecting no response as he searched through the ornate rods of the courtyard's fence.

Best not to respond anyway.

"Albie, Ruckus is in the castle stable, yes?" I asked instead.

"Aye, My Queen, but you'll have to wait until dark for that reunion. Ah, here he comes now."

Delagos, he meant. Indeed, a stouter, rosier-cheeked version of Albie waddled across the pruned lawn.

"Alb! You made it!" The Captain of the Cove jangled iron keys, extending a hearty handshake through the fence bars. "Queen Merrin, wonderful to see you." He cast an uneasy glance back toward the castle, voice dropping. "Alb told me what happened last time. My sincerest apologies. The situation here's grown...delicate. Never imagined she'd go so far as to..." He clapped his hands decisively. "Well, we'll ensure it doesn't happen again. You have my word, Your Majesty."

"Thank you, Captain Delagos. I'm sure you understand why I felt it necessary to check on Queen Beau myself."

Delagos swung open the gate with a lengthy creak. "Of course. Queen Sestilia will be thrilled to see you on her birthday. You're all she's talked about for weeks."

"*Wonderful.*" Excessive, really, how tightly I smiled.

"Any word on the Spirite lass and youth?" Albie asked as we hurried across the courtyard strewn with perfectly trimmed hedges.

"Not a lick. Only Spirites we've seen are the two traveling with you."

Hardly reassuring when Spirites could morph their appearances to suit their needs—though it comforted me knowing Edius and Windley would sense any surge of their power nearby.

The castle loomed before us, precisely as it had appeared in the vision Vita showed me when we were still on southern soil.

"Be on your guard, Merrin. The destroyer is near."

I gave the goddess a subtle nod of resolve before following the guards into the Cove's grand castle. A castle where handmaids scurried like frightened mice. A castle where more mysterious deaths had occurred than the records would ever admit.

A castle that would soon claim someone precious to me.

17

MY DEAREST FRIEND

Through sleek, dark halls gleaming like obsidian, echoing with the tiptoes of stewards hidden in shadow—amplifying their hurried steps like distant cries for help—Delagos led Albie and me to a chamber in a distant wing, far from other guests. This wing, still untouched by Sestilia's lavish tastes, was bright and inviting, furnished with rich mahogany, tasteful fabrics, and comforting greenery.

Just as Albie had requested.

"You stay here, My Queen. I'll see about your dress."

Albie left me in the care of the two cavalrywomen stationed outside, while I hurried to arrange the room's potted flowers into a protective cluster—in case of emergency.

Not five minutes later, a knock at the door startled me. I wasn't expecting company, so I positioned myself defensively behind the makeshift floral barricade before answering. "Come in."

"My, what's all this?"

I knew that voice—as I knew the silken ponytail slipping

around her neck, and the pretty, freckled face peeking through the doorway.

"Beau! Beau, Beau, Beau!" I leapt over my potted defenses and yanked her fully into the room, wrapping her tightly in a much-needed embrace. "I've missed you terribly!"

"And I you!" She squeezed me tenderly, carrying with her a cloud of jasmine perfume.

Then I noticed her attire. "Whoa, Beau! You look *sinful*."

Indeed, the graceful queen was draped in a glittering black gown hugging her slender hips and accentuating the soft curves of her décolletage.

She hugged herself self-consciously. "Yes, well, my choices were slim."

"This gown is definitely Sestilia's doing." Gently, I pushed her arms away. "Don't hide yourself; you look amazing. But it absolutely reflects the tastes of our host. You haven't met her yet, have you?"

"Haven't had the pleasure." Beau gave an exasperated sigh, glancing down at herself before remembering there were more pressing matters than modesty. "But enough about me. Tell me everything. Where have you been? What's happened with the echoes of the forest? Poor Rafe was nearly frantic when he found us!"

"Beau." I took both her hands, holding tight. "It's not good. There's...a lot. But before we get into it—do you know?"

She tilted her head, confused.

Carefully, I rested a hand against her belly.

"O-oh." Color rushed to her cheeks beneath her careful rouge. "I do. I do now, anyway. I had my suspicions, but Rafe... he confirmed it."

"Do you hate me for it?"

"Hate you?" Her brows lifted in surprise. "You mean because of that deal with the sun?" She frowned softly. "'Deal with the sun'? How absurd, the things we've grown used to saying." She shook the thought away. "Of course not. What other choice did we have? I don't know what's to become of the sun's child, but if it's his...I'll protect it fiercely, as my own."

Love.

It shone clearly in her eyes as she cradled her belly through the gown. It lingered on her lips as she chewed them thoughtfully, and echoed through her heart as she considered all Rafe had done to shield their unborn child from wraiths who sought it.

"Magical twins, Beau."

She laughed to herself, almost as if trying to swallow disbelief. "I know."

"You'll be a wonderful mother."

"And you a wonderful aunt."

An aunt was all I could ever hope to be, should my current path continue.

"Foolish queen," Beau said assuredly, placing a palm against my cheek. "As if I could ever hate you."

If only she knew how this story had ended the last time around.

"Come, Beau." Gingerly, I guided her to sit at the edge of the bed. "There's much to discuss, and not much time to discuss it."

But enough time to share every steamy detail about Windley, naturally.

"Oh, Merrin!" Beau's eyes were wide with guilt. "This burden —it isn't yours to bear! It was my bloodline that swore to keep them locked away. It's my fault the role of oracle fell upon you. Had I known—"

"You still would've bedded Rafe," I said knowingly.

"T-true."

I waved her guilt away. "It doesn't matter what brought us here. I'll finish this for the both of us. When it's done, you and your bloodline will never again need to fear the darkness in the shadows. I already have Vita's half of the Crown. Once I reclaim Exitium's half, I'll send that snake to the end of days where she belongs."

"But how, Merrin? How will you accomplish something so great?"

"That's...a great question."

Her brows inched together, humor gone. "Which is to say—you don't know?"

I suspected I was the only one capable of making her look this way—but now was hardly the time to brag.

"I'm taking things step by step," I explained. "Our next step: Windley and Edius—that's the ripped one I told you about—will subdue Sestilia until dawn, when Vita will help me absorb Exitium without drawing in the ghosts surrounding her."

"The ghosts," Beau repeated, clearly unsettled to realize the echoes, at their core, were just Exitium's fallen devotees. "And this...Edius. You trust him?"

"I do."

"Because you fancy him?"

I fixed her with a flinty stare. "You know precisely how I feel about Windley—there's hardly room for another."

She studied me knowingly with those deep, pool-like eyes. "Just because your heart belongs to one doesn't mean your body won't desire another. They're separate beasts. I only mention it because of how you flushed when describing him."

I'd flushed? Not intentionally, surely.

"My beasts already found their prey in Windley," I said. "Edius earned my trust purely on merit."

Beau gave a princess-like laugh behind her hand. "You sound so certain. Very well—I'll trust him too. How can I help?"

"Stay as far away from it as possible. Once things begin, lock yourself safely away with Rafe."

"I couldn't possibly—"

"I mean it, Beau. You'd be doing me a favor. It's not that you can't fight—I know you can—but if you're there, my thoughts will be consumed with worry for you. I fear my wits won't be as sharp."

"I understand." She placed a protective hand against her stomach. "I'm compromised, after all."

"Compromised isn't the word. Think of yourself as protector of something precious. Lock it away safely, out of harm's reach, and guard it fiercely."

Which reminded me—"Get a transfer ready for Rafe, and I'll sign it tonight. If you're comfortable with it, I'll also inform Albie of your secret. Perhaps we can arrange a pairing with one of the Crag's kin as a cover. I know a few who would happily play mate for appearances. My second cousin, for example—he keeps entirely to himself and would expect nothing from you if left to his diversions."

"Yes, I've thought about all that." Sadness lingered in her expression, understandably so. The idea of hiding your love away was hardly pleasant.

"I've struggled with that myself," I confessed. "Wondering how things will work out between Windley and me once this is over. Rafe, at least, is discreet, but Windley..."

Windley would be a much dirtier secret to hide.

"Oh, if there's a way, that boy will find it," Beau said with an indulgent laugh. "It's how he managed to charm himself into my private guard in the first place. One look at you was all it took."

Unbearable.

My fondness must have been showing in my smile.

"You love him." Her tone settled, rich with understanding. "It practically radiates from you. I'm happy for you both."

"I do love him, Beau," I said quietly. "In a way that frightens me. Lately, I've been having thoughts I never imagined. Thoughts about being a queen, about my role in the world, about what lengths I would go to for him."

"You're not alone in that. Royalty is as much a gift as it is a shackle." Beau pressed her forehead reverently to mine. "Tonight, when the time comes, I'll stay safely aside. Thank you for taking this burden from me, my dearest friend. I shall owe you forevermore."

"There are worse fates than being beholden to the Clearing's most irresistible queen."

"Ugh! Enough teasing. I already feel naked as it is."

"Bet Rafe enjoys it," I teased further.

"Well, yes, he was a fan."

"If you feel uncomfortable, feel free to check the closets here. Sestilia's dearly departed sister had far finer tastes, though her clothes might be too big on you."

"No, no, I wouldn't want to offend the Queen of the Cove. I'll manage." Beau eyed me critically, tapping her rosied cheek in thought. "Speaking of which, Merrin—why do you look like that?"

"Albie took me to some ghastly boutique where they painted all this on." I waved vaguely toward my face.

Beau continued tapping thoughtfully as she examined me. "It's not that it isn't lovely—it just isn't you. I could fix it, if you'd like? Keep it formal, but less..."

"Painted? That would be fantastic. *Thank* you, Beau."

"And your curls—I know at least one guard who'd prefer them free from these clips."

"Do it, Beau. Do whatever you please with me!"

With a gentle smile, fashionable Queen Beau set about making up for my deficiencies, wiping away layers of foundation so my natural skin could shine through and refining my eyeliner to "better reflect my personality."

But when she reached my hair—

"Merrin, this is absurd! How did a leaf manage to get tangled in here?!"

Everyone deserves a friend like Beau.

As she worked her magic, we talked of goddesses, Spirites, and everything that had transpired. We speculated about tonight's events, the uncertain future, and finally—

"So," she began carefully.

"So?"

"Have you...?"

"Have I what?"

"Have you and Windley...?"

"Oh. No."

She swiveled from behind me, trying to glimpse my expression. "And why does your voice carry such dismal disappointment?"

Reluctantly, I explained the conversation between Spirite men I'd overheard.

"Psh!" She laughed outright. "As if that boy would ever harm you! He'd cut off his own hand before letting it cause you pain."

Yes, I believed that too, but still...

"Oh, I expect he'll lose a bit of control—but only in the ways you'll enjoy." Beau squeezed my shoulders reassuringly. "My dear, you may be too dense to notice, but his devotion was obvious to the rest of us for years. He pined for you day and night. I often found him gazing out the castle windows toward your queendom."

Her voice mellowed, earnest and sure. "He loves you with a rare, precious love, Merrin. I may not understand his kind deeply, but I know him. When it comes to you, his heart will always overcome any cravings. He's just anxious because he's finally getting what he's longed for all these years."

She leaned closer conspiratorially. "You'll be devoured in the best possible way—and I cannot wait. Rumor has it he's a rather experienced lover."

She paused just long enough for—

"A-ah! My dress!"

I tackled her to the bed in an exuberant hug.

"Stars above, Beau—I missed you!"

"Merrin!" she squealed, laughing despite herself. "Now we'll have to redo your eyeshadow—you've smudged it all over me!" Yet her arms wrapped tightly around me, smearing beyond repair and giggling all the while.

My dearest, dearest friend. Her embrace did feel like coming home.

The next knock was Albie, delivering my dress. Beau helped lace up the back, and when it was through—

"Oh goddess, Merrin! You look radiant!" Her eyes sparkled mischievously. "O-on second thought, we might need to keep Windley very, very far away from you."

From the corner, Albie made a sickly, disapproving noise.

The woman reflected in the mirror was both me and not me. Embarrassed yet proud, my skin tingled at the thought of Windley seeing me like this—beneath the dark castle's dim lights, against candle flames that would set my gown glittering like stardust.

Beau had sharpened the tips of my eyes, giving them a sleek, cat-like shape reminiscent of Edius's.

"I'm sending him out to tend to your stag," Albie grumbled. "Sending both of them. Every man between the ages of twelve and seventy."

"You will not, Albie! We'll need everyone here for tonight's events. Rafe will guard Beau, and you, my knight—will you stand guard at Sestilia's door once the Spirites begin their work?"

Albie wasn't fully listening. "This is your doing, isn't it?"

He shot Beau an accusing look, and she merely lifted her shoulders in helpless surrender.

18

THE GOLDEN DRESS

I found him waiting, lounged casually against the wall at the far end of the hall, clad sharply in a guard's formal attire and looking scrumptious as ever. His posture was effortlessly cocky, as if he were a nobleman awaiting a carriage, his hair a bold shade that proudly displayed his disregard for the world's conventions. But the instant he turned and glimpsed me, all composure vanished.

"Ma...jesty?"

It was silly, but this had been the longest we'd been apart in days. The mere sight of him sent warmth racing beneath my skin.

"Give us a moment, would you, Albie?" I said.

The bristled knight emitted a petulant grunt from somewhere deep within his throat, his narrowed eyes fixed on Windley's loosened jaw.

I rested my hands against Albie's lapels, offering him my sweetest look. "Surely there are worse men out there. Surely Windley isn't so bad."

"No, he isn't *so bad*," Albie conceded grudgingly, "but you deserve the best, My Queen. And I don't like how he's lookin' at you all hungry-like."

Ravenous, Rafe had once called it.

True, Windley had looked at me many ways before, but the way he was looking at me now...

There wasn't a word for it. Love and desire mingled openly with awe and uncertainty, as though he'd stumbled upon a rare, fleeting sight and was terrified of frightening it away. His heart thundered so fiercely I was half certain it would shake the chandeliers above.

The cavalrywomen who'd stood guard at my door waited just ahead. Carefully concealing my eagerness, I gathered my gown and passed them, approaching the Clearing's naughtiest guard.

"My, my." I kept my voice low and teasing. "Who knew a royal guard could clean up so nicely?"

Windley didn't reply.

Strange—unlike him not to seize a chance to flirt, especially after being apart all day.

"Wind?"

He swallowed hard. "Fuck."

I laughed at his awe. "Windley, it's still me under all this."

He kept staring, groping for words. "You're...the most breathtaking thing I've ever seen, Merr. Feels like I shouldn't even touch you."

Not long ago I'd felt the same about him. Slipping us out of the traffic of guests, I caught his hand and pressed it to my waist so the silk crinkled beneath his palm.

"Cloak or ballgown, I'm still the girl who curled up beside you in that drafty tent," I murmured, echoing his old promise. "There's nothing to fear here—be easy with me anywhere."

His gaze dropped to our joined hands, lower lip caught between his teeth. "Hrn."

Oh, how I loved making him—the confident, swaggering, sex-driven Spirite—nervous.

There had once been a time when I couldn't imagine calling Windley darling or walking arm-in-arm with him at a gala. But that had been another Merrin, another life. Now, nothing felt more natural than pulling him close, looping my arm through his, and following behind Albie and the cavalry-women as Windley looked down at me in a manner wholly inappropriate by refined social standards.

We weren't exactly discouraging the cavalry's rumors.

"Wait," Windley whispered, stopping abruptly at the end of a dim hallway. "A word, Queen Merrin?"

Queen Merrin. So strange to hear it through his lips.

"Round the corner," I instructed Albie and the others. "My personal attendant needs a moment."

A word, he'd said, but the second they were out of sight, Windley cupped my face and kissed me fiercely, saying everything words couldn't.

"Sorry, darling. Missed you already from being apart all day. And seeing you like this... I wasn't prepared."

His kiss ignited something in my chest, and suddenly I was the one claiming his mouth, pushing him against the wall, letting him know we stood on even footing.

Speaking candidly, Windley had always been hot, but witnessing his hotness wrapped in polished elegance was another thing entirely.

"Nice hair, pinkie," I teased breathlessly.

"I figured I'd dress for the frivolity of the event." His mouth twitched. "Or at least, that was the idea. But seeing you like this..." He closed his eyes, drew in a deep breath, and his hair darkened swiftly to brown. "This suits your dress better."

"You intend to be at my side all night, then?" I asked.

"Try and keep me away."

There it was—his trouble-loving, ready-to-kidnap-me charm clawing back through any nerves or uncertainties.

Queen and guard, perhaps. But we were far more than what the world would ever let us be.

"If you'd stop distracting me with your unparalleled beauty," he said, "I actually did want a word with you."

"Unparalleled?" My fingers skimmed his collar, easing it down a notch. "Confess—what do you hope to gain with compliments like that?"

"Merrin." His hand closed over mine, velvet-soft warning in his voice. "Touch me like that again and we'll never reach the ballroom."

Albie loudly cleared his throat from around the corner, signaling the imminent end of his patience.

"I'm serious, love," Windley murmured, easing back just enough to lace our fingers together. "We've got to be clear on the plan—has anything shifted?"

"Only the timing," I confessed. "Vita insists we wait for dawn, when she says my inspiration—and her help—will be strongest."

"But we still knock Sestilia out beforehand, right?"

"The moment you can," I confirmed. "Any sign of Charm or Pip?"

"Nothing," he said, mouth tightening. "Almost too quiet. And Exitium?"

"Vita can feel her circling, but hold off on taking Sestilia down until we're sure the destroyer's fully latched on."

"At your command, then..." His voice drifted; something unreadable flickered in his eyes.

"What?" I asked, catching the look before it slipped away.

Instead of answering, he gently pressed his lips against my forehead, leaving them there long after the kiss had ended.

"By the way," he murmured, mouth still against my skin,

my hands trapped warmly against his chest, "have you seen chap yet?"

"Rafe?"

Windley snorted, pulling back with a roguish grin. "Just wait until you do."

It didn't take long to see what he meant.

At the stewards' entrance to the Cove's ballroom, Albie replaced Windley, properly taking my arm to quell any arising rumors.

And then we entered.

Like the rest of the castle, the ballroom was vampirically ornate, with vaulted ceilings, stained-glass windows framed by pointed arches that revealed glimpses of the night sky, iron chandeliers dripping wax from countless candles, and fires roaring at either end more ferociously than any lion's call I'd ever summoned.

A fair number of guests, adorned in varying degrees of finery, clustered along the walls, sipping from crystal glasses or whispering quietly, none eager to dance to the haunting notes of the string quartet.

No sign of Sestilia yet, but I spotted familiar faces—Beau's cavalry in their scarlet sashes, and Beau herself hovering a polite arm's-length from one very disgruntled magician. I slipped free of Albie's escort and hurried over, slowing only when something about Rafe made me blink.

"Rafe! What in the realms happened to you?"

Silver dust frosted the tips of his dark-brown curls—an effect that might have suited Windley but looked utterly misplaced on solemn, buttoned-up Rafe.

"Hello, Your Majesty." His dry tone conveyed just how much he appreciated the attention.

"Now, dear, people will pay it less mind if you do," Beau murmured candidly to him.

"I can't believe I let you drag me to this," he grumbled.

So strange to hear them speaking as an actual couple.

"It doesn't look that bad," I lied. "But honestly, Rafe, what happened?"

"It was Luna," Beau said. "She chased after him, spewing goddess-knows-what concoction at him—"

"Splooge, Your Majesty," Windley interjected smoothly, appearing beside us. "We've established it was moon splooge."

"Of course you would think it was something like that, Windley," Beau said primly. "Anyway, by the time he found us, he was completely coated in it. We simply can't get these last bits out. I've assured him it doesn't look nearly as dreadful as he imagines."

"Aw, chap, it suits you." Windley slung an arm around Rafe's neck. "Should I match you? We could match. Imagine us —twinsies." He glanced from Rafe to Beau. "Too soon?"

I clapped before either could respond. "Isn't this exciting? Think of all the times we'll have at the forest fortress now it's finally out in the open!"

"This one will be more annoying than ever," Rafe muttered in a jaded tone, shrugging Windley's arm off as if swatting away a pesky fly.

"Come on, mate. Admit it—you missed me."

With arms crossed, rolling his eyes dramatically, Rafe marched away.

"He did miss you," Beau assured Windley prettily from behind her hand before trailing after him.

Windley rested his elbow on my shoulder, as he always did. "The queen's looking rather foxy tonight, hmm?"

"Right?" I smiled. "I love it."

"And I love you," he whispered in my ear.

"I think you just like that saying it now feels dangerous," I teased.

For a heartbeat the music, candle-glow, and Windley's closeness blurred the mission's sharp edges. I might almost have believed we were simply guests—until Queen Sestilia swept into the room, and every hidden knife of purpose slid back into focus.

Ugly soul or not, she remained the most beautiful creature I'd ever laid eyes upon. Her fitted silver gown shimmered brilliantly against smooth, dark skin, and silky silvery hair fell around her like a silken shroud, crowned by a sharp, jeweled tiara. Yet nothing compared to those piercing blue eyes, crystalline and icy, like forbidden gemstones pulled from some ancient cavern.

"May I present Queen Sestilia of the Cove," an attendant's voice echoed—to tepid applause and hushed murmurs.

I held my breath as the flawless figure strode regally across the room to a throne framed by cascading curtains of crystal beads, waiting for the goddess within my chest to move, for any inkling—

"The destroyer has found her mark."

"You're sure, Vita?"

A swell of the goddess's breath filled me, distorting my view so the room appeared muted, dull colors through which I glimpsed a shimmer of light from myself and shadow clustering around Sestilia.

"I wonder if she knows yet. If she doesn't, we may handle this with little trouble for her."

Inside me, turbulence stirred.

"Vita? What's wrong?"

"I apologize, little royal. I did not mean for you to feel it. I lament the injustice done to this soul."

"What injustice? Did something happen to Sestilia?"

"It is not my will for you to know; however, I fear we have

less time than expected. The spider queen bears wounds the destroyer will quickly seed. You must subdue her soon."

But it would appear suspicious to act now. We needed to wait until the crowd around her thinned and more wine was consumed. Already, a reception line had formed before the queen's throne, hostage royals presenting lavish gifts to the intimidating matriarch.

"She's occupied for now," Windley said quietly. "But you can't hide from her forever, not looking like that. See? All eyes keep drifting your way."

"Oh, please. They do not."

Yet they did. When my gaze met theirs, guests hastily averted their eyes. My gown truly sparkled vividly beneath the ballroom's candlelight.

"Windley! Did you see that?"

Mid-scan, I'd caught a hooded figure slipping behind the quartet, notably out of place among Sestilia's guests.

Windley followed my line of sight. "One of the queen's assassins? We knew they'd be lingering. Sir Albie mentioned he spotted them tailing him earlier."

"You aren't worried?"

"Not when my girlfriend can drain life with a mere touch. Besides—" He patted his jacket.

"You brought your hatchets?!"

"Where else?" he shrugged.

I should've known.

I continued scanning the room for more assassins, dismissing fleeing glances until my gaze snagged one pair that didn't look away.

"Edius!" I trotted toward him, ignoring stares and whispers. "Well, don't you look fancy. Any word on Charm or Pip?"

Instead of replying, he slowly eyed me from head to toe without emotion before turning his back.

"E-Edi?"

"No word," he said flatly. "You look nice."

"Nice?" Windley shot him a sidelong glance. "Why not tell her what you really want to say?"

Edius turned, brawny arms folded. "You look stunning. Now, kindly stop bothering me." He poked me gently in the forehead before sulking off.

I rubbed the spot he'd touched. "What's that about?"

Windley shook his head. "As I've said before, anyone who can't handle your merciless, soul-capturing stare doesn't deserve it. Now go. You've lingered by me long enough—the courtiers will start whispering. Don't worry, I'll be watching."

With a parting nudge he vanished, slipping through the gaggle of cowering guests before I could protest.

A blur of curtsies, clammy handshakes, and syrup-sweet compliments followed while Albie paraded me about, proud as a peacock. I smiled, nodded, and kept one eye on the throne, the other on my two Spirites.

Because I was watching, I caught it at once—the moment they both lurched forward, eyes snapping to the queen.

"Albie!" I hissed, tugging his sleeve. "I need to—"

I pivoted toward the startled royals he'd been introducing. "Forgive me—so lovely to meet you."

Gathering my gown, I hurried toward the Spirites, whose hushed voices bore troubling urgency.

"What is it? Do you feel them?"

Edius and Windley exchanged a grim glance.

"Yeah. We just felt Ascian," Edius admitted. "But the thing is—"

Windley finished darkly, "It's coming from your favorite queen."

19

A GIFT FOR THE QUEEN

By now, Rafe had noticed our gathering and swiftly approached, Beau close behind him. "What's happening?" he asked, hand resting warily on his sword's hilt.

"These two think they feel Ascian—but it's coming from Sestilia," I said.

"Wait, what?" Rafe's hand fell from his sword.

"But that isn't Charm, right?" Windley was asking Edius. "The mannerisms—?"

"No," I said firmly. "Vita showed me beyond the mortal veil; the echoes were within that person. Exitium can only root itself in royal blood." I paused, pressing my finger to my temple. "Vita? Is that really Sestilia up there?"

"The spider queen is royal and not a beastling. Of this, I am certain."

I reemerged to reality. "Vita confirmed. It really is Sestilia—not a Spirite in disguise."

"I don't get it," Edius voiced what we all felt. "Have we

sensed her this entire time? But it feels exactly like Ascian's power."

"So, does this mean Charm and Pip aren't in the city at all?" I asked.

"Well, we never actually felt either of them—only Ascian—and Lady Life insists he perished," said Windley.

Reassuring, because it meant facing only one enemy at a time—but troubling, as we truly had no clue about their whereabouts.

"I don't know what to make of it," Beau admitted as a lone violin began to wail softly, threading its sorrowful notes above murmured conversation. "But the line is short enough now that we should pay our respects."

Like soldiers marching into battle, two queens, two Spirites, and a magician stepped into a reception line none of us wanted to be in—to wish a spider queen happy birthday and discover what was truly unfolding.

"Edius, Beau. Beau, Edius," I made quick introductions as we waited.

"Your friend's cute," said Edius.

"He means your cake. Or frosting. Or both. Who knows, really," I said.

Edius lifted a lip. "Cake?"

Windley tossed me a grin before quickly masking it, resuming his scrutiny of Sestilia.

"And Rafe, you've...reacquainted with Edius?"

"Yes," Rafe replied curtly, clearly still harboring ill feelings about being impersonated.

Edius didn't seem offended, tipping his nose upward to sniff discreetly at the air, perhaps seeking remnants of his former coven.

Sestilia's throne approached like a gallows.

"You take the lead," Windley whispered. "She likes you best."

She certainly did. Upon seeing me, she leapt from her throne, throwing aside the gift on her lap to gasp: "M—!"

"Sestilia!" I opened my arms wide. "You didn't think I'd miss your birthday, did you?"

"Merrin!" She fell into my embrace like a lover returned from war, her shimmering hair cascading everywhere. She was indeed breathtaking, gripping me with her sharp red nails adorned with bits of dangling silver chain and crystals. "I thought, after last time..."

"Yes, such a shame we had to leave so early," I cooed soothingly, patting her back. "I did say at dinner we'd leave before dawn, but I regretted it immediately."

Best to gloss over the unpleasantness; perhaps her assassins had reported the same.

Edius and Windley exchanged uneasy glances, the only two who could glimpse the darkness coiling inside Sestilia's soul.

"It is indeed lamentable for a soul to twist this way," Vita intoned gently. *"Be kind, Merrin. She is drawn to your spirit as darkness is drawn to light."*

Kindness was my intention, though it would lack sincerity —for I too was imperfect.

Sestilia squeezed me tightly before finally noticing Beau behind me, who was also crowned—though simply, from court reserves.

"You're the Queen of the Clearing?" Sestilia released me at last. "The one I'm to meet tomorrow?"

Beau nodded warmly. "A pleasure, Sestilia. You have a lovely castle."

Sestilia didn't seem to care about Beau's compliments. "I

see you've already met Merrin. She and I are the best of friends."

"Is that so?" Beau's expression was carefully pleasant. "How nice."

Windley slid that same wary look to Beau now, as if passing along a silent warning.

Sestilia didn't notice; she'd started swatting at her head as if warding off gnats.

"Is something wrong, Sestilia?" I asked.

"Oh, just a ghastly headache." She flicked a venomous glance at Beau. "Ever since she arrived."

Good news: Sestilia perceived the echoes only as a headache. Bad news: she knew exactly when they'd arrived. Beau and Rafe had carried them here.

"I'm so sorry," Beau offered quickly. "Merrin has a remedy for headaches if you'd like—"

"Merrin!" Sestilia cut Beau off. "Look at my nails. I had them done this morning. Notice anything?"

"Exquisite, just like everything about you."

"I knew it! I knew you'd notice." She wrinkled her nose cutely. "The secret to making them so shiny—"

"Of course," I played along, noting Sestilia's eyes darting toward Beau as she whispered:

"It's blood. It must be human. Stag blood is far too sticky."

A steward by her throne shifted uncomfortably, adjusting bandages at his cuff.

"H-how unique," Beau fumbled for polite words.

"You don't get it." Sestilia looked to me. "She doesn't get it. Merrin, none of them do. It's like we're the only two lily pads in a great wide lake."

"Or gravestones in an endless field," I suggested.

"Yes!" Her smile glittered brightly, perfectly, as Beau gave a faint noise behind us.

Resting her head comfortably against my chest, Sestilia hummed softly to the quartet's plucked notes. "Oh! What have you brought me for my birthday? I just know your present will be best! You know, I asked for pets, yet so far, I've received none."

At least the people of the Cove had the good sense to deny this girl any pets.

"A-actually, Sestilia, I did bring you a pet of sorts—two of them, for tonight only, mind you, as you know how I like to play."

I wriggled tactfully away from her embrace, beckoning Windley and Edius forward. The two Spirites promptly shoved each other like schoolboys, neither eager to go first.

"Spirites!" Sestilia's eyes sparkled dangerously. "And two this time!" She nudged me with conspiratorial glee. "You bad girl—wherever do you find them so willingly?"

So willingly being the key phrase here.

"How about I tell you in the morning, after you've tried them out?" I said lightly. "Perhaps you'd enjoy them after dancing—"

"Now."

She yanked Edius down by the collar and kissed him hard. He gave me a blank, resigned stare over her shoulder, then shrugged, slid a hand to her waist, and leaned into it. When she let go, his irises burned red.

"Splendid!" sang Sestilia. "You next."

She reached for Windley, but he gracefully evaded her hand, setting a fingertip lightly to her glossed lips.

"I prefer to work in private," he purred darkly, leaning closer, teeth brushing her ear. "Where's your room, darling?"

That one was tough to watch—especially with him looking so formal. I wished fervently it had been my ear he whispered into.

"May I?" asked Sestilia, glancing at me uncertainly.

"By all means," I said, forcing a polite smile that pulled too tight at the corners of my mouth. I'd brought them for her pleasure—or so I pretended.

Sestilia drank in the sight of the two Spirites, all bright-eyed wonder at her unexpected birthday magic.

"Cardory!" she snapped. "Tell the staff and court that anyone who bothers me tonight spends a week in the box. Chambermaids too. Hallway patrols only. Understood?"

Whatever "the box" was, the bandaged steward at her throne eagerly nodded. "Yes, Queen Sestilia! Immediately!"

Fortunate for us, the staff were thrilled for a night away from her. Few queens would have been permitted such liberty, alone with two strange men.

"By all means," Edius echoed, his voice edged with irony—an unspoken reminder that I owed him for this—before letting himself be led away. Windley, meanwhile, offered a rascally wave behind her back.

Across the room, I locked eyes with Albie and gave a firm nod for him to follow.

"She's not quite all there, is she?" Beau murmured, forcing a veneer of diplomacy. "What are we to do with her? The region will crumble under such rule."

"One crisis at a time, Beau. Once this is over, I'll gladly testify to the other sovereigns."

"Oh dear," Beau fretted under her breath. "I feel badly for Windley...and the other."

"That one deserves whatever he gets," Rafe said, thoroughly unsympathetic. "Both of them."

"You don't mean that, Rafe," I chided.

"Don't worry," Beau whispered. "He speaks fondly of Windley in private."

Just as I'd suspected.

Without Sestilia in her throne, ballroom murmurs swelled, and the fires at either end blazed as the quartet continued its eerie song—until Sestilia's steward stepped forth.

"I regret to inform Her Majesty's guests that Queen Sestilia has retired for the evening. Please remain and make merry in her honor."

Few waited for him to finish, moving swiftly for the doors. We needed them to stay; a packed castle meant better distraction.

"Please!" I stepped forward beside the steward. "I am Queen Merrin of the Crag, joined by Queen Beau of the Clearing. We've traveled far to honor your queen and would be delighted if you continued to celebrate in her name. Though *surely* she'll not rejoin us tonight—"

Key emphasis.

"Honored residents, show us the legendary hospitality of the Cove!"

Only a few still slipped away; the rest stayed, coerced or curious.

"Rafe, the music?" I implored.

He stared blankly.

"Not the best choice," Beau said sensibly, taking his arm. "I'll handle it."

She moved off, setting a livelier tone, while I drifted near the doors, anxious over how long it would take to subdue Sestilia.

"Merrin?"

"Yes, Vita?"

"I do not wish to speculate, but I have a thought."

"By all means," I replied—hearing Edius's mocking voice. "Speculate away. I'm restless waiting for the men anyway."

"So—our young beastlings sensed their master's power radiating from the spider queen?"

"That's what it looks like."

"*And their master died in the destroyer's presence, yes?*"

"Right. When I lost control and the echoes escaped."

"*Remember, the destroyer hoards souls. If the master offered his in death, it could be trapped just beyond the veil, tethered to her.*"

"You're saying Ascian himself might be one of the echoes?"

"*That is my suspicion.*"

From what I knew of Ascian, it sounded likely—clinging desperately to power, even in death. "Vita, you're a genius!"

"*I'm a goddess.*"

"That too. But if you're right, once I absorb Exitium, the echoes—"

"*They will have nothing left to anchor them and will pass naturally, including the lavender-eyed man.*"

Then many problems were solved! Charm and Pip weren't nearby; that ring theory had been wrong. We could save that fight for later. Tonight required only extracting echoes from Sestilia, eradicating Ascian's lingering spirit for good.

And Sestilia had already fallen right into our trap.

"Wonderful, Vita! I'm so relieved—I might even enjoy myself."

Perfect timing. The music quickened, and a tap came at my shoulder.

I turned, meeting a white mustache. "Albie? What are you doing here?"

"The lads are busy. Might take some time, so I'll stay with you till they return. Best not to be alone. I trust the cavalry, but we're outnumbered here, and Rafe's eyes are on the wrong queen lately."

"Thank you, my knight."

"And now, My Queen, might I request your first dance?"

Albie knelt gallantly before the crowd—harder on his knees

now than in Mother's days. Refusing him would disrespect his honor.

I took his hand, holding so many stories, secrets, and lessons. "I'd dance with no other."

Albie guided me across a polished floor, perhaps untouched since Sestilia's kindhearted sister had danced here. He placed one hand behind my back, gathering my fingers gently in his. "Remember the steps?"

Of course—he'd taught me beneath starry skies, Mother Poppy clapping the rhythm.

"I won't step on your feet this time."

"I wish you would," he said, weary and bristled.

"Albie..."

His eyes avoided mine. "Feels like you're slipping away, stolen by men who've yet to learn proper manners."

"You taught me well, Albie. I know my worth and won't surround myself with anyone who lowers it—men or hounds."

"Glad to hear it. You'd give 'em hell anyway."

I blinked hard, tears threatening. "I don't think I've ever seen you look so dapper, my knight."

"Pish posh. You've seen me at balls and festivals."

"Yes," I laughed, "usually in full armor."

My heart brimmed with memories made possible by my mother's beloved guard. Now I understood the moisture in my eyes—Albie had long been home, yet lately, I questioned whether I wished to return.

"I love you, Albie. Someday, I'll repay you for all the worry I've caused."

"I love you too, my dear." His heartbeat affirmed his fatherly affection. "You look beautiful, Queen Merrin. Can't blame the hounds for staring." He paused. "Take care of her."

"Who—?"

Albie wasn't speaking to me now. He was addressing the one behind me, who had entered and offered a hand.

"I will always take care of her, sir," said Windley firmly. "You have my word."

"Good lad." Albie released me. "I'll see you at dawn."

Windley smoothly took Albie's place. "Care to dance, lion queen?"

"Funny, I saw you decline a dozen offers. Thought you didn't dance."

"Oh, I dance very well." He lowered his mouth to my ear. "But only with queens."

20

THE KISS

W indley's hand settled upon my waist differently than Albie's—or anyone else's I'd ever danced with, for that matter—and *goddess*, he was right. He truly was an excellent dancer. He pulled me close, our bodies nearly flush, leaning in to whisper words meant only for me, spoken in a tone saved only for me.

"I suspect every man in this room is jealous of me right now. Some of the women, too."

"Psh. Flattery will get you nowhere."

"Are you sure about that?" His fingers slid subtly along the curve of my back—just enough for no one else to notice.

But I noticed. His touch sparked a thousand tiny fires across my skin, each nerve alive beneath his fingertips.

"You can't do that here," I scolded in secret. "I'll collapse in front of everyone."

"Maybe," he said, perfectly guiding me along with the quartet's tempo. "But I'd catch you."

"I'm surprised you have any charm left at all, after satisfying a queen with an insatiable appetite."

He laughed quietly into my hair. "Eh, Ed did all the work."

It was my turn to lean forward, whispering against his ear. "Then why is your top button undone?"

"To seduce you, obviously," he said, pulling me tighter, his voice dropping to a husky murmur. "Is it working?"

I fought a smile. "Hardly. I find you repulsive. You're working against impossible odds. Besides, how do I know this is even your true appearance? Your magic can alter your clothing, too—Charmagne did as much when impersonating you at the beach. For all I know, you're utterly unkempt beneath this disguise."

His mouth curled deviously. "Guess you'll have to inspect every layer yourself."

Then, without warning, he spun me around and drew my hips back against him, swaying us both from side to side, his chin nestled in the curve of my shoulder.

"W-what kind of dance is this?" I managed, flustered.

"How we do it in the south." His lips brushed my ear. "But since I don't fancy your knight's ancient heirloom sword through my belly—" He twirled me neatly, returning us face-to-face.

Several other pairs had joined now, including Beau and an especially stiff-looking Rafe. When Beau caught my eye, she lifted her brows approvingly.

"Do you think Beau's cavalry will find it odd that we're dancing together?" I asked discreetly.

Windley shrugged easily. "I think it's expected. Who else are you going to dance with, if not your guards? The Cove isn't exactly overflowing with eligible royals."

"Because they've all conveniently 'fallen' to their deaths," I muttered beneath my breath.

Windley barked out a laugh, briskly smothering it behind a

cough. "Goddess, Merrin, that's one of the many things I love about you."

Love. It shone plainly in his gaze as it held mine, radiated through the gentle press of his hands below my shoulder blades, and pulsed clearly from his heart into my own. Love made forgetting the rest of the world dangerously easy.

But we couldn't afford to forget.

"She's down, though, yes?" I pressed, grounding myself.

"Out cold. We were...liberal." His eyes flashed sapphire, and I hastily looked away, careful not to be ensnared.

Yet a pang of jealousy pricked my chest at the thought of those eyes capturing someone else, his hands on Sestilia's perfect skin.

I inhaled, caging the jealousy where it belonged—later. *Focus.*

"By the way, I have good news." I launched into Vita's hopeful theory about Ascian and the echoes.

"That son of a bitch!" Windley flared, then amended quickly at my look, "Sorry. Antiquated expression. I'm sure his mother was lovely."

"But it's a relief, isn't it?"

"Yes," he agreed, relaxing slightly. "We still have to confront them, but at least now we can breathe a little easier." His fingers traced over the exposed skin of my upper back, sending pleasant shivers through me. "The real question is— how shall we occupy ourselves until dawn?"

I caught his meaning at once. My stomach fluttered, breath hitching, and though nerves fizzed beneath my skin, every part of me—innocent or not—wanted precisely that.

"Cards?" I managed, voice airy with anticipation.

"Cards, she says." He chuckled softly, his voice dipping into smoky promise. "If we're playing games tonight, my queen, I assure you—they won't involve cards."

Swoon.

Oh, swoon.

As the music slowed, I rested my cheek against his chest. It was reckless, but I was helpless to resist. His warmth, his scent —they drew me in, and I sighed contentedly into him.

"I'm hopelessly in love with you, my knave," I whispered.

His hand tightened at my back, holding me firmly against him. "Oh, my queen," he breathed, voice a velvet murmur against my hair. "And I with you."

Rocking together like boats on a calm sea, we moved as one. I played absently with the silk-fine hair at the nape of his neck, his hands cradling me protectively. Surely anyone watching could see the truth. Surely everyone noticed this was different. Special.

I didn't care.

Maybe society's greatest flaw was its insistence on restricting something that felt this natural, this perfectly right. Maybe the world would be kinder if we could simply love openly, without fear or shame.

Another song flowed seamlessly into the first, slow and languid, until our bodies were flush, my head tucked perfectly under his chin, his heartbeat strong and steady beneath my ear.

Finally, Windley's hand cupped the back of my skull, thumb stroking tenderly over my hair. "I have to go, Your Majesty," he mused regretfully. "No amount of mead will dull what they're seeing. I can't endanger your reign."

"Stay, Windley," I whispered, squeezing him tight. "Please, stay."

He squeezed my hand in return, pulling back just enough to meet my gaze, love and determination incandescent in his eyes. "I'd do anything to protect you—even if it means letting go right now. Dance with someone else. At least one other person, alright? I'll be waiting."

The "someone else" turned out to be Phylo, who looked as though he'd rather flee—but whose impeccable manners prevented escape.

Afterward, I settled against the wall, watching Windley flirt his way through the ballroom to throw off suspicion, strategically choosing partners who seemed distinctly uninterested in men. Maybe he had a knack for sensing it. He wound his way around the room, diligently playing the role of carefree playboy, while I stayed back, pretending to sip wine and chatting aimlessly with any guards or royals brave enough to approach.

But I wasn't really hearing them.

Under the orphic glow—the kind that makes everything feel slightly enchanted—Windley's frosting gleamed like spun sugar. As he slipped by, he skimmed a hand along my waist and purred, "Tonight, I feast."

Goddess help me, those words consumed every thought for several dizzying moments.

In fact, I was so thoroughly ensnared by Windley's whispered promise that I barely noticed the shift in the ballroom around me—the guards' watchful gazes, the music's change in tempo, the hushed murmurs swelling in number.

It wasn't until another Spirite approached that I remembered my existence had purposes beyond being utterly captivated by Windley.

"Edi." I snapped from my daze. "I see you survived your run-in with the Queen of the Cove."

"That bitch is scary."

"So, you've changed your mind about 'hunting down your own queen,' then?" I smirked.

He narrowed his eyes. "What?"

Oh goddess. He wasn't supposed to know I'd overheard that.

"Uh, Vita," I hastily lied, whispering an apology under my breath. "Sorry, Vita."

"It is fine, Merrin. You may use me to conceal your indiscretions."

Edius seemed satisfied, suspicion fading as he crossed his arms.

"Thank you, Edi. I feel awful about offering you up like some back-alley dalliance. Was it terrible?"

His lips twitched. "A back-alley dalliance? Where'd a northern queen pick up a phrase like that?"

"Windley."

"Ah. Figures." He leaned casually against the wall, eyes drifting toward the ceiling. "Wasn't terrible. Honestly? Felt good blowing off some steam. We can get...pent up." He shot me a sideways glance. "But something felt off about her spirit."

"How so?"

"Reminded me of mine. Windley's. Charm's. Just strange for someone pampered in a castle to feel that way." He let out a knowing breath. "Know you said she tried taking out your kneecaps, but...I kinda feel bad for her."

I considered that, recalling how Sestilia had clung to me, desperate as if we were the only "two lily pads afloat on an endless lake." Something raw and wounded simmered beneath her regal façade. And goddess help me, I was starting to feel for her too.

Edius groaned, sensing my mood. "Aw, come on. I can practically taste your sympathy. You've enough to worry about without adding her to the list."

"I'm not sure I can help it."

He gave a low, rueful chuckle. "Suppose not. Look, they sent me over to dance with you."

I clasped my chest dramatically. "Is the forest thug asking a queen to dance? How scandalous."

His hair was swept back low, dark strands slipping free to frame his jaw. The sleek, tailored suit looked striking on him— far better than it should. Windley once called him a "city boy." Perhaps that explained the precise, refined cut. It suited him entirely too well.

"Nah. Not a dancer." Edius's elusive smirk returned, metered out as though amusement was a precious commodity. "Sent over to stand exceedingly still."

"That's all right," I laughed. "I was jesting anyway. I prefer the wall. Keep me company?"

"With pleasure." He leaned back beside me, arms folded loosely, one boot nudging the floor. His presence felt steady— surprisingly comforting, not unwelcome at all. "Windley told me about your goddess friend's theory. About Ascian."

"It's good news, isn't it?"

"For you guys, sure." He sighed, rubbing his jaw. "Means shit for me. I need that ring, Merrín. Gwen... I don't even know how much life she's got left on account of..." His voice dropped, grief edging each word, something deeper than despair.

I hesitated, because he was right. For all we had solved, his troubles remained.

"On account of...?" I coaxed kindly.

"Never mind."

But his heart betrayed him—thudding anxiously, fearfully. While I'd been distracted imagining Windley's whispered feast, Edius had privately mourned someone he cared about.

"I'm sorry, Edius," I said, heat stinging my cheeks. "I wasn't thinking."

"It's fine. You've got your own shit."

I placed a hand on his arm in reassurance. "I meant what I promised. After we're done here, Charm's next on the list. You're not alone."

He stared at me, like no one had ever told him that before. Then, abruptly, his heart pulsed in a way I recognized.

I stepped back. "Edius, don't."

He frowned. "What'd I do?"

"I warned you," I said, regretful but firm. "If you open your heart to me, it'll stay unrequited." I turned, letting the ballroom shadows hide my face.

He pressed a hand to his chest in discomfort. "You don't know what you're talking about."

He knew I did. But maybe it was better left unacknowledged. Foolishly, I acknowledged it anyway.

"Edius, this isn't about you," I said, holding his gaze. "A human heart can trip over itself a dozen times, but a Spirite heart only wakes once—and stays awake. I won't be the reason yours strays off-course. I treasure our friendship, so let's leave the line where it is. Fair?"

He blinked, the weight of my words landing. A muscle leapt in his jaw, then eased.

"You're brutally honest," he said at last—yet the note beneath it sounded closer to admiration than complaint.

We let the silence spool, watching poor Phylo blunder through another stiff dance.

"I'm not *trying*, you know," Edius muttered after a moment, rubbing the spot over his heart. "Whatever you're sensing in here—plus that damned nuzzle—it's...reactive."

Again with the nuzzle.

"And I don't *want* it," he finished, voice tight but sincere.

"Okay," I said, gentling my tone. "Good."

Quiet settled—heavy, humming with things neither of us dared name. His brows pinched, as though he were arguing with himself. Then he shifted closer, exhaled hard, and—

Before I could move, before I could even *think*—

He bent and pressed his lips to my forehead.

A kiss.

A *Spirite's* kiss.

Warmth blossomed, a soft pull that felt intended to comfort —or maybe say goodbye. I had no chance to sort out how I felt about it or why he'd done it so abruptly—because out of the corner of my eye, I saw Windley.

The instant I met his gaze, I realized he'd witnessed everything. Fury sparked in his eyes like a struck flint. Before I had time to question why a forehead kiss would set him off so violently, he was already shoving a startled Phylo aside, striding across the room in swift, deadly focus.

Without warning—without a word—he seized Edius by the collar and punched him square in the face.

"Windley!" I gasped, pressing my hands against his chest, half in shock myself. Around us, guests froze, alarmed.

"Shit!" Edius hissed, rubbing at his nose. Blood smeared his knuckles. "Look, I didn't mean—how am I supposed to resist her?"

Windley's breath heaved, anger crackling from him in waves. *"You just do.* Like I had to. Try holding out *eight goddess-damned years*—then preach to me about resistance."

Guests scattered, muttering amongst themselves. This wasn't going to help any palace rumors.

Windley kept his glare nailed to Edius, but his words knifed sideways to me.

"And *now* I'm worried."

"Windley," I hissed, trying to calm him. "In the hall. *That's an order*."

His jaw clenched, and he stormed out, radiating heat. I was still reeling from his outburst—so sudden over such a simple forehead kiss—when:

"Gods damn it." Edius dropped his hand from his nose and

backed away, eyes downcast. "Sorry, highness. I shouldn't have done that. I—didn't think."

He brushed past, looking more embarrassed than anything. I followed him into the corridor in time to see Windley shove Edius against the wall again.

"What the hell, mate?" Windley snarled, still seething. "Right in front of me?"

Edius flung up both palms. "You think I'd do that there if it meant something? I'm just readjusting—I slipped. She was being nice—"

Windley's fury swung toward me. Clearly "nice" wasn't what he wanted to hear.

I lifted my hands. "Oh, no. Leave me out of it. I was only dissuading him. I felt his heart—"

"You aren't helping, highness." Edius shot me a rueful look.

I swallowed, forcing a centering breath. "Someone explain. *Now.*"

Windley jabbed a finger in my direction. "You, *little minx*, are in no position to demand—"

"Little minx?" My brow rose dangerously. We came from different worlds, and right now, they were clashing.

Before I could snap back, Edius cut in, planting himself between us. "Be furious at me if you like, Windley—but think it through. She doesn't know what it means, not the way we do. I slipped—I'm out of practice. Haven't had to hold myself in check around a human I actually..."

A flush climbed his cheekbones; he cleared his throat. "Point is, you managed eight years of restraint. She didn't do anything wrong—she was just telling me her heart's already yours."

Windley's fist sagged, the anger draining into something like shame.

He faced me then—remorse and raw frustration crowding

the spark of his eyes the instant he registered my tight-drawn brow. "Merrin..." His voice snagged on the word. He stepped in, resting a careful hand on my arm. "I'm sorry, love. You're human—I reacted on instinct."

I could have bitten back, but I remembered how freely he'd forgiven me the night our worlds first collided at Flora's cottage.

"Stars." He scrubbed a hand over his neck, gaze skittering aside. "This is on me. I never explained, didn't want you thinking I was...claiming you. But where I'm from, a forehead kiss is serious—practically a vow."

"The forehead? Really? Why?"

He gave a faint shrug. "Your court keeps rabbits, right? They rub their chins on everything—scent-marking. It's like that. For us, accepting a forehead kiss is basically a marriage pledge."

My hand flew to my forehead, realization crashing down. "So...when Edius was poking me—?"

Edius glared at the ceiling as if willing it to collapse. "That was me trying not to mark you," he muttered, ears reddening.

My jaw dropped. "But—you're engaged."

He winced, letting out a pained click of his tongue. "Y-yeah, I see why you'd think that."

"Because you literally said so!" I retorted, exasperated.

Windley shot Edius a pointed glare. "I knew what he was doing, and I was okay with it—so long as he didn't follow through. Call it a gentlemen's agreement."

"A gentlemen's agreement," I repeated flatly. "About me."

Windley flinched. "I—look, logically, you didn't cheat. You had no idea what it meant. But my instincts were screaming 'You're mine,' and—" He trailed off, at a loss.

I folded my arms. "Windley, you've kissed my forehead a dozen times without telling me any of this. The first time was at that woodcutter's hut—before..."

He grimaced, color crawling across his cheeks. "We were in the south! I just...wanted them to know you weren't up for grabs. It was a precaution."

"So you were marking me."

Windley groaned, casting me a woeful look. "Merr, it's mortifying enough without you looking so smug."

"Oh, I'm smug. You basically proposed before you even admitted your feelings?"

Edius cleared his throat. "She has a point."

Windley's gaze cut sideways, one brow hitching as he flicked an imaginary speck from Edius's lapel. "My feelings were obvious. Besides, that vow wouldn't hold in your world. I was just..." He exhaled hard. "Trying to protect you, alright? Couldn't stand the idea of losing you to another spooky Spirite."

I fought laughter. "So...a forehead kiss is more intimate than a kiss on the mouth?"

"Yes," Edius answered with a tiny cough.

"Than a kiss anywhere?" I pried.

Windley's voice dropped an octave. "Not anywhere. But we're drifting off-topic." He exhaled hard. "I'm sorry. I shouldn't have lashed out. If anyone's at fault, it's the two of us. You did nothing wrong—I let instinct drive me." Taking my hand, he sank to one knee. "Forgive me, my queen. I have royally—and quite literally—fucked up."

Unimpressed, I lifted my chin.

Edius gingerly rubbed his jaw and cleared his throat. "I messed up too—jumping you like that was low." He grimaced. "I'm a cad."

Windley snorted. "A monumental cad—and you're not getting within arm's reach again without a chaperone."

"Overkill," I muttered, then leveled a finger at both of

them. "But no more back-room *gentlemen's agreements,* understood?"

Windley's eyes went wide. "Goddess—*I'm* the cad here, aren't I?"

Now that the heat of anger had cooled, the absurdity left me fighting laughter. "So a forehead kiss makes an incubus blush? How scandalous must it look when Albie kisses mine?"

Edius let out a helpless breath and spread his palms. "She thinks it's funny."

Windley rubbed a hand over his mouth, half-groan, half-laugh. "She thinks it's hilarious."

"No," I corrected, stepping closer, voice dipping suggestively. "I think we've a few hours till dawn. Plenty of time to figure things out."

Windley tilted his head. "Figure what out, exactly?"

I leaned in, whispering something private in his ear.

A shiver ran through him, fingers tightening around mine. "So...you're not mad anymore?"

"No." I grinned, letting my hand roam up his chest. "If anything, I'm relieved. I've wondered why you never get jealous. I do—more often than you realize. It's nice, knowing I'm not alone in that."

Windley's eyes glinted with something dangerously enticing, his lips parting enough to show a hint of fang. "Oh, I get jealous," he promised in a tone that set my heart racing. "You have no *idea* what I've imagined doing, if anyone else tried to run off with you."

His words—and the hungry way he spoke them—sent a thrill down my spine. A lump formed in my throat.

Edius huffed dramatically. "I need to clear my mind."

"Find someone to bed, mate," Windley called after him. "You'll feel better. Just be sure you meet us at the queen's chamber before dawn."

Edius waved a hand, a rueful frown tugging at his mouth. "Yeah, yeah—enjoy your night. I'll catch up before dawn."

And with that, he disappeared.

Windley wasted no time. He scooped me into his arms as if I weighed nothing, voice dropping into that silken, dangerous register that sent slow, heady warmth pooling deep within my stomach. "Best get to it, then, if we're to answer your question." His lips skated along the curve of my ear. "After all—" his grip on me tightened, "I wonder which places might be more intimate to kiss than a forehead."

21

PULLED LACES

Windley carried me only a short distance, then set me gently in the empty corridor.

"Hey," he murmured, eyes steady. "We're... good?"

"I'd tell you if we weren't."

He searched my face.

"We survive this," I added, tracing a slow crescent along his cheekbone with my knuckles, "by recognizing our differences. You've done that for me more than once. With so little time, let's not spend it on anger."

Relief softened his features. "I'm sorry, Majesty—for not explaining, for giving you something without its meaning. I never meant you to think it was more than a kiss."

"In my world a forehead kiss is protection, affection...innocent." I rose on tiptoe and pressed one to his brow. "Now we're even."

The candle-lit hall caught the faintest rose-tinge across his cheeks; he glanced away, suddenly boyish.

Adorable.

"You know," he murmured under his breath, "I'd do it properly, if I could..."

I assumed he meant he'd propose. My chest tightened, silencing my reply.

We stood in the expectant stillness, eyes full of one another, in a space suddenly more enchanting than eerie—the candlelight dancing over polished floors, the distant hum of ballroom strings, the towering doors arching overhead.

"Come on," he whispered, lacing his fingers through mine and leading me deeper into the castle's still halls. With every step the music receded, replaced by the muted cadence of our shoes meeting stone.

"Since we're speaking plainly," I began, voice low but sure, "I'm not interested in a love triangle."

He cast me a sidelong, teasing glance. "Triangle? Between you, me, and Ed, you mean?"

I gave a hesitant nod.

"Easily fixed," he shrugged. "Do you love him?"

"Not in any sense of the word."

"And does he love you?"

"No. I don't think so."

"Then I see no triangle." He walked on, thumb tracing circles over my knuckles, watching me carefully. "But you're worried, aren't you? Because you're attracted to him?"

Again, I hesitated.

"It's natural, Merrin. I'm sure you felt attraction to Pip and Ascian—and even Charm, perhaps. But a lust triangle is nothing to fear." His eyes darkened mischievously. "Especially when your chosen paramour is a *master* of lust."

We arrived at the door to my chambers, feeling less like a doorway and more like a threshold—one that promised to change everything.

Yet, despite our flirtations, I couldn't bring myself to grasp the knob.

"How long until dawn?" I murmured instead, eyes darting toward starlit windows at the corridor's end.

"A few hours yet," Windley said softly.

Silence stretched between us. I shifted anxiously beside the door.

"We haven't been alone like this in some time," I said, stalling.

His palm found the wall beside me as he leaned in close, eyes glinting playfully. "You aren't nervous, are you, lioness? After all your bold declarations?"

I was nervous—frighteningly so—of the quiet, of being alone, of things we'd teased but never done. Beneath skin that once held a lion's roar, I felt the whiskers of a timid mouse.

His teasing smile ebbed at my expression. "Oh, darling," he murmured, tipping my chin with practiced ease. "I'll take care of you. I'll make you feel good."

"I know you will," I breathed, the words quivering. "It's just...the unknown."

His tone mellowed, gliding over me like silk. "Then not tonight. Let's simply revel in this solitude. Who knows when we'll steal another moment?"

He eased me back against the wall, cracked the door, brushed a kiss to my cheek, and slipped inside. I hovered outside a heartbeat longer, mustering my courage.

My fear wasn't of Windley.

Never Windley.

When I finally stepped in behind him, I quietly locked the door. He froze at the subtle click, ears twitching, gaze darting around walls that had suddenly become a cage.

Drawing a steadying breath, I approached, sliding my hands boldly over his chest until they rested lightly at his collar.

"O-our first time behind locked doors," I murmured, attempting sultriness but faltering slightly as my confidence slipped. "I wonder how long before someone comes looking for me."

Windley retreated a step, smothering a strained sound—not disgust, but the effort of holding back something primal. His voice emerged uneven, a rasp edged with barely restrained desire. "O-on second thought, perhaps we should find some cards," he muttered absently, eyes drifting to the moonlight shimmering across my dress before finally returning to mine. "Merrin, if you're not ready, I strongly suggest you stop *baiting the predator*."

He was right; I was sending mixed signals, caught somewhere between lion and mouse.

Yet deep down, I knew exactly what I wanted.

It was just...

"I don't know what I'm doing," I confessed, settling against the wall beside my guardian plants.

He settled opposite me, his gaze melted with quiet affection. "You don't have to. You only need to know you're ready. That's all I care about."

"But...I want you to enjoy it."

He laughed, the sound rich with genuine fondness. "Trust me, queenie. I'll enjoy it plenty."

Windley peered out the window, silver moonlight limning his features in a delicate glow. In another moment, I might have cursed Luna's intrusive brilliance, but right now it felt strangely comforting.

After a beat he murmured, low and earnest, "Would it help to know I'm nervous too?"

"An experienced incubus? Nervous?" I teased. "With defenseless me?"

"*Defenseless?*" He scoffed, tossing his hatchets aside and shedding his coat and overshirt. My breath caught at the sight of him standing before me in only a thin undershirt—sleeves rolled carelessly, lean muscles accentuated, mischievous hair now a striking shade of pink.

"Oh goddess, Windley—you look adorable! What are those?"

He blinked. "These?" He tugged at the straps. "Suspenders. Keep my pants from falling down. Never undressed a man before, have you?"

I stared, enthralled.

"You like them?" His delight turned wicked.

"You look positively impish—like a traveling circus rogue." My heart fluttered as I approached and slipped my finger beneath one of his suspenders, feeling the heat of his skin.

His voice dipped seductively. "Care to take them off?"

In a startled rush, I let go—snapping the strap back against his chest.

"Ouch," he chuckled, rubbing the spot, amusement lingering in his eyes until I slowly turned around, offering him my laces instead.

"I—" My voice faltered, cheeks heating fiercely. "I'll need help out of mine." When he didn't move, I glanced back over my shoulder. "Wind?"

"Savoring, love," he murmured, gaze tracing slowly down the length of my back, igniting shivers beneath my skin.

With deliberate care, almost ritual tenderness, he untied the first ribbon.

"Windley," I breathed.

"Yes, queenie?" His voice thickened with desire.

"I like being alone with you."

His eyes flashed. "Dangerous words to utter, my queen."

He tugged me backward by the loosened ribbon, his mouth finding the sensitive skin at my nape. A sigh escaped me as his palm flattened over my stomach, pulling me flush against his chest. When his teeth grazed the edge of my ear, I spun around, capturing his mouth in a fervent kiss.

"I am ready," I whispered breathlessly. "Lead me, Windley. Show me."

His throat bobbed. "Show you?"

"What it means...to be yours."

A flicker of caution carved through his usual easy confidence.

Truth is, you're not ready yet—and that's all right. I've already waited years for this moment. Now that you're mine to cherish, I want to savor every breath along the way. If it takes a lifetime, I'll wait a lifetime.

I slipped a suspender off his shoulder, tugged his shirt free of his waistband, and flattened my palm against the heat of his stomach. "I want you, Wind," I assured him. *"Tonight."*

He shuddered. His reply came on a ragged breath. "Dangerous words."

He kissed me deeply, backing me against the wall, his hands weaving possessively through my hair as each kiss burned brighter, deeper, pulling us together until nothing separated us.

His initial caution swiftly dissolved into urgent, mutual need. Breathlessly, we fumbled, clothes falling away, barriers shed piece by piece. He pivoted me artfully, fingers sliding deliberately down my spine, loosening the last of my laces as his mouth pressed searing kisses across every newly revealed patch of skin. Each touch sparked embers of desire, leaving me gasping.

A final tug released my gown, and I clung to him, pulse racing at the electrifying heat of his bare skin against mine.

With infinite care, Windley lifted me onto his hips, carrying me effortlessly across the room before gently laying me onto the bed. Hovering above me, he paused, eyes dark with longing, chest rising and falling heavily as desire warred with caution.

"I want our first time together to be without magic," he confessed, his voice raw with honesty.

My fingertips glided along the faded scars that marked his back, and his breath snagged, muscles shuddering beneath my touch.

"Tell me to stop at any time. Tell me if it hurts." He pressed his forehead deliberately to mine, breaths coming slow and cautious. "You're sure?"

For a heartbeat, something wavered in his eyes—a flash of old pain threatening to dismantle his resolve. I felt the weight behind it—the self-doubt lurking beneath his practiced composure.

But just as he had all the faith in me, I had all the faith in him.

Calm your soul, breathe, and try again, lion queen.

Carefully, I cupped his jaw and drew him closer.

"Tent-floor or featherbed, we're still us, Wind. You would never hurt me—*never*. I trust you. So trust yourself...and the wild thing we've made together."

The words slid past every wall he'd ever built. Something inside him shifted—quiet, profound—and the last strand of hesitation unraveled. Years of uncertainty liquefied, replaced by an unhurried smile steeped in relief, yearning, and quiet devotion: a promise of everything we had waited for, everything we had earned.

"I do not take this lightly," he whispered, lips brushing my ear. "I'm no royal, Merrin, no gentleman—but I promise to care for you until my life runs out."

I believed him.

I felt him.

As his lips caressed my skin, his hands framed my waist,

drifting downward—skimming sinuous over my ribs, along the supple curve of my stomach, toward the forbidden heat of my thigh—

"W-Windley! Th-that's your mouth—"

...

...

...

It was beginning to feel good.

It was beginning to feel really good.

It was beginning to feel incredibly good.

Each languid stroke of his tongue was a revelation, pulling soft, breathless gasps from deep within me, sparking nerves I never knew existed.

"Oh goddess—" I murmured, fingers clutching desperately at the sheets, every thought scattering beneath the warmth of his mouth.

"*Yes, Merrin?*" Vita chimed innocently inside my head.

"Not now, Vita!" I hissed, embarrassment flooding my cheeks.

Windley froze, lifting his head curiously. "Did you just say, 'Not now, Vita'?"

"Shh—just kiss me." I reached down, hungrily guiding him up from between my thighs to reclaim his mouth. His laughter muffled against my lips as I silenced whatever teasing retort he'd prepared.

"*Ah, you are procreating,*" Vita observed cheerfully. "*You know it will not work. For practice, then? I shall retreat to the other realm and rejoin you before dawn.*"

Thank you, Vita, I thought, internally this time.

Windley's body was already pressing close against mine again, hands gliding slowly up my thighs, lips teasing my earlobe, my throat, my mouth—anywhere he pleased.

He was, as Beau had promised, experienced—and he knew

exactly how to touch me. Whatever face I made brought forth his quiet, naughty smile.

"Feels good?" he murmured.

I swallowed, nodding shyly, too embarrassed to speak.

"It's all right to say so." His mouth grazed my ear, voice a molten purr. "Say so."

"It feels good," I whispered into the dark.

His gaze flared, intense and primal. He caught my wrist, pinning it beside the pillow, settling his weight over me. The expression on his face was something I'd never seen before—dangerous, hungry, savoring every second.

A predator with his prey.

There was no escape.

I didn't want one.

His mouth claimed mine, deep and possessive, kisses turning confident, passionate, eager—until our movements synchronized naturally, each touch blending seamlessly into the next.

His eyes met mine, silently asking again. I answered with a whispered "Yes," and then he pressed slowly into me, uniting us completely.

The discomfort was fleeting.

Afterward, our bodies moved together instinctively, as though we'd done this countless times before. Windley gripped me fiercely; his sweat mingled with mine, and his kisses eagerly swallowed every breathless cry.

I rolled with him, moved with him, breathed with him—until he shifted above me again, sharp teeth sinking into my shoulder as I dug nails into the lean muscle of his arms.

And though he'd promised otherwise, I distinctly remember his eyes flashing emerald at least three times.

...

...

...

It was beginning to feel good.

It was beginning to feel really good.

It was beginning to feel incredibly good.

A swell was building, like a wave cresting, ready to break over me.

Windley saw it in my eyes and smiled.

"I love you, queenie," he whispered.

Whatever sound escaped me, it wasn't graceful—it was raw, helpless, as though my mind had plunged into warm, syrupy sweetness.

Windley, however, seemed delighted by it. His smile was new—relaxed, utterly content, as though savoring a delicious secret. He drew me close, pressing unhurried kisses to my forehead, each touch brimming with affection, care, and a reverence that said, without words, how deeply I was cherished.

"Well, that was..." Windley cleared his throat. "How do you feel?"

"Hated it," I teased, out of breath—though anyone could tell by the fevered color in my cheeks precisely how I felt.

In truth, I loved it—not just the physical pleasure, but the intimacy, the closeness, the sharing of ourselves in a way deeper than touch.

He sighed softly, fingers threading affectionately through my hair. "I was scared at first."

I brushed his bangs back tenderly. "I know."

He let his thumb drift in solemn awe across my cheek.

"I didn't have to hold back. Not once."

The words carried every nightmare he'd harbored—that he

might lose control, that the monster in him would break me—and every ounce of newfound relief that it hadn't.

"Because you never had to," I murmured, stroking the vein at his wrist. "You know how to handle me like it's second nature."

His chest expanded on a long, quiet breath, as though he could finally believe it.

I rolled onto him, tracing soft circles on his chest while I studied his relaxed expression.

"Can we do it again?"

His palm slid to the curve of my waist, thumb idly stroking the dip just above my hip. "Again already? Thought you'd ask for some cuddling first."

"Spoonery is out. This is in. Is it something we can do more than once in a night?"

A lazy, decadent smile spread across his face. "Gladly."

I tilted my face up toward his, ready for another taste of him—but suddenly, his entire body tensed, his head snapping toward the door.

"Windley?"

"One moment, darling." His brow knitted, features suddenly drawn tight. Carefully, almost apologetically, he eased me aside, blankets pooling at his waist as he sat upright.

Then—a violent jerk. He pressed fingers tightly to his temple, every muscle rigid.

When he turned back to me, his eyes flashed emerald, wild and blade-bright.

"*Shit.*"

He was out of bed in an instant—in all his bare, glorious beauty—scrambling for his weapons. Clothes were hastily gathered, hatchets strapped into place with swift precision. Anxiety coiled in my stomach at his sudden shift in mood.

"Did something happen?" I asked, voice strained with worry.

He halted, eyes darting to me. The sight seemed to wound him—my hair a wild snarl, sheets clutched to my chest, confusion and dread etched across my face. The pause stretched, and I sensed how deeply he despised leaving us with this as tonight's memory.

His jaw locked. "It's Charm and Pip," he said, voice stripped of any comfort, gaze turning feral. "They're here—close. I can feel them."

22

IN THE SHADOWS

W indley and I tore through the castle, tugging sleeves and fastening buttons, racing toward Sestilia's chambers—not her main rooms, but those she used for play.

"This isn't what I want to be doing right now," Windley complained, voice echoing through the tomb-like halls. "Worst fucking timing."

I bit my lip, stealing a hesitant glance at him. The flushed skin of his neck vividly reminded me of our intimacy, sending a fresh flutter of uncertainty—and shy curiosity—rippling through me.

Drawing a breath, I ventured softly, "I...believe I saw your pleasure face."

His mouth crooked into a sly, wolfish grin.

"Oh, you definitely did." Mischief flashed in his eyes as he added, "Though seeing yours has given me some dangerously creative ideas for next time."

Warmth flooded my cheeks. Assurance filled my chest. "You did...enjoy it?"

Windley sighed dreamily, as though recalling something exquisite. "Enjoy is far too gentle a word, love." His voice dipped lower, rich with sincerity. "It was everything I hoped for —and far more."

I glanced at him sidelong. "You're getting poetic."

He flashed a grin, devilish charm restored. "If I were being poetic, I'd still be in that bed, making you forget your name. Wait until you see what else awaits us."

Heat climbed my neck. "You mean there's more?"

Windley's smile lengthened into a slow, decadent curve— promise pooling in his gaze.

"Much."

I couldn't imagine what.

But his smile faded swiftly, replaced by quiet seriousness. His eyes darkened, shifting seamlessly from playful intimacy to something more urgent and protective. "But let's survive this first." His voice grew sober. "If we followed Ascian's power here, it's likely Pip and Charmagne did the same."

"Be on your guard," I read.

He gave me a nod of camaraderie.

By the time we reached the wing housing Sestilia's second chambers, Edius was already there, shifting impatiently beside Albie.

"My Queen!" Albie pulled me protectively to his side.

"Things are in motion, my knight." I looked past him. "You felt it too, Edi?"

"Yeah. Both of them."

"I just returned from a sweep," Albie said.

"Good. Stay here with the queen," said Windley. "I'm going after Pip."

I jumped forward, cutting him off. "Not alone, you aren't."

"Merrin, you have work here. Take care of Exitium. I just need a chance alone with Pip. If I can get him away from

Charm, I know I can reach him. He keeps releasing bursts of power—like he wants me to find him."

"That sounds like a trap."

Windley spun his hatchets. "I'll be fine. Besides, I don't plan on going alone. It's the salty magician's turn to get cock-blocked."

"But Beau would be unprotected!" I wouldn't allow it. "Albie! Go with Windley and stay with Beau once he retrieves Rafe."

"Out of the question! I'm not leaving your side!"

"Albie, please. I don't want to command you. You're the only one I trust to keep her safe as you would me. I can handle myself."

"Argh! You'll be the death of me, Your Majesty!" With gritted teeth, Albie accepted my wishes and followed after Windley, but not before—

"May I?" Windley asked permission this time before brushing his lips to my forehead in a protective kiss.

Edius watched the knights sprint away through the dim corridors. "You don't want me going with them?"

"No, Edi. I need your brawn. We must move Sestilia somewhere within view of the dawn."

Edius oriented himself. "Which way's the sun come up?"

"That way." I pointed. "But first, we retrieve Sestilia. Ready to reenter the web?"

Edius gave a firm nod, following me into chambers befitting a beautiful spider. An enormous canopy bed sat at the center like an island amid a glassy sea, sheer black fabric cascading down. Walls glittered with embedded gemstones, as if we'd stepped into a miner's cavern. Blankets and robes sprawled across velvet chairs, a settee, and a vanity. Tall windows cloaked by heavy curtains provided ample shadows for hiding.

I tapped across obsidian floors, Edius at my side, until—

"Wait." He took my wrist.

"Ed?"

He leaned in as if he might make another mistake, but instead of marking me again, he merely sniffed with quiet reverence.

"A-are you feeling badly? Don't. Windley is beyond it." I smiled to myself at the flutters in my stomach. "He's surely happier than ever. O-oh! How are you?" I took his chin, tilting his face. "Your nose seems healed."

"Y-yeah."

He was harder to read than usual. "You're good?"

He nodded slowly.

"I'm glad. I never meant to hurt either of you. Come," I urged in hushed entreaty. "Help me lift her." I hurried to the bed where arguably the most beautiful queen lay, peeling away the curtain and leaning over her.

Sestilia.

"She really is stunning, isn't she, Edi? Sweet, in her own deranged way. It would be best if we did this without her know—"

"Merrin! That is not the spider queen!"

Vita's warning arrived too late—after the mattress creaked, after the sudden, lancing pain had already pierced my gut.

Because I, mighty queen of the temperamental coast, had just been stabbed.

By an impostor.

I staggered back, clutching the wound. My knees buckled, and I collapsed against Edius—who stood ready to catch me. Edius, who remained silent, eyes empty.

Edius, who was clearly part of this trap.

"I'm sorry, Merrin!" Vita's voice was frantic. *"I was slumbering to allow your procreation practice! Merrin! Can you hear me?!"*

I heard her, but responding was impossible, my breath strangled as blood trickled from my abdomen. My limbs trembled, vision wavering, as the impostor rose from the bed, contempt in every step.

"Well, that was entirely too easy, cupcake."

I should have known better. Should have paid attention. My weakness was my young heart, caught in emotions I'd never felt—distracted by devils.

Edius's strong arms wrapped around me, lowering me gently to the floor, his expression curious and detached.

"You must save yourself, Merrin—drain the beastling or perish!" Vita urged desperately.

Drain...Edius?

He tilted his head, observing me. "Does it hurt, queen lion?"

It did, so terribly that I couldn't speak. Vita's voice faded before I grasped her meaning. Edius's breathing deepened, savoring something unsettling.

With effort, I lifted a trembling hand to his face, my fingertips cold and numb as shadows encroached at the edges of my vision. At my touch, something beneath his skin shifted subtly. The sharp angles softened, replaced by wide, youthful eyes, round cheeks, and a familiar, innocent gaze.

Realization struck like lightning—this wasn't Edius at all. It was Pip, carefully disguised, betraying my trust in the cruelest possible way. Strangely, even as my blood slowly pooled around me, relief flickered briefly through my pain-clouded thoughts. At least Edius hadn't truly betrayed us.

"I am trying to sustain you, Merrin, but you must use your power!" Vita shouted urgently. *"I will not allow you to perish! If your vitality runs dry, then I shall wield your power for you!"*

But I couldn't drain Pip, just as I couldn't have drained Edius. Trading one life for another was not a power I wished to hold. All

I could do was breathe, following Pip's breath as a shaky guide. His thumb brushed lightly over my forehead, lingering curiously on the spot kissed earlier by two separate predators tonight.

Wearing Sestilia's body like a gown, Charm snapped from the bedside. "What are you waiting for, Pip? Finish the job!"

"But..." Pip glanced up uncertainly. "They both marked her, Charm. Before, it was just Windalloy, but now it's Edi too."

Charm's eyes narrowed dangerously. "Because she's a fiend, Pipsqueak! She tricked them both!"

"No." Pip's voice deepened slightly, anger simmering beneath the surface. "Edi said he'd never mark a human. Only his wyrdbound one. You saw him earlier—he looked...happy with her. He's never happy."

Charm sneered coldly. "You idiot. Spirites don't have soulmates. It's a fairytale meant to keep fools hopeful."

"We do!" Pip snapped back through Edius's mouth, his voice cutting and defiant. "Windalloy told me they're real! He read me stories before he left. And if she's both of theirs...what if she's mine, too?"

Charm pressed fingers irritably to Sestilia's temple. "This, dear boy, is precisely why you shouldn't roam freely. You'll fall prey to any pretty-smelling bitch. Kill her, and break her spell over Windalloy!"

"Pip," I rasped desperately, forcing my voice through the pain. "Listen to me—"

Slowly, Pip met my gaze. His grip tightened protectively, laden with solemn devotion. "She's scared," he murmured, his voice suddenly ancient, weighted with unexpected authority. "I feel it in her heartbeat."

I didn't deny it—I was scared.

"Please, Pip," I pleaded in a whisper. "Join us. Help me."

Charm laughed cruelly. "Why would he ever do that? Pip, you know what must be done."

But Pip didn't move. His hold remained firm, eyes locked on mine as though he could see beyond skin and bone, straight into the core of who I was. As our gazes held, his expression subtly shifted—innocence dissolving into something older, darker, and unfamiliar. It was as if a mask had slipped, revealing someone else entirely. Someone I'd glimpsed briefly before, back in Ascian's cursed manor.

Charm's amusement abruptly hardened into warning. "Pip."

He flinched visibly.

"Put her down. Now."

Pip swallowed, grip adjusting. I braced myself for the worst.

But instead, his voice emerged fierce, resolute, entirely unexpected. "Give me the ring, Charm."

Charm went rigid. "What?"

"Master's ring," he repeated forcefully, voice vibrating with determination. "Give it to me."

Charm's jaw tightened. "No."

Pip's hand pressed more firmly against my bleeding wound, yet with unmistakable restraint. "Give me the ring, or I'll call Bobbin!"

"You wouldn't dare—"

"Give—me—the—ring!" Pip's throat worked as though fighting to suppress something clawing desperately within.

Little did I know, his monster had already slipped its leash. A hundred eyes blinked lazily from the darkness, silently observing our struggle.

Charm hesitated, mouth open in shock, uncertainty flickering across her stolen features.

Pip's gaze narrowed dangerously, voice lifting into an eerie, singsong croon. "Oh, Bo-obbin..."

In the corner of my eye, something massive shifted.

Charm recoiled instantly, disgust and rage twisting her expression. "ARGH! Fine, you sniveling little shit!"

A blackstone ring clinked sharply onto the floor.

Charm hissed bitterly, "Heal her, then. Ruin our plan! And then what?"

"I'm going to talk to her." Pip's voice was firm, unyielding, stripped of hesitation.

Charm sneered contemptuously. "Pointless! Don't come crawling back when she shoves shadows down your throat. She'll kill you once she sees the monster tied to your soul."

Pip shifted behind me, retrieving the ring. I heard the faint scrape of metal against skin, felt his sharp inhale. With tempered care, he tipped my chin up, words spilling in a low, insistent rush: "Drink it in, queen lion. You must breathe it for it to work."

Ascian had hexed countless souls, but one breath was more potent than any other—strong enough to mend wounds mortal or magical. If only I'd realized then whose breath that truly was...

I gasped weakly as Pip leaned down—but the face hovering above mine wasn't the Pip I knew. Youthful innocence vanished, replaced by mature features, angular cheekbones, eyes darkened with secrets and ancient predation.

His lips opened inches from mine, and all I registered was a strange, unsettling wrongness—until I inhaled.

Magic.

It curled between us, warm and golden, ancient and famil-iar, independent of Pip, Edius, or even Ascian himself.

I didn't merely breathe it—I devoured it.

Darkness retreated from my vision. Pain dulled, edges smoothed.

Pip's hands trembled as I absorbed his magic, drawing deeper breaths to knit torn flesh.

Yet through the healing haze, unease whispered at my awareness. Behind Pip's wide eyes stirred something older, deeper—something powerful and restrained. As though the innocent youth I saw was not the entire truth of him.

I recoiled, chest heaving. "Th-thank you, Pip."

My wound still ached, but was no longer deadly.

Vita flared, incandescent with warning. *"Now leave! This place isn't safe. Next time, do not hesitate to take life if needed!"*

"No." My voice was hoarse but resolute. I wouldn't trade another's life for mine. That path was a slippery slope I'd already stumbled down once before.

Pip withdrew abruptly, scrubbing his mouth as if to erase my touch. Youth quickly reclaimed his features, innocence slipping back into place as though whoever had emerged was safely hidden once more.

"Sorry, queen lion," Pip whispered shyly, eyes downcast. "You're too scary at full power."

Charm barked, "Put her down, Pip! She'll get you!"

Pip's grip faltered. I tucked my face into my arm, avoiding his gaze before emerald flashed again in his eyes. "Listen to me, Pip. Queen Sestilia—the real one—is dangerous."

"I know," he murmured quietly. "Master Ascian is inside her."

"Not just Ascian. She loves Spirites. She'll gobble you up if given the chance. I'm a good queen; she's a bad one. I'm trying to protect us all. Please, don't beguile me—tell me where she is."

He hesitated. "You're still scared." His fingers brushed

lightly over my chest, barely touching, sensing my heartbeat through bone and breath. "I can feel it."

I was scared—but not for myself.

For him.

"I am scared, Pip. You matter to Windley. I want to protect you, too."

"She's lying, Pip!" Charm circled like a vulture. "Show her your monster. She won't like you once she sees it."

Pip stiffened, his expression shifting mournfully. "She's right. You have to meet Bobbin. I need to know if he likes you first."

Bobbin.

Dread knotted my stomach. Bobbin wasn't just a name—it was nightmare made flesh, a creature bound irreversibly to Pip's soul.

The wraith Edius had described as a spider with "a few extra legs."

Eleven, to be exact.

And really, why eleven? An even number would have made more sense—not that a twelfth leg would help me now.

Spiders had never been my favorite among Vita's creations.

"They're essential for life's balance," Vita murmured, serene despite the tension. *"Artists weaving intricate webs to decorate the world."*

I had no patience for poetic sentiments—least of all now.

Pip's grip tightened painfully as he dragged me toward the darkest corner. Charm leaned smugly against the vanity, arms folded, watching intently.

I stumbled along, my wound raw, limbs weaker than I wanted to admit. Desperately, my eyes scanned for anything useful—Charm had a blade, both of them wielded magic.

I had nothing. No dirt, no greenery, no source to summon Vita's strength.

I was trapped in shadow.

My gaze flicked toward the door, silently begging Windley and Edius to realize the earlier power flares had been bait, praying they'd burst in before it was too late.

But before hope could bloom—

A spined, bristly leg slammed down before me.

From the darkness, something monstrous stirred. A hulking mass unfolded from shadow, countless eyes blinking open at once—glassy, reflective, soulless orbs arranged in too many rows. Chitin gleamed wetly, joint after grotesque joint flexing beneath an oily shroud of darkness. It didn't merely look alive; it seemed impossibly, hideously aware.

Pip's voice mellowed into a coaxing lilt. "It's okay. He won't hurt you."

My blood froze solid.

I had no chance to react before the monster lunged, limbs slicing violently through the air.

I made the mistake of screaming.

"You hate him!" Pip cried, panic rising. "You think he's ugly!"

"Told you, Pipsqueak!" Charm laughed, delighted.

I scrambled backward, but another leg slammed down, cutting off my escape. The creature loomed, countless limbs forming a cage around me, eyes glittering with predatory curiosity.

"*Run, Merrin!*" Vita's voice sharpened with succinct urgency. "*This foe is ancient and fierce!*"

I spun toward the door, but a massive limb crashed down, blocking my way.

"*Around it, Merrin!*"

Easier said than done. A leg whipped forward, nearly impaling me, anticipating every movement.

"Can I not drain its life?" I cried desperately, stumbling away.

"*You cannot,*" Vita warned. "*The fiend is not of the living.*"

Charm's laughter rose, shrill and vicious. "You were right, Pip—this is a far better way for her to go! Looks like she lost her shadow sorcery, exactly as you predicted!"

Pip had sensed the echoes' absence? He'd felt their power thriving inside me once—and now, he felt their loss just as keenly. No wonder they'd chosen this moment to strike.

The wraith closed tighter, suffocatingly near. Pip and Charm hovered just beyond its grasp—untouchable.

"Vita, what can I do?" I reached frantically for her strength, but it danced uselessly beyond my fingertips. Even golems needed dirt. If only I'd brought a guardian plant! Compassion had become my weakness. In sparing Pip, I'd sealed my fate.

Yet as fear clawed at my chest, gentle warmth blossomed.

"*Close your eyes, Merrin.*"

"Vita?"

"*Close your eyes. It will be over soon.*"

"I—I don't want to die." My own voice shocked me, fragile, trembling, far weaker than a lion's roar.

Charm cackled savagely.

"*You have nothing to fear,*" Vita murmured softly, her voice calm but resolute. "*My light fills you. Hush now. Be still.*"

The line between hero and villain is rarely clear; darkness and light often blur where they meet. I'd been foolish to hope Windley, Rafe, Edius, or Albie might burst through the door at the last possible second, racing valiantly to my rescue.

No one was coming—no guards, no saviors, nothing but the press of shadow.

Yet, in that breath between surrender and oblivion, a savior did arrive—not a knight, nor a man, not anyone I could have imagined.

"EXITIUM!"

A tidal wave of shadow surged violently into the chamber, roaring like an ocean unleashed. Darkness—richer, deeper, infinitely more powerful than anything I'd ever known—erupted through the entrance, devouring the wraith in blistering fury.

The creature shrieked as shadows consumed it, limbs dissolving into ash, chitin cracking as tentacles of darkness tore it apart piece by piece, until nothing remained but swirling dust and smoke.

When at last the chaos receded, Pip and Charm had vanished.

Standing before me, draped in raw, terrifying power and midnight shadow—

Was a queen.

A fearsome, breathtaking queen.

My breath caught painfully. "S-Sestilia?"

23

THE DAWN'S LIGHT

L ater, the scattered pieces would finally fall into place.

Charmagne and Pip, like us, had answered Ascian's silent summons. They arrived at the Cove first, believing their master awaited them. The "assassins" Rafe and Albie caught tracking us through the city hadn't been assassins at all.

Like us, Charm and Pip exploited the distraction of Sestilia's birthday festivities to infiltrate the castle. Like us, they sensed Ascian's dark essence residing within the Queen of the Cove. Like us, they'd planned to ensorcell her—but Windley and Edius unknowingly revealed our intentions, granting Charm the perfect chance to strike first.

Yet here, our paths diverged sharply. Charm and Pip drained patrolling guards to fuel their transformation spells. Pip, disguised flawlessly as Edius, convinced Albie to search elsewhere. They imprisoned the real Sestilia, leaving Charm free to assume her place.

Then Pip cursed the party guests, ordering them to attack

Edius and Windley—delaying my true allies when I'd needed them most.

But Charm and Pip hadn't counted on one thing:

Sestilia now wielded the same power I once held.

Just as bloodlust ignited within me to protect those I loved, it had fiercely awakened within Sestilia.

I shouted her name desperately, but she didn't hear, encased within swirling shadow from another realm.

"Vita! How do I stop it?"

"Give her my light, as I gave it to you in your darkest hour."

Before I could take a step—

"My Queen! Get away from her!" Albie's voice rang out as he hurried toward me, Faylebane ready. "The lads are behind me!"

"But Beau—"

"Rafe's with her! Couldn't reach them, not with guests after us. Come!" Albie pushed me toward the doors.

"No, Albie! Only I can stop this! If I don't, we'll all perish!"

Even at his age, Albie was stronger. He'd have succeeded dragging me away if not for Edius and Windley rushing in, pursued by innocent guests they desperately tried not to harm. Windley slammed the door shut behind them.

Sweat-coated, he reached me instantly. "Merrin! Thank goddess! It was a trap, wasn't it? Both of them? I was careless—I didn't think to scent him. If I'd paused for even a moment, I would've known it wasn't Edius!"

"I'm fine," I reassured him quickly. "I don't know where they fled, but I'm fine."

"Gods!" Edius cursed, noticing Sestilia's trembling, shadow-drenched form swelling. "Not again!"

She looked like ruin incarnate, corrupted entirely by Exitium.

And now we were locked inside with her.

"I thought we had time! Didn't you say it had to mature in her first?!" Edius demanded.

"You forget—their spirits aren't alike," Windley said grimly. "Merrin resisted it longer."

"No! She did it to save me! Pip unleashed a monster, and I couldn't escape—I must reach her! She doesn't have Vita's radiance like I did! I must share mine!"

"Merrin." Windley's grip was firm but respectful. "You didn't witness Ascian's end. Those shadows will devour you." He held me as one grips a kite against fierce winds.

"We have no choice. Trust me, please—I can do this."

"I know," he breathed shakily. "If anyone can, it's you." Still, his fingers hesitated, struggling to let go.

Albie saw it too, dread deepening his wrinkles.

"I'll be fine, my knight. Have faith, as I have faith."

Windley took charge, urgency taut in his voice. "Ed, Sir Albie—help me get some daylight into this goddess-forsaken chamber."

"Careful, highness," Edius urged.

The Spirites sprinted toward heavy curtains, but Albie paused.

"If I turn my back now, promise you'll be there when I look again?" Albie's voice trembled with emotion.

"Yes, my knight."

"...You're not the same gal you once were."

"No, my knight."

"That unruly spirit of yours finally broke free. Your mother'd be proud. Only one smile like yours remains—I can't bear losing it again. Careful, Merrin."

He dropped my title, and tears shimmered in his eyes. "Live for the both of you—the two women I cherish most."

With an aching look, Albie hurried away, yanking open curtains to reveal dawn's fragile glow.

I stepped toward Sestilia.

Her eyes were pitch-black, shadows streaming wildly around her. Dark veins pulsed beneath her skin. I'd once looked this way—terrifying and lost in shadow—and Windley had shielded me from that truth.

The room brightened as more curtains parted, dawn glinting off embedded gemstones.

Dawn painting the air anew.

Dawn dispelling night's grip.

I didn't paint, but if I did, I would have painted in the dawn.

I didn't write, but if I did, I would have written in the dawn.

I didn't sing, but if I did, I would have sung in the dawn.

Vita's voice resonated tenderly within me: *"Feel my breath within you, Merrin. Embrace the warmth of creation."*

"The darkness surrounding her—will it harm me?"

"It will not, as long as my light shields you. Do you feel it?"

I did. It surged through my veins, calling forth memories as my armor.

Albie guiding my small hands on a fishing pole, his reassuring whispers as patient as the river itself.

Beau, cross-legged on the fortress belvedere, charcoal-smudged fingers sketching the horizon we swore never to forget.

Windley racing me barefoot through the orchard, laughter weaving through leaves as I fell breathless to the grass.

My mother's gentle voice, pages turning softly, reciting poetry crafted just for me—a memory newly remembered.

Vita's breath flowed outward, enveloping me.

"Lion queen! You're glowing!" Windley shouted, tearing open another curtain, ushering dawn's first light.

"To enter the destroyer's shroud is to face despair. Cling to

your most beloved memories. Shield yourself from shadows, as you've done before."

Just as I'd once quieted echoes with memories of those I loved, I summoned them now.

Mother Poppy wrapping me in a woolen throw, thick with hearth smoke and whispered stories.

Windley, holding me close in darkness, murmuring sweetness into my hair.

Steeled by these memories, clutching my mother's necklace, I felt the earth's pulse beneath castle stones, the breath of life in courtyard grass beyond.

"When you walk into darkness, know I am with you. You are not alone."

Trusting Vita fully, I stepped into Sestilia's storm.

Darkness poured thickly, swirling upward without escape. The queen was merely a vessel for Exitium's wrath. How swiftly she'd succumbed—yet all for my sake.

"Sestilia?" I drew closer, imagining her at a great ravine's edge, as I once had been.

Otherworldly voices whispered mournfully around me. "SeSTilia... Seeeestilia..."

"How can I hear them? They aren't bound to my soul." The glow dimmed slightly.

"Turn away from their distraction!" Vita warned swiftly.

"They sound...sad. Is this Sestilia's sorrow?"

"It is the spider queen's loneliness."

Loneliness—she'd never known true warmth. Vita meant for me to share my light, as others had shared theirs with me.

"Armor yourself! Shadows strengthen!"

"Sestilia." I drew her into a careful embrace. "You're not alone. I offer you the warmth you lack. I don't know what made you this way, but I will try to understand. Feel the love around me, and accept it."

Vita's divinity poured from me into her, feather-light as moth wings, ringing with the delicate chime of Vita's laugh.

"Release Exitium, Sestilia," I urged, voice low. "Cast her into me. Share your burden."

But darkness still surged.

"If Exitium wins, there'll be no feasts, no galas, no joy. Reject that fate, Sestilia!"

Darkness battered our fragile shield.

"Surmount this, and you, Beau, and I will be forever bonded—the only three queens who overcame this trial. Release her!"

Energy pulsed violently outward, striking my chest, hurling me back.

"MERRIN!" Windley's anguished cry pierced through the chaos.

Yet something extraordinary unfolded.

Darkness collided with Vita's brilliance, dissolving into glittering emerald sparks.

Countless souls freed at last. Ascian's twisted soul flared bright, defiant—but faded at last into oblivion.

As Vita's radiance surged forth, Exitium's shadow was devoured, dissolving into golden sparks that drifted into nothingness.

Yet the strongest impact was the force Vita had purposefully allowed through.

It barreled into my chest, a familiar darkness settling within.

"Hello, Merrin," a slippery voice whispered. "Do you remember my name?"

I did—but I refused to utter it. Never again would I yield to the silky deceit of a fallen serpent.

That shadow lingered only a heartbeat before Vita's brilliance surged again, devouring the darkness until nothing remained.

I exhaled slowly into the residual warmth. "Thank you, Vita."

I had reclaimed both halves of the Nemophile's Crown—this time without absorbing Exitium's warped echoes.

I should have asked then. Should've demanded the meaning behind "delivering the destroyer to the end of days."

But I was foolish. And careless.

"You did well, little royal. Rest now, regain your strength. But first—you must open your eyes. Your companion fears you are lost."

My eyes snapped open, finding three anxious guards leaning close. Arms supported me fervently, but they weren't Windley's. He stood back, granting space out of quiet respect for Albie.

"My Queen! Are you hurt?" Albie's voice shook.

"I'm all right, my knight." I strained to see past him. "Sestilia?"

"Alive," Windley answered quickly, stepping forward at last to cradle my face. His touch lingered with tenderness before he slipped away, lifting Sestilia's crumpled body with practiced care into his arms.

Exhaustion settled deeply into my bones. My wound still throbbed, my strength frayed. The day had been punishing, yet there was no time to rest.

"Edius, have you sensed either of them?"

He shook his head, frustration evident. "They drained guards down the hall—that's what started it. We felt pulses all over—including here—but strongest near the ballroom. Seems Pip marked guests throughout the night, activating their curses remotely." He grimaced. "Can't get the stench of hex off me."

"We must pursue them before we lose this chance." I gripped Albie's arm, steadying myself. "But we can't leave the castle like this. These people still have breath—I can't drain them as I did the townsfolk. We must push through and end this now."

"Alright," said Edius. "Any thoughts on how to bypass the mob without—hey, what the hell?"

Before I could even turn, Albie's hand shot out, uncharacteristically seizing my throat and throwing me roughly to the ground. Faylebane's blade hissed free, hovering inches above my pounding heart.

"Albie!" I gasped, eyes wide in disbelief.

But in his stare, there was no recognition—only bleak, terrifying emptiness.

24

MY MOTHER'S
NECKLACE

There are moments—captive ones—that burrow so deep
they stain the pale edges of memory. I would earn two
on this journey.
This was the second.

And the one responsible—well, not truly responsible, but the
final domino in a tragic chain—was someone who neither
wished for it nor intended it. Someone who caused my heart
greater pain than it had ever known.

It all happened in mere seconds—too quickly for compre-
hension.

Albie stood over me, eyes devoid of love or light, and drove
his trusty sword—Faylebane, hardened by countless battles—
straight into my chest.

Charm had been determined, it seemed, to pierce me one
way or another: first as Sestilia's impostor, then through my

beloved knight. A bitter twist of irony threaded through my pain.

Albie knew precisely how to strike a killing blow, which was why—despite my agony—I knew instantly he'd resisted at the very last moment. His sword had missed my heart by inches, piercing deeply but sparing me from immediate death.

"HE'S HEXED!"

Windley and Edius shouted simultaneously, realization crashing through them both. Windley, burdened by Sestilia, was too distant to intervene quickly. Edius, closest, acted without hesitation. Perhaps it was instinct. Perhaps panic. Either way, it happened too fast for thought or remorse.

Edius lunged, stabbing Albie brutally enough to halt Fayle-bane mid-strike.

Weapons clattered to the ground with a harsh clang, echoing through stunned silence.

Albie staggered, disbelief crossing his worn face, then collapsed heavily beside me.

A scream caught in my throat, soundless with horror.

"S-SHIT!" Edius recoiled instantly, staring at bloodied hands as if only now realizing his actions. "I—I didn't know what else to do!"

Beside me, Albie gasped weakly, breaths shuddering softly.

Desperation surged. I reached toward him, willing life back into him, silently begging Vita for guidance.

"Me...rr...in," Vita's voice trembled, distant as death closed in. "Save...self...power...and...take..."

Windley dropped to my side, urgent, tears streaking his cheeks as he clutched me tightly, staining himself crimson. "Merrin! Stay with me!"

"GIVE...TAKE...MERRIN!" Vita shouted, frantic now. Realization struck cruelly—Vita demanded I drain Albie to save myself. Yet somehow, after all this time, she still didn't understand me at all.

I could never take Albie's life into my veins.

Vita insisted he would die anyway—but I couldn't bear it being by my hand. Yet the choice slipped beyond my grasp—stolen, beyond my control.

Exitium had twisted my words before, but Vita had never breached my free will. Never before—and never again after this moment.

"She has the power to give and take life. Connect the hume's hand to hers, and it shall be done."

My voice. Not my words. Not my will.

Windley's fists shook, anguish and rage warring openly across his face. He knew what I wanted, knew I couldn't live with Albie's blood on my hands—yet he couldn't let me die.

"I'm sorry, Merr," he choked out, voice wounded. "Forgive me."

Yet Windley hesitated, paralyzed by agony. Another stepped forward instead—one willing to bear the terrible weight neither Windley nor I could carry.

"Forgive me, highness," Edius whispered hoarsely, eyes dark with grief. "I can't let you die."

He took Albie's weathered hand—fingers that had once brushed away tears, taught lessons, held fake tea with utmost dignity—and pressed it firmly to mine.

Vita seized control. A surge of brilliant green radiance flared around us, swirling with desperate urgency as it forced my hand to siphon Albie's life into my veins. Betrayal and grief clashed bitterly—wounds no magic could heal.

This was no healing hex like Ascian's ring. It was merely a transfer, just enough to ensure my survival.

As that shimmering aura sputtered and dimmed, so too did the light in Albie's eyes.

Movement stirred beside me. Windley's arms tightened, shaking with quiet sobs.

"Merr? Goddess, Merrin..."

Yet I couldn't face him. Couldn't face anyone.

Because Albie—my beloved knight, protector, family—lay motionless at my side.

"H-Help me, Vita!" I pleaded in a choked hush, my heart screaming. "You said I have the power to give life! Help me give it back! Bring him back to me!"

Her voice came gently, heavy with regret. *"I'm sorry, Merrin. Life, once lost, cannot be returned."*

The others couldn't hear her—but they witnessed my despair, the quiet sobs shaking me apart.

Windley, ever adept at comforting words, found none. Even Edius stood broken, haunted by his deed.

Windley's fists clenched tighter, trembling. "GODDESS-DAMN IT, PIP! How could you do this? They've watched us —you knew exactly how deeply this would hurt her. How much it would hurt me!"

"Kid's mind is gone, Windley," Edius murmured bitterly. "You keep wanting to reason with him, but he's been wiped too many times. And Charm—she's broken too. I'm guessing this was her doing."

"No. Both of them." Windley squeezed my shoulder with unspoken understanding, then stepped toward the door, pressing his forehead against it. He pounded once with his fist, voice raw with grief and anger as he shouted, "Pip! Hear me—I hoped we might reconcile, might still be brothers. But after this, I'll never forgive you. *Never.*" His tone turned coldly danger-ous. "Release these people, or I promise—your pain will eclipse Merrin's tenfold."

A heavy silence settled.

Then the distant thud of bodies collapsing—the hexed guests finally freed, dropping unconscious as curses lifted.

Edius bolted from the chamber, desperate to find the culprits. Sestilia rested, regaining strength. Windley tried coaxing me away from Albie, but I couldn't move—not yet. My chest tightened painfully with each breath, grief gripping my lungs like claws. I needed one final memory, one last tangible connection to the knight who had given everything for me.

As my shaking hands smoothed Albie's armor one last time, my fingertips brushed against something delicate and unexpected. A thin chain had slipped free from beneath his shirt in the struggle, pooling against the crimson-stained metal.

My breath caught sharply, burning at the back of my throat.

A pendant.

Identical to mine.

By the way, that necklace was a gift from your father. The pendant's genuine crystal coral. He had a matching one— brought them for your mother all the way from the Crystal Sea.

My heart stilled, then shattered all over again, grief driving deeper into my bones. A new uncertainty took root, constricting my chest further, stealing air from my lungs.

Was I, Merrin of the Crag, bearer of the Nemophile's Crown—only half-royal?

25

A BREAK, I THINK

T hank you, captive ones, for toughing it out. I imagine some of you saw it coming. And for those who've experienced something similar—I am truly sorry.

My heart beats alongside yours. Loss is never easy, is it? But pain shapes us, captive ones. It molds us into something stronger, even if we can't see it yet.

Stay with me. The worst is behind us.

After the events in the gem-studded cavern, bathed in dawn's light, Sestilia's castle descended into chaos. Windley carried me swiftly through halls in search of a healer, stepping over incapacitated guests now freed from their hexes. Along the way, he alerted Rafe and Beau, and though I protested their leaving the safety of their chambers, they followed.

Beau commanded her cavalry to secure Albie's body and initiate a search for Charm and Pip—two enemies notoriously elusive, able to change their appearances at will. And they weren't hiding their power. Windley tensed repeatedly as he carried me, eyes anxiously flicking over his shoulder.

He waited until I was safely settled in the castle's healing chambers, laid carefully in a bed near Sestilia.

She was alive but weak, exactly as I'd been after releasing Exitium. She would recover, and I would see her in a new light. Unstable or not, she had merit, as I'd told the echoes days ago. Even the darkest souls held the potential for redemption.

"I need to go after them, love," Windley murmured, voice soothing as a lullaby.

I knew it, yet couldn't voice it without breaking.

"I'll be back before you wake, I swear," he whispered, pressing his forehead to mine.

Be careful, Wind. I couldn't speak, but he saw it clearly in my eyes.

"I'm always careful." His usual confidence failed him; he couldn't even muster a faint grin. Instead, he lowered his lips to my ear, breath warm and reassuring. "I'll help you through this, as you've helped me. Whatever it takes." His kiss on my forehead lingered, imprinting his intentions, as if leaving protective armor to shield me from the dangers still lurking beyond these walls.

Then, he slipped away.

Beau stayed by my side—beautiful, regal, freckled Beau. "Oh, Merrin. I'm so sorry." She eased the stray locks away from my forehead, a comforting, motherly gesture. "Sir Albie loved you dearly. I can't imagine the ache in your heart."

Rafe stood quietly nearby, sword still simmering with faint fire, dark curls tipped in silver. He didn't speak but placed a steady hand atop my head, standing statuesque as Beau wept— for me, for us, for the great loss both our queendoms had suffered.

Albie had been dear to many.

Hidden in my pocket was a token taken from his body. Proof, perhaps, that I wasn't who I believed myself to be—that my ties to Albie ran deeper than I'd ever imagined.

I only loved poetry because Albie had read it to me, in his grizzled voice, on countless nights when sleep refused to come.

But whose poetry had he shared with me all those times?

Through all this, Vita tried to comfort me, but I pushed her away, too bruised to accept the comfort she offered. I knew it was for the best. I knew Albie would want me to survive—it would've been senseless for both of us to fall.

My heart was broken—but my spirit endured. Albie would want me to carry forward. And so, I would.

I had promises yet to fulfill—to deliver the destroyer to the end of days so this story might still reach a happy ending.

Yet peace felt out of reach, knowing I'd never again see my knight. My heart was broken, but my faith endured—scarred, yet standing.

I wasn't alone in my grief.

Edius carried guilt heavier than chains, desperate to atone, driven to fix the unfixable. He was both hero and villain, as so many of us were, tangled in the intricate web woven from the crossings of our stories. We were driven to choose lesser evils, forced again and again to reckon with our choices, our courage, and our faith.

And Edius—he was fighting desperately for something precious, fragile, and pure.

Gwen.

I'm sure you'd love to hear all about Gwen. But that story won't come today. It's been a long, hard journey, and I think we could both use a rest.

Perhaps tea—those curled flowers that unfurl slowly in hot water. Or a bath. I do enjoy baths.

I know there are still questions. I know this isn't the ending we hoped for. But stories, like lives, have seasons of loss and renewal. Stay with me, captive ones—the brightest dawn always follows the darkest night.

Hold your darlings close. Until our next meeting—know you're never alone.

With all my love,
Merrin

MEET BRINDI QUINN

Brindi Quinn is a Minnesota-based romantasy author best known as "the genie author" behind the wildly swoony Come True series—and for weaving sparkly worlds where romance, banter, and reluctant attraction collide. Since 2011, she's penned 20+ YA and NA novels that blend fantasy, paranormal, sci-fi, and comedy into page-turning mashups filled with morally gray protectors, forced proximity, and plenty of swoon.

Her earlier titles are currently retired while she gives her backlist a full, professionally edited revamp—so for now, her available reads are the Come True series and The Crown Saga.

When she's not plotting meet-cute mayhem, Brindi can be found biking with her soulmate, gaming with her dog, or chatting all things bookish online. She is represented by Eva Scalzo of Speilburg Literary.

Find more at Brindiful.com.

Brindi Quinn

Magical books for magical people.

facebook.com/brindiful

instagram.com/brindiful

tiktok.com/@brindiquinnbooks

goodreads.com/brindiful

bookbub.com/authors/brindi-quinn

youtube.com/@brindiquinn

amazon.com/author/brindiful